D1808195

Becky Bexley
The Child Genius
2

Good and Bad Times at University

Diana Holbourn

Fun, interviewing a celebrity's brother,
the paranormal, and stress at university

Windy
Seaside
Publishing

Good and Bad Times at University
Copyright © 2023 by Diana Holbourn

This is a work of fiction. Names, characters, places, and incidents either are the product of the author's imagination or are used fictitiously. Any resemblance to actual persons, living or dead, events, or locales is entirely coincidental.

All rights reserved. No part of this book may be reproduced or used in any manner without written permission of the copyright owner except for the use of quotations in a book review. For more information, please contact the author via www.DianaHolbourn.com

Cover design, book design and formatting by Gareth Southwell (art.garethsouthwell.com)

First edition August 2023

ISBN (paperback): 978-1-7391809-5-9
ISBN (ebook): 978-1-7391809-4-2

First published 2023 by Windy Seaside Publishing

Contents

1. Becky and Some of Her Family Talk Over Ideas   1
    For Spare-Time Activities She Could Do At University

2. Soon After Going to University, Becky Advises   7
    a Psychology Tutor She Finds Crying In His
    Room Over Marriage and Family Problems

3. Becky and Her New Group of Entertaining Friends   23

4. Becky Tells the Story of a Horse That Lots of   43
    People Were Convinced Could Do Arithmetic

5. Becky and the Students With Her Tell Each   51
    Other Funny Stories and Discuss Such Things
    as Faulty Psychology Research

6. Having Fun Doing a Show at a Local   71
    Community Radio Station

7. Becky Gets to Interview the Brother of a   89
    Famous Pop Star for her Radio Show

8. Good Times Having a Laugh With Friends   99

9. Becky and Her Friends Spend an Evening   121
    Chatting About the Paranormal

10. Bad Times at the Psychology Department   227
    Christmas Party and in the Days Afterwards

11. Becky's Friends Try to Cheer Her Up With Some   297
    Comedy, and They Have a Bit of Serious
    Discussion Too

12. Fun At Christmas   315

Acknowledgements   325

About the Author   326

Other books in this series   327

Chapter 1

Becky and Some of Her Family Talk Over Ideas For Spare-Time Activities She Could Do At University

Becky Bexley could be described as an oddity, having been a genius from birth, and making it to university to study psychology and media studies degrees when she was only ten years old. Most people didn't call her an oddity though; some people, at least, used politer words to describe her.

(Yes, it does stretch the bounds of credulity to imagine she could have achieved what she did so young; but this story is similar to a legend in some ways . . . in that legends wildly exaggerate people's achievements, or just make stuff up. This story does contain a lot of accurate information though, comfortably nestled within the freak setting.)

Becky had impressed people around her all her life, bossing her mum around before most kids learn to talk, giving some of her teachers advice about giving up smoking, noisily criticising anything she thought seemed illogical, and doing all kinds of other things like that. She'd been a popular girl at school, because she could make good jokes, and she'd given a lot of people who needed a bit of help some good advice, including giving the headmaster some new ideas for improving the school's anti-bullying strategy. He hadn't realised he needed the help, but he was grateful.

When she got into the upper sixth form at school when she was allegedly nine, she carefully investigated what was on the psychology and media studies courses at some universities, thinking it would be nice to do degrees in them at one when she finished her A levels, which she thought there was a high probability of her doing when she was just ten, her being a genius and all. She'd read things that had made her think there might be a huge variation in the quality of teaching at them, and wanted the best.

But then her mum told her she'd like her to study at a university near enough to home that she could come back every evening, so she could make sure she was eating well, sleeping enough, and not associating with people who were going to cause her problems.

Becky wasn't too happy at first, but she didn't mind too much, since she thought it would be nice to be with her mum.

When she actually went to university though, while she loved the courses she was on, sometimes the students did things late into the evening that sounded fun, so she sometimes felt she was missing out by living at home rather than at university.

Her uncle Steven, her mum's older brother, felt sorry for her, and said to her mum, "She's got the brain of an 18-year-old;

why not let her do things that other 18-year-olds do; if she wants to go out and get drunk out of her mind, why not let her? She needs to learn how to get drunk sensibly anyway for when she gets older."

Steven might have been a bit the worse for drink himself when he said that.

Becky's mum asked sarcastically, "Getting drunk out of her mind would be drinking sensibly, would it?"

Then she objected: "Steven! She has got an advanced brain for her age – and I'd like to keep it that way, thanks! I don't want her brain cells destroyed by alcohol. And she's got a ten-year-old liver that's still developing; I don't want that destroyed by drink. And I don't want Becky to be in situations where she could get caught in the middle of fights and who knows what, because she's too drunk to have her wits about her and out late at night! Besides, she needs her sleep at night!"

Uncle Steven had to agree that his sister had a point, so he said, "Yeah, I suppose you're right."

But he thought it would be nice if there was at least something Becky could get involved in, to relieve the awfulness of a life dedicated to homework – at least, he presumed it must be awful, going by his own experiences of slogging through it . . . or not doing so and getting detention after detention as punishment.

Becky's mum agreed. They wondered what she could get involved in.

They discussed it with Becky. Some students did do fun things in the afternoons they thought she might like to join in with.

Her mum said, "Would you like to do sailing?"

Becky said, "Why would I want to do that? It's an old-fashioned technology; it went out well over a century ago! What would be the point of doing it now?"

Becky's mum said, "What about horse riding? I did a bit of that when I wasn't much older than you; it was fun."

Becky said, "That's just as old-fashioned! That was what they had to do before cars were invented! I don't see why anyone would want to do it now! I'd like to drive a racing car!"

Her mum smiled and said, "I don't think anyone would trust you to be let loose in a racing car!"

Becky said, scratching her head in mock puzzlement, "That's funny. Why would they trust me to go on a horse but not to drive a racing car? I mean, I might not be able to kill quite so many people on a horse, but I could still do damage; I mean, what if I galloped it into a supermarket and it knocked things off shelves left, right and centre, gobbled up things all over the place, and barged into everyone in its way? Imagine if people panicked for aisles around and there was a great stampede to get out and people got trampled . . ."

Becky's mum interrupted, saying sternly, "I've heard quite enough of that, thanks! I don't suppose anyone would trust you to ride off just anywhere on a horse; there would probably always be someone with you, and a horse would be easier to stop quickly than a car."

Steven was still thinking of alternative things that Becky could maybe try, and said to her, "How about canoeing? I saw people doing that in the swimming pool at the university I went to, having great fun!"

Becky said, "What? That must be worse than sailing! An old-fashioned technology, but this time, you have to work a lot harder with all that rowing! I'd like to learn to fly!

I'd like to zoom across the country, piloting a plane myself at hundreds of miles an hour!"

Becky's auntie Diana had just walked into the room and heard the last bit of the conversation. She said as a joke, "Or for the real extreme experience, if we have a nuclear war in our lifetime and the world gets blown up, how about asking permission to sit on top of one of the missiles when it gets fired off? You'd go thousands of miles in minutes! Just think how exciting that would be, at least till the end; way, way more of an adrenaline boost than any fairground ride!"

Becky's mum and Steven didn't find that funny. Steven said, "Shut up Diana! Why do you always have to say such depressing things?"

Becky thought it was funny though, and it gave her an idea. She said to her mum and Steven, "Why are you only thinking of me doing more activities with students? Mum! Tell you what I'd like: Take me on more trips to fairs! Let's go on more days out to fairgrounds and places! How about we have a special day out to a funfair once a month when the weather's warm enough? And we could go out to other places too, so we go out somewhere every other week."

Becky's mum agreed, and Becky was happy.

They didn't quite manage to go out as often as Becky suggested, but they still found places to go out to quite a bit, and they enjoyed themselves when they did.

And Becky made a group of close friends at university her mum ended up trusting and being happy for her to stay out with in the evenings sometimes.

Chapter 2

Soon After Going to University, Becky Advises a Psychology Tutor She Finds Crying In His Room Over Marriage and Family Problems

Becky Bexley was only ten years old when she started at university . . . Well, something like that anyway, perhaps. It's possible there's a touch of exaggeration or lunacy in a few of the claims these books make about her. Still, off she toddled to university, hoping to hold her own among students a fair bit older than her.

She was doing two degrees at once, psychology and media studies. But she still did well, keeping up with the other students who were only doing one degree, and she even had spare time sometimes, though some days she worked a lot later than a child of her age should have done.

(The reason she could fit all the classes for two degrees in was because in psychology, there were only half a dozen lectures and other classes a week; the students did most of their work through personal study for essay writing. And Becky could do most of her study and write her essays when she chose to – provided she did them quickly enough to hand in on time, naturally. In media studies, students did most of their work through personal and group projects, and didn't have many classes at set times either, so each group could do their teamwork when it was convenient for everyone in the group; and the course wasn't all that intensive.

Not many of Becky's media studies and psychology classes clashed with each other. But when a psychology lecture was on at the same time as a media studies class, the psychology tutors would record it for her, and she'd listen to it later.)

One day in the early evening, Becky was walking through the psychology department at the university when she saw the door of the room of one of her tutors standing ajar. She was surprised, because she'd thought they'd all gone home, but decided to ask him about something on the course she found confusing. She pushed the door open and looked in.

To her surprise, she found the tutor slumped over his desk, head in hands. He straightened up when he saw her coming. He looked as if he'd been crying.

Becky asked what the matter was, and why he hadn't gone home. She asked if there was something she could do to help.

Tears started running down his cheeks again, as he said he didn't think there was anything she could do.

Becky asked if it was a psychological problem, saying that if it was, he was at least in the right place, since there were lots of books around with advice on how to solve problems related to that, and being a psychology professor, he must know what a lot of them said anyway, so he wouldn't even need to look at them.

The psychology tutor wiped the tears from his eyes, and confessed to her:

"I'm not sure whereabouts to look to find books that would help. The psychology I teach is no good; it's junk really. I just teach it to make money. It never did many people any good, and I don't suppose it ever will. I've overheard students saying it's a waste of time, all that old-fashioned stuff about Freud and other early psychologists who they think were really just experimenting and making up wacky theories and trying them out on people."

Becky said, "Those early psychologists might not have been as bad as all that. Anyway, if you don't think it's worth teaching what they thought, why not learn up about another kind of psychology and start teaching that instead?"

The psychology professor sighed, and said he just didn't feel as if he had the energy to make the effort, since it might take quite a bit of work, and at least he knew what he was currently teaching well so it was easier.

Becky said that might be true, but that he'd be almost certain to get more satisfaction in life if he did make the effort and started teaching something worthwhile.

The psychology tutor started crying again, and asked her if she was yet another of the students who thought his lectures weren't worth listening to.

She hadn't seen the point in them, but she didn't want to be tactless and say so. So she said, "Well, they can at least be interesting sometimes. You seem to have dedicated your life to them anyway; they seem to be keeping you here late! I expected all the tutors to have gone home by now."

The psychology tutor unexpectedly confided, as he wiped his eyes and stopped crying: "I haven't gone home because I'm scared of what my wife will say. She's always criticising me, saying I'm no good, telling me I teach a worthless subject and I should find a better career, and that she doesn't find me attractive any more. She despises me especially because I can't deal well with our children when they misbehave. But it's not easy! Whenever I try to tell them off, they just ask questions like, 'Would Freud be raising his voice like this? Would Freud say that? How would Karl Jung be dealing with this? I bet he'd have dealt with it better than you. What would he say if he knew you nag us sometimes?' I know those psychologists might well have dealt with it better than me, so I just get embarrassed and ashamed, and then the kids get away with whatever they're doing.

"Or when I ask them if they'll help with the housework or other things, they ask, 'Would Freud expect us to help with the housework when we want to go and do homework, or when we want to play with our friends so we can develop our social skills as young people? You know that's important, don't you!' And I don't know what to say, and we end up in a discussion about what psychologists who lived decades ago said, and then they go away and never help with anything!

"Then my wife yells at me because I can't control them. But she doesn't do much better! She just yells and yells at them, and that doesn't work either, but they just yell back and get aggressive. She smacks them sometimes, but I've noticed that every time she smacks the oldest one, he gets more aggressive, and bullies the younger ones for a while, smacking them sometimes. Then they get into fights, and scream and yell. It's horrible at home! I like to stay here to escape. But then my wife shouts at me for coming home late. I hate it there nowadays!"

Tears began to fall from his eyes again.

Becky said, "I think modern psychology can help you with those problems. For a start, I know of a comeback line you can use with your kids whenever they ask you questions about what Freud would do when you try to tell them off or ask them to do things. You don't have to be ashamed; after all, Freud probably wouldn't handle things any better than you do! And you don't have to discuss things with them – after all, it sounds as if they're not asking because they're genuinely interested, but just because they know it'll end up with them getting out of helping, or avoiding a telling off.

"So whenever you tell them off or ask them to do something, and they ask whether Freud or someone else would say what you just said, you could try saying back to them, 'Regardless of whether Freud would do anything different, do . . .' whatever you're asking them to do. Whatever they say, don't allow yourself to get drawn into an argument about it, but use that kind of phrase. So if they say something like, 'It's not fair!' you could say, 'Regardless of whether it's fair or not, do . . .' such-and-such. Even if their accusations against you sound embarrassing or unfair to you, don't fall into the trap of complaining or discussing them, because that'll be just what they want, since they'll think making the accusations is a good way of making you change the subject so you stop talking about what you asked them to do, or making you argue till you get fed up and stop asking them to do it. So even if they call you a stinky old hippopotamus or something, you could say, 'Regardless of whether I'm a stinky old hippopotamus, go and do . . .' whatever.

"I'm not saying don't ever tell them the reasons why you're asking them to do things; they wouldn't like it if they felt as if they were just being ordered around. I mean, it would be only fair to say to them every once in a while things like, 'All I'm asking you to do is to help with the washing up; it won't take long; you'll still have lots of time to do your homework and enjoy yourself before you've got to go to bed. It's only fair that you help us a bit with the housework, since we do most of it, and pay for all the food you eat and the clothes you wear and so on. We like to enjoy ourselves too in the evenings after working all day, you know. So if we all work together, we'll get it done sooner, and all have a decent amount of time to spend relaxing or whatever before the day ends.'

"You know, I'm saying you can appeal to their sense of fair play sometimes, to help them sympathise with your point of view more. But you can always use that 'regardless' phrase as a backup.

"And when you tell them off, it'll be best if you talk to them in a firm but calm tone of voice if you can, not shouting or sounding hot-and-bothered; if you seem agitated, it might just make them think they're getting to you, so they might know that they just have to play you up a bit more and you'll get upset and storm off or something, without making sure they do what you've asked them to. Or worse, it'll get their adrenaline going and make them feel aggressive, so they'll behave worse because of that.

"And if you often shout at them, they might get into the habit of behaving badly, because their adrenaline will always be being hyped up by being aggressively yelled at, and they'll pick up the habit of yelling from you and their mum, thinking that's just how people behave in life so it's acceptable. Either that, or they might think they'd better do what you want, if they think you might do something worse if they don't, but they'll have a bad opinion of you, which might last for decades, no matter what nice things you do for them.

"So even if you don't feel calm, it can help to put on a slightly deeper, calm but firm voice, and look at them steadily when you talk to them. That'll probably have more influence than if you just yell, or get bogged down in discussions of how fair you're being to ask them to do things, because it'll sound like the voice of authority.

"But you'll need the backing of your wife, to make sure she never takes their side. I think you need a good honest discussion with her. It'll be best if you wait till she's in a good mood, and you've got quite a bit of time for a discussion. When you begin, don't start criticising her, since that'll only make her want to defend herself, and it'll probably quickly turn into a shouting match that just ends up with both of you angry. Instead, you could tell her you'd like a good talk with her about the future. Try to make sure you don't say anything that gives her the impression that you're blaming her for what's gone wrong, since again, she'll want to defend herself then, and it might turn into an angry argument. But you can talk with her about how you'd like the future to be."

The psychology tutor felt hopeful for the first time in ages, and began to cheer up. But he became conscious of the fact that any student walking past might hear what sounded like him being bossed about or taught psychology by a ten-year-old, and that embarrassed him. So he got up and gently shut the door, before sitting down to listen to the rest of what Becky had to say.

Becky continued, "You could tell your wife you'd like things to change, and that you'd like to sit down with her to make some good solid plans about how to improve the marriage and your family life. You could say you think you've got some good ideas. If she agrees to talk things through with you, you could start by saying you've got some new plans about how to handle the children when they're naughty, and tell her about the phrases you can use that mean you don't need to be drawn into an argument with them whenever you're telling them off like you used to be, and that she doesn't need to resort to yelling to try to get them to do things, like she has up until now, because whatever they say, you can both just say, 'Regardless of whether that's true', and repeat what you asked them to do.

"If your wife makes a spiteful sarcastic comment about how it was about time you thought of something new, try not to get drawn into an argument with her even if what she says annoys you, but try and keep your mind on what you want to achieve by having the conversation, and just say something like, 'Let's not argue about the past; let's look forward to the future, and just plan how it could be better.'

"Besides recommending that you both start using those new phrases with the children, tell her what I said about the quiet, calm but firm voice of authority it's recommended that you use when you tell them off, and encourage her to use it too. You don't have to tell her a ten-year-old told you about it. If she stops yelling at the kids, and you stop letting them get away with everything, they'll probably start behaving quite a bit better, and you and your wife will both be happier. And then your wife might not criticise you so much, and she'll probably think more of you."

Just then, they both heard a snippet of conversation, as two students walked past the door, one saying to the other, "Well everyone knows psychologists are as nutty as the people they say they want to help! I heard about one who . . ."

Just what he said the psychologist did, they never found out, because the conversation faded away. But both Becky and the tutor ignored the insult to psychologists, and Becky carried on:

"You could tell your wife you'd like the two of you to have a fresh start, to revitalise your marriage. If what you say sounds optimistic and gives her a spark of hope, she might agree. Then you could make it more likely that the optimism will continue, by suggesting that one good thing to do would be if you both look out every day for the good things the other one does, and compliment each other on them, either right then and there when the good things happen, or by writing the compliments down in a spare moment and giving each other what you've written when you can relax together in the evenings. If you look out for things about each other that please you, your opinions of each other might start to change for the better, and you might want to be nicer to each other. If your wife starts to think more of you, you'll probably get more confident and happy, and then she might like you even more.

"And you could tell her you'd like to plan ways with her of arguing less. You could try thinking about what tends to start off arguments, and plan to make changes.

"For example, if you find you argue most before dinner after a day's work in the evenings, when perhaps you're both a bit hungry and tired, and that's making you more short-tempered than normal, you could tell her you think it would be good if you had a new rule that says no arguing before dinner, so anything either of you wants to bring up can wait till afterwards.

"I read about someone doing that and finding it worked for him. He realised that when he got home from work, he was always tired and in a bad mood, so conversations were much more likely to turn into arguments then than if they happened when he was in a better mood later on in the evening. So he recommended to his wife that they always waited till after dinner before they said anything controversial to each other in future. She agreed. It turned out that when they had the kinds of conversations after dinner that used to lead to arguments when they'd had them before, he was in a much better mood, and just didn't feel like arguing so much, so they could have them without them turning into arguments.

"And I read about a couple who'd always argue about money on Friday evenings, and it would always put a dampener on their weekend. But then one Friday, one of them said, 'How about we argue about this on Sunday evening instead, so we can enjoy the weekend together first?' The other one agreed. They enjoyed their weekend. When it came to Sunday evening, they'd enjoyed each other's company so much that they were in too good a mood to argue, so they didn't in the end.

"So maybe that kind of thing could happen for you and your wife.

"Or if you notice that certain phrases irritate one or both of you, and set you off arguing, you could both have a go at using different phrases instead. For instance, if you tend to accuse each other of 'always' doing a certain irritating thing, or 'never' doing something such as helping with a certain thing, but then you tend to get into arguments about how fair the accusation is because it's not quite true, you could try and get your wife's agreement for you to both make a commitment to dropping those words, and try using less extreme ones that might be more accurate.

"Or if you blame each other a lot, or nag and criticise each other, you could try both making a commitment to phrase things differently, so instead, you don't complain about what's going wrong, but ask nicely if a certain thing could be done differently in the future. For instance, instead of saying, 'I hate the way you always leave your dirty socks to pile up by the bed' – just supposing either one of you does that – you could instead say, in a nice tone of voice, 'You know, I'd really really appreciate it if you could try to remember to put your dirty socks in the washing bag at night from now on instead of leaving them next to the bed.'

"That kind of thing has a few benefits: One is that you'll be being precise when it comes to letting the other person know what you want, rather than just complaining that they don't, say, do enough housework or something, which wouldn't make it clear just what you'd like them to do more of, because they might not know what kinds of housework you'd like them to do. Also it means you're not making an accusation that might immediately put them on the defensive, but you're being polite, which will come across as nicer, so they'll be less likely to argue. And you'll be making them think about how to change in the future, which might start them planning, instead of making them think about what they might or might not have done wrong in the past.

"Couples have used other ways of trying to make sure they argue less too. I'm reading a book by a therapist who recommends that people try to think up inventive ways of doing things differently when arguments begin that might stop them, maybe by surprising the person they're arguing with so much they're lost for words or something. It says one man came up with the idea that he and his wife should make it a rule that whenever they argued, they should take all their clothes off. He thought that would hopefully stop them arguing in public, or when it was cold, so it would reduce the number of arguments they had. Since all their children had left home, his wife agreed.

"It turned out that it worked really well. When their first argument started after they'd decided on the rule, while the husband was making serious points, getting into the argument, he took one of his clothes off with each point he made, and threw it on the floor.

"At first, his wife was surprised. But then she started laughing, and she laughed more and more the longer he kept on doing it. He was laughing as well, trying to argue at the same time.

"Eventually, they realised they actually more or less agreed with each other, so the argument stopped.

"They laughed with each other about what had happened over the next few days, and the man's wife said she didn't think she'd ever be able to keep a straight face in an argument with him again! So maybe you could try something like that.

"But you won't necessarily have to do anything as dramatic as that.

"Once arguments start, they kind of fuel themselves, since the two people arguing will be making each other angrier by what they say and the way they say it, although they might not fully realise what their own contributions to the arguments are, because they won't necessarily know how their tones of voice are coming across to whoever they're arguing with, or have time to think about what they're saying enough to make sure it's really fair before they say it. So the person who starts an argument can't really be blamed for the whole of it.

"Sometimes, just doing something a bit differently during an argument can stop it getting worse. The book by the therapist who told the story about taking clothes off during an argument says she's a marriage counsellor who's helped quite a lot of people improve their marriages; but even after everything she's learned about how to do that, it seems she still has arguments with her husband. But she says in the book that she has learned ways of sometimes avoiding them, or stopping them getting worse once they start.

"She says sometimes, people can irritate other people without meaning to, not because they're doing anything wrong, but just because the person they're talking to happens to get irritated by the kind of thing they're doing. She says one example is that when she and her husband used to be in the middle of an argument, he would often walk away to his workshop or somewhere, and she used to get annoyed about that, because she used to think he was just avoiding the problems she wanted to discuss, and she hadn't finished talking about them, so she used to follow him, still talking. But she found that just made him more annoyed, so the arguments got worse. She says that kind of thing happens with a lot of couples, where men get up and walk away in the middle of an argument, and women want to carry on talking and follow them, but then the arguments get worse.

"She found out that the men were walking away because they were beginning to get really stressed and felt as if they really needed to cool down before they could carry on talking. She realised it was better to talk to them when they were calmer anyway, since then they'd be able to think more clearly. So she started just letting her husband go and cool down for a while when he walked away, and she advised people who came to see her for counselling to do the same.

"She found out that that worked a lot better for her than what she'd been doing before, since her husband would go away and think about what they'd been saying, and come back some time later, realising she'd been right about some things, or suggesting a sensible way of dealing with the problems. So the arguments didn't start up again, or weren't so bad.

"And there's a story in her book that's another example of how just doing something differently from normal can help, about a woman who realised that arguments with her husband would often start after he would go quiet, and she thought he must be annoyed or upset with her, and she'd ask him what was wrong. He'd say nothing was, and she'd say she was sure something must be wrong. He'd say nothing was and ask her to stop asking, but she'd say there must be something wrong. Then he'd get annoyed with her, and an argument would start.

"Maybe unbeknownst to her, he was being thoughtful when he went quiet, and her asking him questions and expecting him to talk to her was disrupting his thoughts, and that's why he didn't like it.

"She didn't understand why he would want to argue with her when she was only trying to be helpful and caring, but she decided to stop keeping on asking him what was wrong when he went quiet.

"The next time he went quiet, they were just about to get in the car to go out together. She asked him what was wrong, and he said nothing was, as usual. She decided not to say anything else, but instead turned the car radio on and sang along to the music as they drove.

"After a few minutes, her husband asked if she minded if they turned it down, because he wanted to discuss something with her. She turned it down, and he told her about his feelings about something that had happened earlier in the day. It was the first time ever in their marriage that he'd voluntarily talked about his feelings about things.

"So that was a real difference! Maybe something small that you do could make a real difference too. If you have a good think about what kinds of things happen just before you and your wife start arguing, or before arguments get noticeably worse, if they do, and you realise there are some things you do that you could change, even if they don't seem to be bad things to you, then maybe you could try doing different things at those times, to see if it makes different things happen as a result that stop some of the arguments."

The psychology professor was sitting up straight by then, interested in what Becky was saying. He thanked her, saying he felt a lot more cheerful, and in a far better mood to brave going home.

He looked happier whenever Becky saw him from then on; and a few weeks later, he met her when there were no other students around, and thanked her for the advice she'd given him, saying his marriage was improving, his children were behaving better, his wife liked him more, and he'd started to like going home again. He also said he'd begun to look at modern psychology books, and thought he might be willing to learn about up-to-date psychology from some of the ones with a good reputation, and start teaching something worthwhile after all.

Becky was pleased that what she'd advised had helped.

Chapter 3

Becky and Her New Group of Entertaining Friends

Becky soon made friends at university, even though she was about eight years younger than the other students; and she started spending quite a bit of her spare time with a group of nice people from her courses and from other ones, and having fun.

No one in the group drank much alcohol, and when they had a pint or two, they were responsible and gave Becky soft drinks, so her mum was happy. In fact, her mum got to trust them so much she let Becky stay with them fairly late into the evening sometimes, or even overnight on rare occasions.

She bought Becky a mobile phone, and they got into an arrangement where on days when Becky decided she'd like to stay out late with friends, she'd phone her mum and let her know, and then she'd phone again when she was ready to come home, or else her mum would phone her up when she thought Becky had stayed out late enough and it was time she was brought back and went to bed. That did lead to some arguments sometimes though, because Becky wanted to stay out late more often than her mum knew was good for her, because she needed her sleep.

But Becky loved being with her new group of friends. They did things that were fun, and had interesting conversations.

For instance, one day they were all having a nice meal together when one student, Adam, told Becky that in his class recently, a tutor had held a kind of auction that he just knew would end badly for a couple of them, and then said afterwards that he'd done it to give them a lesson in how people can get carried away into making bad decisions when they want something. Adam said to her:

"He auctioned off a £20 note. Before he did, he said it didn't matter how much less than it was worth the person who ended up with it paid for it; they could still have it. But he said there was one special rule people had to obey: The second highest bidder – the one who'd just lost out to the winner – would have to pay the tutor all the money he'd bid, for nothing in return.

"At first, everyone loved the idea of getting money for virtually nothing, and people started bidding things like a penny, not stopping to think that they'd hardly be likely to get the money for that, because lots of other people would probably want to try to get it for almost nothing too. People bid more and more until the bids were over £10. Then quite a few people dropped out. By the time the bidding got to over £15, most people had dropped out, since they must have realised that if they carried on, even if they ended up win-ning, they might have to pay over £20 for the £20 note, so they'd really be losing money. By the time the bids got to £19, only a few people were left in the auction. Most of us were sniggering, knowing that soon, people would start bidding more for the £20 note than it was worth.

"But two people didn't want to stop. They both knew that if they stopped and the other person won the money, the rules meant that they'd have to pay the tutor quite a bit of their own money for nothing. So even though they were bidding higher and higher amounts so they were risking having to pay more and more if they lost when the bidding finally did stop, they didn't want to. There was a laugh when the first person bid over £20 for the £20 note. They probably thought that if they won, they'd only have to pay a little bit more than £20, whereas if they lost, they'd have to pay the tutor over £20 and get nothing in return.

"The bidding went up and up, past £25, and then past £30, and even up to £40. Some of us were sure it had to stop soon, but the students still bidding tried and tried to outbid each other, till they got to just over £65! They must have been feeling so keen to outbid their rival that it seems they hardly noticed, because neither of them seemed to be losing much enthusiasm. Neither of them started looking worried, even though the one who lost in the end was going to have to pay over £60 for nothing, and even the one who won was going to have to pay over three times what the £20 note was actually worth to get it! So really he would be losing £45 he wouldn't have lost if he hadn't been so keen to take part and win.

"At last, it seems one of them did realise that if he carried on bidding he might bankrupt himself! So he must have resigned himself to losing an entire £65, and stopped bidding. I don't know how the other one felt, paying over £65 for a £20 note! Part of me felt sorry for him; but I suppose it must have taught him a lesson."

"That was an expensive lesson!" said Becky. "What was it supposed to teach people?"

Adam said, "The tutor was teaching us that we ought to have a good think before trying to get things we like the idea of, instead of rushing into it. His lecture was about things such as how if people let feelings control them, such as an urge to snap up something in a popular sale in case it soon disappears because other people buy all the ones on offer first, they can make bad decisions in their rush to get what they want; he said some people end up with a whole lot of stuff they later realise isn't that good after all, because they get things before taking the time to examine them to find out how good they really are, since they're worried that they might be really good and they'll lose out if they don't get one quickly before everyone else gets them all.

"Or they pay much more than they'd intended to when they left their house in the morning, because they get things they think are bargains, only to realise later that they're not as good as things they could have got that they'd have wanted more if they'd shopped around and found them, and that they've actually spent more of their hard-earned money than they would have done if they hadn't been so keen to chase bargains that they bought things without really thinking about whether they were likely to use them enough to make it worth it!

"The tutor said people can be so focused on the one thought of getting something for a bargain or before the shop runs out of the items in the sale that they can get carried away with an exciting feeling of competing with other people to get one, not stopping to think, 'Do I really want this, and do I really want to spend this much money on it?' He said some salesmen and shops deliberately create conditions where people feel as if they're competing for things, like by advertising that there's a sale on, but saying offers must end soon, so people are more likely to buy things without stopping to think, because they feel as if they need to be in a rush and might lose out if they're not quick enough to get one before the offer ends. So the shops make more profit, but it means some people end up with things they realise later they could have done without, or things that aren't as good as things they might have discovered in other shops, or even in the same one, if they'd looked around for longer."

Becky asked, "Does your tutor often play tricks on his students that make him money?"

Adam said the tutor told the class he held an auction like that every year with a new class, and always got similar results, but that he gave the money to charity.

Then he told Becky something his tutor had told the class, about a real auction where two people who should really have known better fell into the trap of letting competitive urges carry them away into making a bad decision. He said:

"He told us that in 1973, the vice president of a television network in America bid well over three million dollars in an auction for one single television showing of a film called *The Poseidon Adventure*, about people trying to escape a shipwreck after the ship got capsized by a tsunami. He was bidding against bosses of other television networks, in an auction held by the film makers. He bid a lot, because he was hoping the film would be expected to pull in high ratings so it would attract lots of advertising, so the company would make quite a bit of money; but bosses reckoned the company lost a million dollars by spending that much on it, even after they got the extra big profits from the advertising.

"It's thought that the reason the vice president got carried away into spending such a daft amount was because for the first time ever, a film was being auctioned in a fast-paced atmosphere of competition, where network bosses were there in the room with each other, bidding against each other, while they were feeling as if they needed to make bids fast if they weren't going to lose out. Apparently, a feeling of real competitiveness took over them. The boss who won didn't have experience of bidding like that, and all the television network bosses were so keen to outbid each other that it seems they didn't stop to think about whether what they were doing made sense, and whether the film was really worth it, especially considering there were lots of other popular films they could show; all they were thinking of was how much they wanted to win the right to show that film and outbid the others. They didn't really have time to think of much else, because the auction would have been going fast, with their competitors quickly making bids.

"Afterwards, the man who won regretted having paid so much, and the owners of his television network weren't pleased. When he was interviewed, he said they'd decided they'd never again bid for a film in an auction. And one of the bosses who'd only just lost out said he was relieved he'd lost, since his own television network could so easily have had to pay more than the winner had if he hadn't at last had the sense to stop bidding. He said it was as if they'd all lost their minds in the competitive fever of trying to outbid each other, with their adrenaline stirred up, and getting what they wanted being the only thing on their minds. He said that after his final bid, he started worrying about what he'd do if he won the rights to show the film and his network had to pay all that money. He said he was relieved not to have won.

"When the tutor told us about that, he advised us that when we notice our own adrenaline getting all stirred up, in whatever situations it might happen to us, and the only thing on our minds is getting something we want, we try to remember to think of our feelings as a warning sign that if we're not careful, we might do something we regret, so we should slow down if possible and stop and think."

Becky said, "I suppose that could be a good idea in all kinds of situations. But wow, you hear about rich people spending ludicrous amounts of money just on paintings and things, and I always thought they must have more money than sense and were uncaring for doing that, because those amounts of money could do a lot for charity; but maybe that's why they do it sometimes – maybe they get carried away by the urge to win and not to lose out, so they end up making daft decisions!"

Adam was thoughtful, wondering if that might be true.

———

The group of friends didn't just chat; they had lovely meals together. Sometimes they'd cook all together, making mostly vegetarian concoctions, with different kinds of vegetables and herbs and spices, suggesting ideas for what they could put with what . . . Occasionally, the suggestions didn't go down too well though:

One day a student in the group called Danny said, "Some-one once told me he was making dinner for a group of people, and he made chocolate pudding with a jug of chocolate sauce to go with it. He got the sauce and the gravy for the dinner mixed up, and ended up putting chocolate sauce on the dinner and gravy on the pudding. No one who ate it said a word. He assumed they were just being polite. But maybe they liked it. Shall we try putting chocolate sauce on our dinner to see if it's nice? We all assume we won't like it, but that might just be because we've always grown up thinking sweet things and savoury things don't mix. Our parents would never have approved of us putting chocolate on our dinners, but maybe the only reason we're sure we won't like it is because we've just accepted what they think without questioning it. That's not a good thing to do. Let's try it for ourselves."

The group laughed, and one said, "Don't be daft! I can just imagine what it would taste like, and I'm pretty sure it wouldn't be nice!"

But Danny decided he wanted to try weird things, even if no one else did. He chose to make a sandwich, just for himself, with a mixture of peanut butter, cream cheese, chocolate chips, marmite and a spoonful of sugar. He made a horrible face while he was eating it, but he insisted that it was nice, though people weren't quite sure if he was serious or joking. Everyone laughed at him. He didn't make any more weird concoctions after that.

———

One evening, one of the friends, Dawn, said, "I was listening to the news on the radio the other day, and it said there was some species of penguin that would be in danger of going extinct because of climate change – either that, or it would mean the penguins would all have to 'abruptly change their habitat by the end of the century.'

"I thought sarcastically, 'Wow, as abrupt as that, eh?' I mean, that would be like a tutor saying to one of us, 'I want you to abruptly get to the lecture theatre, and I want you to make sure you make it there by at least midday tomorrow!' "

Some of the group tittered. But one of them, Angela, protested, "It's not fair to just have a laugh about the wording giving a funny impression, and not to be concerned about the real problem though! I mean, what if some penguins really are going to have a hard time surviving?

"I've heard about people thinking more about the wording than the problem before. What you said reminds me of something in a book I read. I can't remember who the author was or what it was called now, but it was an autobiographical book about how when the author was a little girl, growing up in Poland, the Second World War broke out, and she and her mum were evacuated to Siberia. I think they might have been Jewish, but I can't be absolutely sure. But one thing I remember the book saying is that one day when they were living in Siberia, an official in the town they were living in told her to tell her mum that 'Ivan the bum' was going to be sent to live with them. Everyone called him Ivan the bum because he was a beggar, who I think liked to sit around swearing and drinking. Not many people liked him. Anyway, she was a bit scared by the news, and told her mum in alarm, 'Ivan the bum's going to be sent to live with us!'

"Her mum replied by saying, 'Don't call people bad names! It's not nice!'

"The author said that felt a bit like the way it must feel if someone's corrected on their grammar while they're trying to warn people the house is on fire!

"I think Ivan the Bum turned out to be just about tolerable in the end.

"Actually, come to think of it, I've just remembered that when I was about ten, I went down a slide and landed with a bit of a clonk at the bottom in some mud. I didn't hurt myself, but it was a bit of a surprise. I said quietly, 'Bum!' That wasn't something I was in the habit of saying. My mum saw me come down the slide, and said, 'Don't use bad words!' It didn't seem to occur to her to wonder why I'd said it."

Dawn blushed slightly and said, "Oh, it's not that I don't care about the penguins . . . Well, actually, I can't really bring myself to care about penguins in general; I'll leave that to environmentalists. But no, it was just that I thought the wording in the news story was funny, because it made it sound as if it wasn't nearly as much of a problem as they were making it out to be, with them saying the penguins would have to move abruptly by the end of the century."

One of the group, Shirley, grinned and said, "Talking of inappropriate wording, have you ever deliberately sung rude words to songs in public, like hymns in church?

"I'm not saying I do that. But I was having a conversation with someone the other day about that kind of thing, and what might happen if a country's entry in the Eurovision Song Contest said rude things about Britain. Then it occurred to me that it's not just foreigners who might sing rude things about this country; if someone was in a crowd of people who were singing the national anthem, just imagine: They could sing, 'God hate the Queen' instead of 'God save the Queen', and I bet no one would notice! . . . Actually, maybe if most of the crowd sang that, no one would notice, since the word hate would sound quite like the word save, especially with the music making the words more difficult to hear. I suppose an anti-monarchist revolution could start right under the Queen's nose!"

(This conversation took place some time before Queen Elizabeth died.)

One of the friends, Monica, said, "Aww, why would anyone want God to hate the Queen?"

Another one of the group, Mandy, said with a grin, "I dunno, maybe they'd ask him to hate her just for fun. Actually, have you noticed, the national anthem isn't very polite, is it! I mean, it tells God to do all these things to benefit the Queen, like saving her, and sending her victorious . . . victorious what, it doesn't say! But anyway, not once does it ever say please! Maybe the person who wrote it grew up with servants he could just order around and they'd do things without being asked nicely, so he thought God must be like that too. So he wrote a national anthem ordering God around."

One of the friends, Gary, chuckled and said, "Imagine someone saying, 'God, I order you to hate the Queen! Why? Well, I haven't got a good reason really; it's just that ordering you to hate the Queen seems like a fun thing to do!'"

Dawn said, "Imagine if it really was possible to order God around! Imagine if God would do anything anyone told him to! . . . That's if he really exists, of course."

Another one of the group, Sharon, said, "Wow, people might order him to do all kinds of things. The world would be chaotic! Imagine if someone asked him to turn their enemy into a pile of compost, and immediately their enemy disappeared and there was a pile of compost right where they were!"

Becky said, "That could be inconvenient if they were, say, standing by the teacher's desk in a classroom. Or imagine if the person the one who told God to turn into compost had been sitting on the teacher's chair! The teacher would come in and wonder why there was a massive pile of compost on their chair!"

Gary grinned and said, "Maybe the teacher could be the one turned into a pile of compost! I wonder how they'd manage to do their teaching then!"

The friends laughed.

Then Sharon said, "I wonder what God would do if people gave him conflicting orders. It could be confusing for him. Mind you, maybe sometimes he could carry them both out at the same time. I mean, say if one person started singing the national anthem and ordered God to save the Queen, and at the same time, someone else ordered him to turn her into an acorn. Maybe he'd turn her into an acorn, but he'd put her on a cushion in a glass display case in a museum where she could be displayed for centuries, and where she'd always be safe from squirrels who might want to eat her."

Becky grinned and said, "Imagine a tour guide taking people around the museum and announcing, 'And this is the Queen!' Or they might quickly bypass that bit of the museum without saying anything about it, because they'd worry about what it might do to their credibility if they announced that an acorn was really the Queen!"

Shirley said, "I don't know; I mean, if people were used to people being turned into all kinds of things just because people ordered God to turn them into them, they wouldn't think there was anything strange about it. Imagine if someone went into the museum and said, 'God, turn all the objects in this museum into mushrooms!' Then from then on, the tour guides who took people around might say things like, 'This used to be a beautiful jewel-encrusted necklace that was found in an ancient Egyptian tomb. Now it's a mushroom. And this used to be a delicate ornate ancient Roman vase. Now it's a mushroom.' 'This used to be a skilfully embroidered amazingly intricate tapestry belonging to Henry VIII's third wife. Now it's a mushroom.' 'This used to be a Second World War tank. Now it's a mushroom.'

"Mind you, someone might think to ask God to turn things back into what they were at first every morning before the museums opened. But imagine if there were battles going on all day between people who wanted them all to be mushrooms and other things, and the people who wanted them to be what they used to be, so a tour guide leading people around a museum would never be sure what they were going to be when they got there."

Mandy said, "Wow, governments could actually turn enemy weapons into other things. Imagine if a prime minister one day ordered that an enemy country's nukes all be turned into peanuts! Imagine how surprised the enemy's nuclear scientists and other military people would be if they went to where the missiles were one day and found they'd all suddenly become peanuts! It would change the face of modern warfare! Imagine them trying to catapult peanuts at us, lamenting, 'It seems this is about as aggressive as we can make our wars of aggression now!' Well, apart from the fact that they could order God to turn them back into nukes. But just think of what they might do to our own weapons!

Imagine if they ordered God to turn all our guns into marsh-mallows!

"But imagine what a disadvantage atheist regimes would be at! They wouldn't believe God could turn things into other things, so another country's weapons would be safe from that strategy if they attacked them."

Another one of the friends, Miriam, said, "Or imagine if a country managed to send nuclear missiles to obliterate us, but while they were on their way, instead of a four-minute warning, messages came over loudspeakers all over the country and on television and radio – or whatever would happen – saying, 'A few minutes ago, a nuclear missile was sent hurtling towards us; but don't worry, the Prime Minister's ordered God to turn it into a giant jellyfish. Oh, and don't get alarmed by that: He especially ordered God to make it one without those horrible stingy things some of them have on them!'

"And then imagine if someone was just walking along in a place where they couldn't hear the warnings, when a massive squishy jellyfish whizzed down out of the sky and splatted down onto their head!"

Dawn said for a joke, "Do you think the world will end in our lifetime? I mean, maybe all it would take would be for the leaders of two countries with nuclear weapons to argue and argue, and then decide that a perfectly sane way of resolving things would be to nuke each other's countries! Hey, shall we take a bet on what year the world's going to end? Then if this country gets nuked, at least one of us can feel triumphant in the seconds before they're blasted into oblivion, and if whichever one of us got the answer most accurate happens to come across another one of us when we're about to be blasted to bits, we can wave and triumphantly say, 'I told you so!', and die happy!"

The others giggled, and Adam said, "Somehow I think we'll all have more important things on our minds at the time!"

Dawn smiled and said, "I dunno, it depends if anyone here's narcissistic enough to think of it as hugely significant and take loads of pride in winning the bet. Hey imagine if some country lobbed a nuclear missile at this one, and while it was on its way, while most people were running around panicking, wondering what to do, one of us was jumping up and down gleefully, loudly boasting, 'Twenty years ago I was at university, and me and some other students had a bet on what year the world would end, and I guessed the year the most accurately, which must prove I'm the cleverest one who was there! Hey, stop panicking and pay attention to what I'm telling you, you stupid idiots! I said I was in a group of students who all bet on when the world would end, and I guessed the closest year, which must prove I'm the cleverest person of the entire lot of them!' "

The friends laughed, and Mandy said, "I don't think there's anyone who's narcissistic enough to do a thing like that here! You'd have to be a bit looney to behave like that! Mind you, maybe there's something to be said for being a bit looney if it can make you happy while you're being nuked!"

Adam grinned and said, "Being a bit looney wouldn't always have that effect though. But just think! You'd have to really care about your image if you were trying to convince everyone you were fantastically clever even while you were being nuked, instead of panicking like everyone else might be!"

Sharon said, "Imagine if there was someone who cared about their image so much, who was so worried about people thinking badly of them, that they easily got paranoid about what people thought of them. Imagine if they were a town planner, and they heard people talking about how some people had hearts of stone, and they thought, 'Stone must be a bad thing then'; so they decided there wouldn't be anything like stone in the towns they designed, so they'd order that everything had to be made of wood or plastic or soft things from then on; so they decided that pavements had to be made out of wood, or the things they make mattresses or duvets out of, and all the buildings would be made out of rubber, and the roads would be made out of plastic, or soft earth with grass growing on it. Imagine what it would be like walking along a pavement that was like a massive soft bouncy mattress!

"And imagine if weeds grew with the grass the roads were made out of, but then the town planner heard that it wasn't thought of as cool to be around weeds, so he ordered a few workers to spend days and days going around all the roads pulling them all up, and the roads were all closed to traffic while that happened, so all the car drivers and lorry drivers and people who wanted to use buses were inconvenienced all that time!

"And imagine if the person heard people on the radio talking about people with cold hearts, or people being cold, meaning they were unfriendly, and they thought, 'Cold things must be bad then', so they turned their fridge off and decided never to have any cold things in their house again. And they heard someone criticise another person, saying something like, 'They never smile or let themselves have a good laugh; it's as if their emotions are frozen!' And they thought, 'It must be bad to have anything frozen then', so they turned their freezer off, because they decided never to have anything frozen in their house again!"

Shirley grinned and said, "They'd get pretty confused if someone came to their house and asked for a cup of tea, and they said, 'I'll just go to the shops and get some milk', and the person asked if they didn't have any in their fridge, and they said, 'Definitely not! I would never keep any cold things in my house! I want people to think this house is a warm, friendly environment when they come here!' and the other person was surprised and asked them how they stopped their food from going off quickly if they didn't use a fridge or a freezer, so they started thinking it might be good for things to be frozen or cold sometimes after all, but they weren't sure."

Miriam grinned and said, "That's if the person who came to their house had recovered enough to talk after somersaulting along the pavements on the soft mattresses they were made of if they couldn't keep their balance enough to just walk along them."

They giggled.

Then Mandy said, "I come across funny news stories sometimes. I read one about how in Germany, a TV licence demand was sent to a sixteenth-century mathematician. The person living in the house he used to live in sent back a letter saying he'd died in 1559. But he still got a reminder a few weeks later. And before that, a letter was sent to a poet who died in 1805, asking him to declare all the radios and televisions in his house, and pay the licence fee."

They talked about funny news stories for a while.

On another evening, one of the friends, Lauren, said, "One of my biology tutors told us a funny thing today. He said scientists are trying to breed cows that burp less, since they say all the cow burps add up to loads of methane being released into the atmosphere that contributes a lot to global warming."

They discussed other weird and amusing scientific things they'd found out, and had a good time.

———

Sometimes, they discussed interesting and useful things rather than amusing ones, and could get quite serious. On one evening, Becky told them about an interesting thing she'd learned on her psychology course. She said:

"We learned that if something bad happens to someone in a crowd, such as them falling ill or being attacked, it's been found that people often won't do anything to help, not because they don't care, but because they wonder whether they should, and they look around at other people for clues about what to do, and they often see the others looking calm, as if they don't think the problem's serious enough to need intervention, or they think someone else is bound to come and help, or that it'll be resolved by the person or people involved in it; so they think things will probably be alright in the end, and decide not to intervene, maybe thinking the person probably doesn't really need their help, or that it might be better if they stay out of things; but the real reason the others are looking calm isn't because they don't think there's anything to be concerned about, but because they, too, will probably be busy looking around to see what everyone else is doing, to try to pick up clues about what they ought to be doing themselves; and seeing no one doing anything, they assume they don't need to be worried, or that someone else will probably deal with it. So they all make the same mistake.

"It's been found that the best thing for anyone in any kind of trouble in a crowd to do is to single out someone from the crowd, and shout at them in a way that'll make it obvious to them that they're the one being spoken to, for instance saying, 'Oy, you with the purple hair!' – well, basically mentioning something that'll identify them, and then asking them to help, and asking them to get others to help too.

"Mind you, I read that, but then I heard that footage from CCTV was studied in a certain place, and it was found that people did intervene when they saw other people being attacked over ninety per cent of the time. So maybe the thing about people not being sure whether to help just applies in certain situations."

The friends found that interesting, and said they'd try to remember the thing about attracting attention to get help, though they hoped they'd never need to.

They talked about other interesting things, and enjoyed each other's company.

Chapter 4

Becky Tells the Story of a Horse That Lots of People Were Convinced Could Do Arithmetic

On Becky's psychology course, she learned a lot of useful and interesting things. But not everything she learned was very good. In fact, she couldn't believe some of the things the students were taught!

One day, a lecturer told the class that an experiment had found that people could be influenced so easily to decide for one thing or another when they were making big decisions that even just having drunk a hot or cold drink could make the difference between what they decided to do or think. A hot drink would give them warm favourable feelings towards people, so they'd be more likely to make a decision in their favour straight after they had it, and a cold drink had been found to make them emotionally colder and more negative towards others, so they'd be more likely to decide against something people wanted straight afterwards.

The lecturer tried to prove what he was saying by playing the class a video where a psychologist gave people a hot drink, and then introduced them to a man who said a few things to them that led to a brief conversation. After the man had gone, the psychologist asked them if they liked the man, and whether they'd give him a job if they ran a company. They replied yes to both questions. Then he gave a different group of people a cold drink, after which the man came in and said exactly the same things as he had before, and they had pretty much the same conversation. Afterwards, the psychologist asked them whether they liked him and would give him a job, and they had a lot of doubts about both of those questions. The psychologist reported that that was proof that just holding a drink of different temperatures could have as dramatic an effect as that on people's choices. Not all of them had even drunk their drinks when they made their decisions.

The lecturer told the students the finding as if it was actual fact. But Becky was convinced there was a problem with the idea. She stood up in the lecture hall, and said in a loud voice:

"You're wrong! These experiments don't show what you're saying they show. Think about it: The participants in the experiment probably knew what the psychologist expected them to say – they would have been able to tell from his body language and tone of voice, and they were probably taking cues from those things to decide how to answer, because they probably assumed he knew best, being someone who they might have assumed would know a lot more about human behaviour than they did. Didn't you notice that when he asked the first group whether they liked the man and would give him a job, there was enthusiasm in his voice? That would have made them think he was expecting them to say yes because he must think it was the right decision, so they probably said what they thought he wanted to hear.

"Then when he'd given the other group the cold drink and asked them if they liked the man and would give him a job, there was doubt in his voice. That probably meant he doubted they'd say yes, because he was pretty sure the cold drink would have made their attitude more negative, because he was already convinced that his theory was right before he even tried it out on them; but they probably interpreted his doubtful tone of voice as doubt that the man was a likeable person and that he deserved a job, so they would have followed what they thought was his cue, and doubted too, again thinking he must know best. It's like what happened with Clever Hans!"

The lecturer was embarrassed, but admitted that Becky might well be right.

After the lecture, one student, Marcus, asked Becky, "Who's Clever Hans, and what did he do?"

Becky said, "We're going to learn about him on the course soon. I was curious about what was coming up on it, so I gave myself a sneak preview." Then she explained that Clever Hans was a horse, who performed to crowds in the 1890s and early 1900s.

She said, "In one of Charles Darwin's books, he said he thought some animals' intelligence was close to human intelligence. Then there were a lot of reports in the press about animals doing intelligent things. One man in Germany felt sure animals could probably even do maths and spelling and things like that, if only they were taught. He thought it wasn't fair that they weren't being given an education. So he tried to prove he was right. He spent thousands of hours trying to teach a cat, a horse and a bear how to read and spell and do maths. The bear didn't like it at all, and the cat wasn't interested, but the horse seemed to be learning."

Marcus chuckled. Becky continued, "After a while the man was convinced he'd taught the horse to do simple sums, and that he was even able to work out square roots and fractions. He was also convinced the horse knew the days of the week, how to spell quite a lot of words, and other things. He took him out to perform in front of the public. The horse became famous, and soon huge crowds flocked to see him."

Another student, one notorious for apparently lacking a sense of humour, overheard some of what Becky said, but not enough to understand the story, and interrupted, saying, "There's a horse that can spell and do maths? Don't talk daft! Then again, I suppose you are only about ten years old, aren't you."

A bit annoyed, Becky said, "Let me finish! Then you'll understand what I'm trying to say!"

Then she continued, "A lot of people thought the horse must have special powers, or that what seemed to be his abilities proved that if only animals had education, they could really get to be as intelligent as humans; in fact, some people estimated the horse's mathematical ability was equivalent to the average fourteen-year-old's. But some thought his owner was using some kind of trickery, which he denied. Some scientists came and tested the horse, and went away feeling sure he really did know maths and spelling. Even when his owner wasn't there, the horse could still answer questions he was asked correctly, in his way."

More students had overheard what Becky was saying, and were gathering around her to listen. She continued,

"The way the demonstrations to the crowds worked was that the horse's owner or someone in the crowd who'd come to watch would ask a question, and the horse would tap his hoof a certain number of times for the correct answer. The horse would almost always tap the right number of times, and sometimes even seemed to be correcting an audience member who answered for him but got the answer wrong, by tapping the right number of times.

"The horse would be asked questions like, 'Today's Wednesday. How many days have we got to go till next Monday?' The horse would tap five, the right number. Or he'd be asked to spell a word, by tapping once for A, twice for B and so on, with pauses between each letter. He would be asked to spell out the names of certain people and other things, and mostly got them right. Or the horse's owner would write out a number and ask the horse what it was, and as if he was reading it, he'd tap out the right number of times.

"Not all the scientists who tested the horse went away satisfied; some were still curious to know what could really be going on, so they gave the job of finding out to a psychologist who had some new ideas about how to test the horse.

"He compiled a long list of questions, so he could experiment a lot by asking the horse things, and testing him under different conditions. After testing for a while, he discovered that the further away a questioner was from the horse, the more difficulty the horse had in answering the questions correctly. And he found that when the horse couldn't see anyone while he was being asked the questions, or when he could only see one person but that they didn't know the answer to the questions being asked, he hardly got anything right at all. He couldn't even spell his own name any more.

"The researchers began to suspect that his abilities had something to do with looking at the people asking the questions; so they began to watch what was going on between the horse and the questioners.

"They discovered that almost always, the questioners, and the people in the crowds, unconsciously displayed body language that was different while the horse was counting and when he'd got to the correct number of taps. While he was counting up, there tended to be a very slight build-up of tension on their faces, because they were in suspense, wondering if he'd get the right answer; and the tension relaxed suddenly when he got to the right number. Also, a questioner tended to lean forward slightly when they asked a question, which it turned out that the horse recognised as his cue to start tapping; and either they or lots of people in the crowd would lean back slightly when he got to the right number, which he must have recognised as his cue to stop.

"If the questioner and a small number of other people thought the answer was something it wasn't, all the people in the audience who knew the right answer would still have that body language, and the horse was watching them.

"So what he'd really learned to do was not to do maths and spelling and reading and other such things, but to understand that their change of body language meant he ought to start and stop tapping. Watching the body language of the majority was what enabled him to do what seemed to be correcting people who were wrong. He must have learned to distinguish between the different kinds of body language over his many

many hours of training, and thought what he was doing was what his owner and the crowds wanted.

"When the horse wasn't getting the body language cues from the questioner or a crowd, he lost all his ability to answer questions correctly."

Quite an audience had gathered around Becky by then. She finished by saying:

"What I was saying in the lecture was that psychologists and other people doing studies and experiments can think one thing's going on, when actually something completely different's happening. So they can write misleading reports about what they've discovered. And people can believe them for years. That's what I've come to think because of things I've read anyway."

A lot of the students who heard Becky thought she'd taught them much more interesting things than they'd heard in their lectures that day.

Chapter 5

Becky and the Students With Her Tell Each Other Funny Stories and Discuss Such Things as Faulty Psychology Research

ecky and the students who'd gathered around her carried on talking.

Becky told them she'd heard some funny stories about how some people who'd done psychological research had thought they'd got certain results when they hadn't really, because they'd misinterpreted what was happening. She said:

"I heard about one study that was done where a psychologist thought he'd found that listening to Mozart makes people more intelligent. At least, reports of his study said he had. Even a scientific journal reported it, without finding fault with the idea. But the study hadn't been done very well, and the psychologist hadn't actually found what he seems to have thought he'd found at all.

"He'd separated the people who took part in the study into three groups: One listened to Mozart, one listened to a relaxation tape which had a monotonous musical droning noise in the background, and one sat in silence. Then they were all asked to cut a folded piece of paper in certain ways, and then try to guess how it would look when it was unfolded. Something like that anyway. The people who'd listened to Mozart guessed most accurately. The study was publicised, and all over the media, it was reported that listening to Mozart makes people more intelligent. One man even bought 100 thousand Mozart CDs for people – I think he was a boss and he bought them for people in his company, hoping to help them get brainier. People started thinking they could make babies in the womb more intelligent if they played Mozart to them, knowing they'd hear the music through their mothers' stomachs.

"But really, the study didn't prove that listening to Mozart's music increases people's brain power at all. Not only that, but the media exaggerated the claims the psychologist who'd done the study actually made – he didn't go quite so far as to say it does do that. But people who read the newspapers thought he did, because it sounded that way.

"The thing is that What happened in the study could have meant something very different from what people and the psychologist who carried it out thought it did. If you listen to a relaxation tape that makes you feel a bit sleepy, or sit in silence where you've got nothing to do, you'll probably get less alert, so you likely won't do so well at a task you're asked to do straight afterwards. So the findings could simply have been showing how well someone with average alertness levels would be likely to do, whether they'd been listening to Mozart or not, and how relaxation can slow down people's thinking a bit. It seems that no tests were done before the people in the study were split into groups to find out how well they did before they listened to anything, which would have been a good idea, since it would have found out if the people who listened to the relaxation tape had been more alert before they did that, and whether the concentration levels of the people who listened to Mozart really were better after they'd done that than they were before.

"It's a bit like something I heard recently about how the top story on the news one day was that dementia's now the biggest killer of old people in this country. When you hear about the headline, you think it sounds really bad, because it sounds as if dementia must be really on the increase; but I found out that although it is increasing, that's because more people are living longer so there are more people around to get it.

"And besides that, the statistic's hiding some really good news – that the reason dementia's now the top killer of old people is because deaths from other big killers like cancer and heart disease have gone down, partly because better treatments have been developed in the past decade or so, and partly because fewer people are getting heart disease and certain kinds of cancer than they used to because fewer people smoke, so they're avoiding what used to be a big risk factor for both; and a lot of people are reducing their risks by living healthier lifestyles in other ways, like eating more healthily and exercising more; and also there are medications that people who are found to be at risk for heart disease often get put on that help prevent it.

"So fewer people are dying from heart disease and cancer in middle age and young-old age than they used to, and fewer people are even getting it, so dementia's overtaken those as the biggest killer. But you might not hear that on the news.

"and actually, I heard that although dementia's on the rise, because there are more old people around than there used to be, the percentage of old people with dementia's decreasing compared to the percentage who used to get it, and that's thought to be because a lot of people live healthier lifestyles nowadays than a lot of people used to, so some of the risks for it are diminishing, because people are more at risk if they live unhealthily, although some risks are beyond a person's control. For instance, just ageing itself is a risk, I think.

"I heard about another statistic that hides good news like the dementia one does. It's another one that sounds bad at first, and it is quite bad, but it hides some good news that people might not realise just by hearing it. If I remember rightly, it's that suicide is now the biggest killer of middle-aged men in this country. I mean, that must mean something's wrong that really needs to be investigated and changed; but it doesn't necessarily mean there's more suicide now than there was before; it might mean there's about the same amount that there was before, but that the reason it's the biggest killer now is because other things that used to kill more middle-aged men than they do now, like maybe accidents at work, in places such as on building sites and down the mines, and car accidents, and heart disease, and maybe other diseases, have gone down a lot; so it's other causes of death decreasing, not suicide going up . . . Unless it's both.

"Anyway, about this study that supposedly discovered that listening to Mozart's music makes people more intelligent: After it was publicised, studies like it were done by other psychologists, and it was discovered that people who preferred another classical composer and listened to him did better in a test straight afterwards than people who listened to Mozart did. Then studies were done in schools that found out that people who'd listened to pop music did better than people who'd listened to classical music.

"Then studies were done that found that people who'd listened to mere bangs on the table did better than people who hadn't listened to anything.

"It was finally realised that it wasn't the music making a difference, but listening to any kind of sound that could cause people to concentrate on their surroundings more so it would increase alertness levels, like any sound that's new or sudden so you'd instinctively pay attention to it might; and the more the sound was enjoyed the better.

"But after all that, I don't know if the findings actually had any relevance to real life! I mean, for one thing, I don't know if they found out how long the effects lasted! And for another, I expect everyone knows it can be easier to slog through something you're not keen on doing if you've got music on in the background to make it a bit more enjoyable, and up-tempo music might help perk you up a bit; but if a lot of random sounds are going on at the same time as you're trying to concentrate on something, or you're having to listen to music you really don't like, it's going to distract you, so it'll make it harder to concentrate, so you'll probably get less work done, or you might do it less well.

"And besides, I don't suppose it would really go down well if a boss came in every morning and banged on the table a few times or something, telling the workers he was just trying to make them feel more alert so they'd do a better job!"

The students listening to Becky thought that was interesting and amusing. She told them a couple of other funny stories about studies and things, saying:

"A lot of studies get criticised because there aren't many people in them, since anything the people running the study think they're discovering could easily be just a result of chance if it's not happening to enough people for anyone to be more sure it's a real effect, and they might not find out quite a few important things they'd find out if they were studying lots of people. Like if they're studying whether a drug has side effects, and whether side effects only show up in some people, none might show up if there aren't many people in the study, because they might all happen to be people who don't get the side effects. But sometimes even when there are loads of people taking part in a bit of research, the results can be inaccurate, because there might be something about those people that sets them apart from other people in some way that means it'll be a mistake to think the study results apply to people in general.

"I read that in 1936, reporters for a magazine in America called The Literary Digest wanted to predict who would win the next election. They ended up predicting that one of the candidates for president would win quite a big victory over the other one. The staff working on the magazine sent out ten million postcards to readers, asking them to send them back with the name of the man they were going to vote for on them. A quarter of the postcards – two and a half million – were sent back, and there was a strong preference for one of the candidates. But the magazine got the prediction they based on that totally wrong – the other candidate won a massive victory.

"It turned out that even though the magazine poll asked so many people, all the people who were asked were well-off; and at that time, there was a lot of hardship and poverty in the country, so a lot more people weren't well-off, and most of those wanted to vote for the other candidate, since they thought he'd help them more, because he was promising to do that. The names of readers the postcards were sent to had all been taken from directories of people who owned phones and cars, or were subscribers to the magazine; and owning a phone or car was a luxury in the 1930s, and anyone with money to spare to subscribe to a magazine would have been one of the better-off people.

"So really, the people at the magazine could have worked out before they sent the postcards that the results wouldn't say much about how the country as a whole would vote, if they'd thought about it."

"Wow, so just one or two mistakes made by people doing a study could mean the whole study's invalid!" said one student, Stuart.

"Especially if they're big ones," said Becky with a smile.

Another student, Matthew, said that reminded him of a mistake a newspaper reporter made, saying:

"I heard that some prankster edited a Wikipedia page about a certain Cypriot football team to say their fans wore hats made of shoes, sang a song about a little potato, and were known as the 'Zany Ones'. One day they played Manchester City, and a newspaper journalist looked at Wikipedia for information about the team, and assumed that stuff was true, and put it in the paper's match reports."

Some of the students sniggered. Becky said, "I think that proves that it's often best to check facts with more than one source of information. I've looked for information in Wikipedia a lot, and there's loads of useful stuff there, but I suppose it could be edited by anyone, who could say anything! Let's hope people don't put untrue stuff in there very often!"

The students smiled and nodded in agreement.

Then some of them started telling the group about things they'd heard about studies that had been reported on as if they were respectable and their findings were true, when in reality they hadn't been done very well at all.

One of them, Kirsty, said, "I heard about a study – or maybe it was more than one – that found that you're less likely to die from things like heart attacks and strokes if you drink alcohol in moderation – say about one small glass a day – than if you don't drink at all. I heard that even some doctors started advising teetotal patients who'd had heart attacks to start drinking a bit, thinking it might be good for them because of that.

"But then another study came out that found that all alcohol's bad for people; and the people who'd done it said the reason the other ones had found that drinking in moderation's better than not drinking at all was because they made a mistake, counting former alcoholics and other people who used to drink heavily but who'd given up drinking because it had given them serious health conditions as non-drinkers. It also included people who'd never drank alcohol because they'd always been too poor to, which meant they were also too poor to buy much healthy food; and they tended not to bother with exercise.

"So more people in those groups were likely to die young than did in the groups of people who drank in moderation, not because they didn't drink at all, but because of their problems.

"The people who discovered what had happened in the first studies said that actually, drinking any alcohol risks putting the blood pressure up a bit, so it means your risk of having a stroke or heart attack goes up that little bit. Alcohol also has other harmful effects on the body.

"Mind you, hopefully none of us need to worry much about effects like that just yet."

One of the students, Debbie, said, "Wow, you would have thought the people who did the first studies would have checked for things like that, wouldn't you, maybe only comparing people who had similar levels of health to begin with!"

The others agreed.

Then Becky said, "I heard about an experiment that was done with people who thought they were drinking a bit too much. As far as I remember, they were given this task to do where lights would flash in front of them, and most of the time a blue light would flash, and they had to press a blue button whenever they saw the blue light. But sometimes a yellow light would flash, and when it did they had to press a yellow button. But especially at first, they often pressed the blue button by mistake when they saw a yellow light, because it was just automatic by the time they'd pressed it quite a few times when the blue light flashed. They practised and practised, and over time, they got better and better at pressing the yellow button when they saw the yellow light.

"The psychologist in charge of the experiment thought that must mean their self-control was increasing, since they were resisting the impulse to press the blue button and pressing the right one instead. And at the same time, they started getting better and better at resisting the urge to have an extra drink when they were tempted, so the psychologist thought the task to improve their self-control with the buttons must be improving it in other areas of their lives too, like by helping them resist the urge to drink.

"I don't know all that much about the study, so I might have missed some details, but I wondered if it really was to do with that.

"What I heard made me think, 'Hang on! What if the reason they got better at resisting the temptation to drink more than they should have was really because of any talks they had with the psychologists who were doing the study about it, or that the very act of thinking more than they normally would about how much they drank made them turn to thinking more about how they ought to cut down, or they felt more self-conscious about drinking than they had before they signed up for the study because they had to report how much they drank each day or week to a psychologist so they tried to drink less, or they just tended to go through phases of drinking a bit more than they should have done, and getting better at the exercise coincided with times when some of them drank less, or they enjoyed their talks with the psychologist and that made them feel as if they had a better social life or that it was nice that someone was taking an interest in them so they just didn't feel like drinking so much; or what if it was something else?'

"I think it's difficult to tell what's really causing the effect psychologists are finding with studies sometimes."

The other students smiled and murmured agreement.

Then One of them, Graham, said he'd been reading about flaws in some research just in the past few weeks. He seemed eager to talk about what he'd learned, for some reason. Oblivious to any sensitivities any of the students he was with might have to such topics of conversation, he said enthusiastically,

"I had a bit of a laugh recently, when I read about a study that was done to find out if women are somehow most attractive to men at the times when they're at their most fertile during the month. The researchers studied the amount of money lap dancers in a club got in tips from clients, and found that the tips were biggest at the times when they were at their most fertile. They reduced towards the times when their periods started, and were at their lowest when the women were actually having their periods. But it wasn't like that for women who were on the pill so they weren't fertile for any days in the month – there was no peak in their earnings.

"So the researchers confidently published the supposed finding that even though people are completely unaware of it, some hormone men can subconsciously smell must make women more attractive to them on the days in the month when they're at their most fertile. They said they thought it must be nature's way of encouraging breeding.

"I think there was a big problem with the research though: It seems the researchers were somehow convinced that if the lap dancers got the most money on the days of the month when they were at their most fertile, it would just have to mean that the males who were watching them were more attracted to them then, which would just have to be because they could subconsciously smell their hormones, which would just have to be making some kind of chemistry go on between them. But they completely overlooked other possible – and actually much more likely-seeming – explanations..."

It suddenly occurred to Graham that Becky, being so much younger than the others, perhaps shouldn't be hearing about lap dancers and things like that. He went bright red and hung his head. He mumbled an apology, and said he shouldn't have mentioned it.

But Becky reassured him it was alright, explaining to him that she'd learned about reproduction in biology at school, and that she'd heard some of the boys joking about how they'd like to go to clubs to see lap dancers, and that she'd looked it up on the Internet when she was eight, and though she didn't understand in the slightest and puzzled over why some grown-ups would get such a big thrill from such a thing, she at least knew they did, and put it down to just one more strange thing she'd learned about grown-ups since she'd come into the world, on a par for sheer weirdness with their strange habit of cooking what must surely be junk food for dinner and then telling their kids off for wanting to eat junk food if they asked if they could stop at a fast-food restaurant on family outings, saying it wasn't healthy, or the odd tendency of some of them to ask their kids to help peel the potatoes, and then tell them off for doing the job slowly, when they should realise that the faster they went, the more likely they would be to accidentally catch their finger with the potato peeler and shave a bit of skin off it.

Then again, maybe it was just her grandma who did that. Still, grown-ups were odd sometimes, Becky thought.

She couldn't understand why Graham had suddenly got so embarrassed, and told him she wanted to know what silly mistakes the men doing the study had made, so she wanted him to carry on talking about it.

So he did, though still looking embarrassed. Becky puzzled over why, but then concluded it must just be another one of those odd things grown-ups – or near-grown-ups – do sometimes.

He said, "I suppose it's possible that there's a lot more to this research than I know about, and that when you hear the full story it makes more sense, and maybe they really did find some kind of interesting effect that's worth knowing about, like the effect of a barely detectable smell of certain hormones or something. But just judging by what I heard, it sounds a bit daft.

"It seems it simply didn't occur to the men doing the study to wonder if something else could be causing the effects they discovered, such as the lap dancers perhaps feeling more self-conscious while they were having a period so they didn't give such a good performance – an effect that could be eliminated if they were on the pill because they could control when they had their periods, so as either not to have one at all while they were working, or to at least have it at its heaviest while they weren't, so they wouldn't have to worry about whether blood might leak out, or whether a man might notice they were wearing something to catch the drips.

"When they weren't on the pill, their earnings might have gone down quite a bit in the few days before they had their periods because they might have been anxious that they'd start one while they were working, and maybe worried that they would even start leaking blood at work before they even realised they had started one, so they might not have performed so well, whereas on the pill, they just wouldn't have had that worry, since it would be possible for them to have their periods when they chose to, like on their days off.

"Also, some women might look a bit bloated in the few days before their periods, or feel irritable and a bit down, so that could mean they didn't make such a good impression, so they didn't make so much money. Or maybe some of them had period pains or felt a bit sick and depressed during their periods, so they didn't perform as enthusiastically; again, on the pill, their periods would be lighter and likely wouldn't cause those effects, so there would be no change in their performance.

"The time when the lap dancers were at their most fertile would have been the time of the month when they could be most certain that their last period was sure to have properly ended and their next one wasn't about to start, because it would be the time when both of those things were furthest away from happening. So it might be the time in the month when they would likely be doing their work with the most confidence.

"So basically, it was the lap dancers' lowest rate of earnings, not their highest, that the researchers should probably have realised was the significant thing, that would have given them the best clues as to what was probably really happening.

"It seems that if only the men doing the study had kept an open mind to possible explanations for their findings other than the one they, for some reason, thought just had to be the right one, they might not have made the mistake they did. But their research was published in respectable scientific journals."

Graham suddenly felt ashamed of saying what he was saying in front of all the females in the group, not just Becky, and decided he'd better get away before he died of embarrassment. He'd noticed some of the female students looking at him in a disgusted or disapproving way, though some were smirking, and it had made him feel self-conscious. He was even more embarrassed when one commented,

"You can tell this study was done by a man, or men. All those things would be obvious to a woman researcher, so they probably wouldn't have even thought of inventing strange theories to explain things . . . Mind you, you're very insightful about it for a man!"

All the female students burst out laughing. Graham said, "Actually, to be honest, I only got to understand it like that from reading comments on it from women; it's just possible I'd have believed the study findings if I hadn't read those."

Then he told the group he had to leave, and walked off at a brisk pace, only to trip on a part of the wall that jutted out, because in his haste, he wasn't looking where he was going properly. He stumbled, and instinctively moved the leg he'd hit the wall with to the other side of the other one to get it out of further harm's way, but then lost his balance, spun around with the momentum caused by the speed he'd moved it at, and tottered back to them before he managed to steady himself. Someone in the group grinned and said, "Hello again."

Graham grimaced, turned back around, and went off at a much slower pace. No mishaps happened to him that time, and he managed to get away without stumbling and coming back again.

Another male student, Gavin, said, "What Graham said reminds me of a joke about bad studies where scientists or psychologists don't look for more than one possible explanation for why things in them are happening, and just interpret things the wrong way:

"A scientist had a frog on the table in front of him in a lab, and shouted, 'Jump!' The frog jumped a metre."

Gavin was about to carry on the joke when a tutor came out of the lecture theatre, and for some reason, he thought he'd better wait till the tutor had gone before continuing, as if there was something naughty or embarrassing about the joke. He was about to continue telling it, and had just opened his mouth to do so, when Becky interrupted him, jokingly asking, "Do you mean the frog understood English and was obeying his command to jump, or do you mean it jumped with fright because he suddenly made such a loud noise when he shouted?"

Gavin was a bit confused and said, "Um, I don't know. It doesn't say in the joke. It's not relevant to the joke anyway."

He carried on, "Anyway, the scientist cut one of the frog's legs off, and then yelled, 'Jump', and it only jumped half a metre. He chopped another of its legs off and yelled, 'Jump', and it jumped a quarter of a metre."

Kirsty interrupted and jokingly asked, "Are you sure this is a joke, not some kind of nightmare you had, or a horror film script?"

Gavin said, "No! Let me finish. The scientist chopped another of its legs off and yelled, 'Jump!' and the frog didn't move at all.

"He then carefully wrote in a book where he made a record of his study findings, 'I have discovered that when you chop three legs off a frog, it goes deaf.'"

A few students smiled. But Marcus said, "Yuck! Must you tell gory jokes in front of Becky?"

Gavin suddenly wondered if he'd just done a bad thing, and looked as embarrassed as Graham had, and covered his face with his hands too. He mumbled something about just trying to illustrate that scientists ought to look for more than one possible explanation for their study findings. Then, perhaps because his mind was clouded with embarrassment, he thought he'd better leave too, but he didn't want to trip over a jutting-out bit of wall and come spinning back towards them again like Graham had, a bit like a human boomerang; so for some reason, he decided to go off in the opposite direction, even though that wasn't the one he needed to go in if he wanted to get anywhere much, since all he'd get to going that way was the end of the building, since the lecture theatre was right near it. Still with his hands over his face, as if he somehow thought it didn't matter that he couldn't really see where he was going, he started walking. Unfortunately, he tripped over a chair and fell over. He wasn't hurt, but he was winded.

Marcus shouted at him, "Jump!"

Gavin didn't feel like jumping up right that second, before he'd even reached a conclusion about how much or little he'd been damaged, so he didn't move. Marcus joked, "Ah, I have discovered that when humans fall over, they cease to understand their own language!"

"Very funny!" Gavin said sarcastically, making a face.

Marcus said, "I bet a frog wouldn't find your joke funny either!"

Becky giggled and joked, "That's supposing the frog really could speak English, like the one in the joke that knew the scientist was telling it to jump." She hadn't minded the joke, so there was no need for Gavin to have been embarrassed really.

Another student, Dave, said, "I don't suppose even a frog would mind hearing that joke much, just supposing it could speak English, unless it had been traumatised by having its own legs chopped off, or by seeing people chop legs off other frogs, to cook for French people's dinners or something."

One of the group, Jackie, asked, "Do you think a frog really would be traumatised by seeing that? I don't know if frogs have feelings. I'm pretty sure some animals don't care about their own kind much – we had rabbits when I was younger, and one had babies, and she ate them! Still, I suppose it's possible she thought she was too young to be a mum, and the responsibility was really stressing her out, so she was just trying to rid herself of the problem or something. Not that that would be an excuse for a human to do it."

All the students thought that was yucky. But Debbie said, "Well I know some animals care about other ones; I've heard stories about chimpanzees and elephants looking as if they're grieving when their friends or family members die, and magpies even seeming to hold some kind of funeral services for theirs."

"Maybe some animals have feelings while others don't," suggested Stuart.

"But I bet none of them would find your joke funny Gavin," joked Marcus with a grin.

Gavin protested, "My joke wasn't meant to be funny. It was just meant to illustrate a point."

"Isn't the very definition of a joke something that's meant to be funny?" queried Kirsty.

"Oh I don't think so," smiled Matthew, who then grimaced as he said, "I've come across loads of jokes that weren't funny at all. A lot of them were just mean. I don't know what kind of people find jokes that are just bitchy funny!"

"But who has to find it funny for it to be classed as a joke, the people hearing it, or the person who makes it?" asked Jackie.

"I suppose it must be the person who makes it," said Debbie, "otherwise what would it have to be called if some people found it funny and some didn't, a semi-joke or something?"

They all smiled.

Dave said to her playfully, with no malice intended, "So does that mean that if I called you an ugly bitch and said it was a joke, it would be classed as a joke, no matter what you thought of it?"

They knew each other quite well, so Debbie knew he wasn't trying to be insulting. She said seriously, "It would depend on whether you sincerely believed it was a joke, I suppose. I think some abusive people call other people names and say other insulting things to them, and then claim they were only joking, just so they can get away with it, because they can say, 'Can't you take a joke?' if the other person complains. I think a lot of people probably make jokes just out of spite, like those blonde jokes on the Internet – I bet they're just made up by people with a big case of sour grapes, because they know they're a bit ugly and that other women are prettier than them, or they're men, and beautiful women don't fancy them, so they're resentful of them, and things like that. And I bet the people who laugh at those jokes are the same. So what they're doing is a bit like gloating; it's not just fun."

"Come on, let's go and get something to eat," called another student, Colin, with a good-natured smile. He hadn't heard all of what Debbie had said, just a bit of it, and joked, "What did you say, Debbie? You'd like to eat a big case of sour grapes? Yuck! Each to their own I suppose!"

They chuckled. They all decided to carry on discussing flawed studies and other things over lunch.

Chapter 6

Having Fun Doing a Show at a Local Community Radio Station

As part of Becky's media studies course, she helped to host a show on a local community radio station once a week for a few months with a few others from her course. They played some records, but most of the show was taken up with interviews of local people who were doing interesting things or trying to promote local events. The students had to write detailed reports for their tutor about how they planned what to do, how they found people to interview, any problems they had on the shows and how they solved them, and all kinds of things like that.

Becky enjoyed her programme. Sometimes she made mistakes while getting used to the radio equipment, but soon things began to go more smoothly. Some of the people she interviewed were entertaining.

She and her fellow presenters sometimes had fun thinking of new things to put on the show. One day, she and the others were in the studio after they'd done a programme when

Becky said for a laugh, "Hey, let's pretend we're broadcasting from a shopping mall one day. We can get sound effects off the Internet, as long as they haven't got any kind of copyright on them, or we could go and record some.

"Let's put the sound effect of a crowd in the background, and sound really excited about this special broadcast we're doing from the shopping centre, and pretend we've set up our equipment in a stupid place like in front of a few shop doorways, and people can't get in or out. Let's get a few people to pretend to be walking past, commenting while we're trying to be all enthusiastic, saying things like, 'Look at those idiots! They've set up broadcasting equipment right in the shop doorway so we can't get in!' And another one could speak to us, saying angrily, 'What is your problem? You've put that equipment right in people's way! You'd better move it quickly or I'm calling the police!' And then someone else can pretend to be a policeman telling us we're in the way and we need to move on, and when we protest, he can say we'd better move or we'll be arrested!"

One of the others, Carla, grinned and said, "Just think about what the tutors will think of us if we forget to tell them we're just pretending!"

They all laughed.

They liked the idea though. One of them, Kelly, said, "And how about if we go to a farm and record some farmyard sound effects, and then we could fade them in slowly during a show so it sounds as if animals are all coming into the studio.

"We could pretend to be shocked, saying things like, 'Oh no, why are all those animals coming in here? What will the tutors think if they find out? What are we going to do?'

"Then Becky could say, 'Don't worry; I expect they just want to join in. Let's let them all sing a nursery rhyme or something, and then they might be happy and all go away again.' We could say that sounds like a good idea and that we'll try it. Then Becky could say coaxingly, 'Come on animals, sing us a nursery rhyme.' We could have played around editing the animal sound effects before, and we could make each noise they do while they're supposedly singing play at a different pitch, and see if we can get them to sound vaguely like a nursery rhyme, to pretend they're singing.

"Then we can fade them out slowly and pretend they're walking out of the studio again, and all say things that make us sound relieved."

The students thought that idea would be good fun, although one, Nicola, said with a chuckle, "If we don't warn the tutors about what we're going to do, they might think we must be in danger and send the police around, and contact the radio station owner, or the environmental health department of the council or something, before they realise it's a joke. Maybe they'll realise we're just mucking around about ten seconds after they've spoken to the police, and have to ring them again straight afterwards to tell them it's just a bit of fun."

They all laughed.

Becky said, "Yeah, we'd better warn the tutors we're going to do it if we do.

"Maybe another thing we could do is pretend one of us keeps falling asleep and snoring. One of us could make the sound of loud snoring all of a sudden, and then they could pretend to wake up with a start, and fall back to sleep and snore half a minute later or something. They could do that a few times, always apologising for falling asleep, and then they could say they'd better go and rinse their face under the cold tap to wake themselves up. We could try to find the sound of a really powerful waterfall on the Internet, or ask if anyone knows where a real one is around here that we could go and record, and we could play that just after the person says they're going to rinse their face under the cold tap, so it sounds as if that's what the tap sounds like."

They giggled, and one of the group, Kim, said, "Maybe we'd better warn the tutors we're going to do that too, just in case they give us lower grades for not being able to stay awake."

"Or in case they contact the radio station owners," said Carla, chuckling, "to warn them we must be doing horribly dangerous things in the studio near their equipment with our own private waterfall."

They all laughed.

Then one of them, Philip, said, "Hey, how about we pretend we're fed up of our microphones because they keep picking up background noise from the studio we don't want them to pick up, so we say we're going to throw them in the bin, and that we'll just play music for the rest of the show without any talking. We could see if we can get hold of some gong sounds, and when we say we're throwing the mikes away, we could play them, and one of us could say, 'Wow, this bin does make a loud metallic noise when you throw things away, doesn't it!'

"Then one of us can say, 'Oh no, they're still picking our voices up, even though they're in the bin! That just proves they pick up things far away from them that we don't want them to. Let's smash them to bits!' Let's try and find a sound effect on the Internet of something really big being smashed, like a whole pile of plates, and play that just after we say we're going to smash the microphones. Then we can talk, and then one of us can say, 'Wow, do you know, those microphones are still picking up our voices, even though they've been smashed to pieces! They must be mega-powerful! Actually it's a shame to get rid of such impressive microphones as these! They're awesome! Let's get them out the bin and start using them again.' We can play a sound effect of picking up broken glass, and say, 'Let's try to fit them together again while we play this record.'

"Then afterwards we can just carry on as if nothing happened."

The others giggled, and Becky said with a grin, "The tutors are going to get worried . . . again, when they hear us say we're going to throw the mikes away. I wonder how long it'll be before they realise we're just messing around."

One of them, Collette, said, "Do you think they actually listen to our show? I wonder if they just take it on trust that we've done it."

They giggled again, and Carla said, "Well I wouldn't want to skive off doing something as much fun as this, even if no one at all listens to it! And imagine if we decided not to bother doing it, only to have to do about ten interviews in a few hours when they told us they wanted to hear them for our exams. Imagine phoning someone up in desperation because it's nearly the last minute, and saying, 'Yes, I know you're in bed by midnight most nights, and it might seem strange that we're asking you to stay up late to give us an interview in the middle of the night when we only want you to tell us about the time you gave your relatives turkey and roast potatoes mixed in with Christmas pudding on Christmas Day one year, telling them it was a special all-in-one Christmas dinner, because you didn't get on with them and wanted dinner to finish more quickly in the hope they'd go away sooner, but we really need you to do this interview now! Please!' "

The others laughed, and Kim said with a grin, "Yeah, we'd better do the shows for real."

Becky said, "The other day my mum was doing some washing up, and when she ran the tap to put the washing-up water in, I thought, 'This sounds a bit like a crowd of people clapping.'

"Wouldn't it be good if we played a record of something where there was an audience clapping at the end, and we mixed the sound effect of washing-up water running into a sink with the clapping, starting it after a few seconds of it, and then leaving it on for a while after the clapping faded out, to see if anyone emailed us asking why there was the sound of washing-up water running into a sink at the end of the record, and if our tutor noticed and asked us what we thought we were doing, or if no one commented!"

The others grinned. They thought it might be fun to try, just for a laugh.

Then Becky said, "I heard a broadcast once where someone had recorded an audience laughing, and they played some music that they'd mixed the laughs with, where bits of laughs were played in rhythm to the music, as if they were some kind of percussion. I loved it!"

Then she said, "Hey, how about we do a funny feature one day where we pretend clocks are coming into the studio all by themselves? You know some songs have a boring beat, where the drums just seem to do a loud monotonous high-pitched tap-tap-tapping all through the record, louder than anything else in the song? How about we play one of those, and pretend that a load of clocks hear it and think it's a clock, and decide it would be nice if they could join in, so they barge into the studio to ask us if they can? We could pretend I speak clock language so I can understand what they're saying.

"We could see if we can find lots of clock sound effects on the Internet, or see if we can think of people we know with loud clocks and ask them if we can record them, and then put all the recordings together into one, and fade the recording in gradually so it sounds like them all coming into the studio, getting closer and closer. Then one of us can say, 'Oh look! There are clocks floating into the studio all by themselves! I wonder what they could want! I hope they're not going to make a nuisance of themselves!'

"Then I'll say, 'I can speak clock language. I'll ask them what they want.' I'll click my tongue quite a bit so it sounds a bit like a clock, and then we can have just one clock making a noise, and we can pretend it's the boss clock and I'm talking to it. Then I'll tell you it's saying they've just heard a clock playing to the music on a record, and they'd like to do that too, so they want us to play some music where they can all join in.

"Then we can play a bit of that record again, maybe about half a minute's worth, and we'll play all the clock sounds at the same time, so it sounds as if they're all joining in.

"Then we could fade the record down, and one of us could say, 'That was nice. It actually made that record sound a lot better.' Then we could play a bit of the clocks again, and I'll tell you they're thanking us for letting them do that. We could say goodbye to them, and one of us could say it was nice of them to visit us, but if they want to join us again, it'll be nice if they knock first to let us know they want to come in."

The students in the group grinned, and Kelly said, "That's given me an idea: How about if we pretend a whole succession of things is coming through the studio. We could find the sound of a steam train, and start by fading that in gradually, and one of us could say, 'Oh no! There's a steam engine coming right through the studio! It could have knocked and asked our permission to come in first!'

"We can fade it out again so it sounds as if it's gone through and gone away out the other side. Then we can play the sound effect of a modern train fading in and a bit later fading out again, as if it's coming into the studio and going out the other side too; and while it's playing, we can shout things like, 'Oy! Train! How come you thought it was alright to come in here without our permission? You're disturbing a radio broadcast!' Then when it sounds as if it's going out, one of us can say, 'Trains are cold metallic things; they don't have hearts, so I suppose it's no wonder they just don't care about doing that!'

"Then we can fade up the sound of a bus and then fade it out, and pretend that's coming into the studio and going out the other side as well. One of us could say, 'Oh no, how many more things are going to think it's OK to just barge in here? The buses and trains of today, they've got no respect!'

"Then we can play the sound effect of a succession of cars coming and going. One of us could ask, 'Why do they think it's alright to just come through our studio like this? They aren't even knocking first! Did someone build a road through here while we weren't looking?'

"Then we could play the sound of a marching band coming through. We could shout things like, 'Oy! Stop that noise! You're humans, not cars; you at least ought to know better than them; after all, you're supposed to be a bit more evolutionarily advanced than cars and buses and trains!'

"When that's gone through, we could play the sounds of children playing, and pretend teachers are guiding a whole coachload of children on an outing through here. One of us could say, 'Honestly! Even teachers have no respect for privacy these days!'

"When they've gone out, we could pretend bicycles are coming through here ringing their bells. Maybe we could find enough bikes around here to record quite a few bell sound effects.

"And then when they've gone, one of us could say, 'Quick, shut the door!' We could have a door-shutting sound effect, and then one of us could say, 'Alright, which one of you left the door open when you came in?' as if they think that was the reason all those things came in here.

"One of us could sound apologetic, saying, 'I suppose it must have been me; I was the last one to come in. I just didn't realise all those things were going to come through here! I'll always make sure I shut the door from now on! We'll have to all make sure we do!'"

The students grinned. They thought that would be fun.

Lastly, Becky said, "How about if one day, one of us announces that they've found out some top-secret information leaked by a government source that forecasts that Armageddon's due to happen next Wednesday at midday. We could say the information hasn't been officially released to the public in case people panic, but that in a few days' time, the Met Office will issue the most severe weather warning they can issue, an Armageddon weather warning. They'll say there's going to be severe hail and thunder and very strong winds, but then the weather will stop altogether.

"We could record that announcement before our show, and we could put music in the background. Then we could play with the file we've made by mixing them together with an editing program on one of our computers, gradually speeding it up, with every ten seconds being slightly faster than the last one, or something like that. It might take a while to get it how we want it, but it should be fun when we have. When we play it on the radio, we can tell listeners that we understand it might be shocking and upsetting for them to find out Armageddon's happening in a few days, and that by the way, if they think the music and our voices were speeding up during the announcement, it's probably because they've got a medical condition we've found out about called speeded-up hearing syndrome, which people can get if they're feeling anxious, because the heart beats faster, and that makes all the other systems in the body go faster, which makes people hear things as if they're faster than they really are.

"We can say we'll put a nice slow soothing record on to calm them down; and we can really put a fast one on. Then we'll say that if they think it was fast, they must have a very bad case of speeded-up hearing syndrome, but that if they just go and have a lie down, they should be perfectly alright again soon."

Becky's fellow presenters grinned and giggled. They liked the idea of doing all those things.

So they did. They did a funny feature every week, and listeners started expecting one. No one seemed to take them more seriously than they were meant.

One of Becky's co-presenters was a student called Andrew White, a young black man. He was in an amateur dramatics group, and was often rehearsing for their next play in the evenings. Sometimes the group members wrote plays themselves. Andrew had recently had an idea for one, although he thought it might make a better film than a play, because it needed special effects that might be hard to do in a live play – a comic horror fantasy about a mad scientist who genetically engineered a load of mice to be more intelligent, and altered their anatomies so it was possible for them to talk if they were taught to. The plot had it that the scientist somehow encoded the alterations he'd made to their vocal cords into their genes, so their offspring would be able to talk too, and then he taught them all to speak English and let them go into the wild.

In Andrew's story, they bred with other mice, and when their offspring were born with the ability to talk, the genetically engineered parent mice taught them to. They went to live in all kinds of places, mainly holes in the walls of people's houses. They would scare the people living there every so often by creeping out and talking about what they were doing.

For instance, a couple had just gone upstairs to bed one night when they heard a spooky high-pitched cackly laugh, and a very high-pitched voice coming from downstairs saying, "These are the special chocolates they got for Christmas! Now I've gnawed through the box, I'm starting on the chocolates! Yum yum!" Mice would talk like that as they ate food in people's houses, like ultra-midget burglars. The play was full of scared and puzzled couples, either hiding, or running about their houses looking for whoever or whatever had been nibbling their things. The mad scientist hadn't made it public that he'd taught mice to talk and released them into the wild, so even when they caught the mice at it, they couldn't believe what was happening!

A boy was doing his homework one evening when he heard a high-pitched voice from under his desk that said, "Yum! These shoelaces taste nice!" He felt something nibbling his shoelaces and looked down. He saw a mouse, and realised it must have spoken, and jumped up in horror and ran out of the room. But he braved going back in the room ten minutes later, only to find the mouse had nibbled through his homework! He said, "Oh no, that took me hours!"

The next day, he told the teacher at school that he was sorry he couldn't hand his homework in, but a talking mouse had eaten it. The teacher didn't believe him and punished him, thinking he just hadn't done it and was making up a stupid excuse. The boy was annoyed, and decided to get revenge and show the teacher the mouse was real. That night, he managed to catch the mouse and put it in a box. He brought it to school the next day.

The teacher was writing on the blackboard when she heard a strange high-pitched voice from behind her doing a spooky long cackly laugh and saying, "Yum! This paper tastes nice!" The teacher was startled, and looked around to see a mouse on her desk, nibbling her notes! She ran out of the classroom in horror, and wouldn't dare come back for the rest of the lesson. The kids loved it. They were all teenagers, and spent the time playing games and chatting. Some of them egged the mouse on to eat more of the teacher's notes. But they weren't so happy about it being there when it decided it had had enough of the notes and started jumping into their school bags to see what it could find there! They chased it out the door, and it ran straight for the school kitchens, and there was a big chase, and it got horribly close to the kitchens before it was caught and put back in the box it came in.

Eventually the mad scientist who'd made the talking mice was arrested. All the mice were rounded up – teams of professional mouse catchers were sent out to get them. They were all put in cages and sent to a country far away, and sold as pets there.

The mad scientist was taken to court and banned from science labs for life, and given ten thousand hours of community service, having to sweep the streets and pick up litter for hours and hours a day for ages, to keep him out of mischief, so he couldn't spend time inventing anything else that would be a menace to society.

Andrew was trying to think of how to turn the story into a stage play, hoping it could be done somehow.

Becky liked to go and watch the plays Andrew was in. And she enjoyed it when he talked over the ideas he had for new plays with her. She came up with a few good ideas for him to use herself.

One day at the radio station, Andrew said for a laugh that if they ever ran out of people to interview, he'd be willing to play the part of someone improbable for fun, and they could do a joke interview. For instance, he'd pretend to be Henry VIII, and Becky could interview him about his life, and they'd both pretend to be very serious, at least till near the end, and they'd see how listeners reacted.

Becky had giggled when she first heard Andrew's surname. He told her a lot of people did that. He'd often seen people looking surprised or trying to stop themselves grinning or laughing when his name had been called in a doctor's waiting room or some other place and he'd got up, and people had seen that the man whose surname was White was black. For years he'd been a bit self-conscious about it, but by the time he went to university, he was used to it, and usually just tried to ignore people's reactions, though he actually found some amusing.

One day he interviewed a woman called Mrs Green for the show. Before the interview, she told him she was surprised to have been told his name was Andrew White, only for him to turn out to be black, not white. He joked, "Well imagine my own surprise when I heard that you were called Mrs Green, only for you to turn out to be white, not green at all!"

She chuckled, and quipped back, "Actually my friends do tell me I've got green fingers; I've got some lovely big plants in my garden! And when I went on a ferry to France once, the sea was a bit rough and I started feeling a bit seasick, and my face might have turned a bit green by the end of it!"

Becky thought it would be fun to interview people who'd ended up with red faces. She suggested they go out and see if people were willing to be interviewed about funny or embarrassing experiences they'd had for the show. The others liked the idea. So they went out to try to find people to interview.

Some couldn't remember any stories. Some could, but they felt way too embarrassed about them to have them recorded and broadcast on the radio. But several people were willing to tell them about amusing embarrassing things that had happened to them, and it turned out to be a good show.

A retired lady called Mary said:

"Once when I was a young teacher, a little boy called Charles came to school with a basket covered by a cloth. 'Look what I've got in here Miss!' he said, taking off the cloth, and out jumped a young rabbit, absolutely terrified from having been brought to school on the bus – thank goodness he didn't escape on the bus! The rabbit hopped frantically around the room, darting under every desk and into every cupboard, hotly pursued by 24 excited squealing children and the teacher! Suddenly a voice spoke from the doorway, saying, 'Whatever is happening here?' It was the rather severe headmaster, who was waiting for our class to arrive so he could take assembly in the hall underneath our classroom, and he had come to find out what all the racket was about. Curbing their excitement, the children followed him out of the room and downstairs, while I was left to catch the rabbit, put it in its basket and take it to the caretaker to look after for the day."

An old lady called Ruth told them some stories, all about things that had happened in the 1950s.

The first was about when she was training to be a nurse. It didn't happen to her, but to another nurse. The nurses who were on night duty had to cook breakfast for the patients, starting with putting bacon on to cook slowly at five o'clock in the morning. Some patients' families would bring them eggs to eat with it, and the nurses would write the patients' names on them so they'd know who to give them to. They were supposed to butter bread for the patients too; they were supposed to do that just before they gave the food to the patients.

But since there was a lot to do, the nurses could feel rushed; and sometimes they buttered the bread earlier than they'd been told to. The matron on the ward was a stern strict disciplinarian, and they didn't want her to find out they'd done it, so they would put it outside on the fire escape so she wouldn't see it . . . Or at least, that's what they thought. But they discovered she'd found out what they were up to. One night, she phoned the nurse who was on breakfast duty, and said with mock politeness, "Could you bring the bread and butter in from the fire escape? It's started to rain, and it must be getting wet!"

Another woman told them that when she was a child, she went on holiday to Ireland with her family. One day they stopped at a petrol garage to refuel the car, and her mum went for a toilet break while they were there. When she was coming back, they noticed she must have accidentally tucked the end of the toilet roll into her tights somehow. As she walked across the garage forecourt, the toilet paper was unravelling and unravelling; there was a long trail of it stretching out behind her, all the way back to the loos. She couldn't remember if her mum was embarrassed; she was too busy laughing.

Another retired teacher said she used to teach in a town where there's a famous horse race once a year, one the Queen and other members of the Royal Family go to watch. She told them that afterwards, they would drive slowly out of the town, and people would come out to wave to them. She said she used to work at a school on the Queen's route out of the town, and she knew the Queen would be travelling past there a couple of hours after the race, because she always did. It was held on a school day in those days.

On the day of the race one year, she told her class of little children that if they came back to the school a couple of hours after school had finished with their parents, and looked out for a black car travelling slowly with flowers on it, it would be the Queen, and they could cheer as she went past.

At breaktime, she went into the staffroom, And the teachers in there heard a great cheering and yelling from outside. They went to see what was going on, and they saw all the children near the school railings, loudly cheering and waving, while a hearse was going by!

The headmistress said, "Oh well, at least the dead person got a good send-off."

A teacher called Abigail said she'd once accidentally tucked her skirt into the back of her knickers after she'd been to the loo at school, and walked into the staffroom like that. She said thankfully there was only one other member of staff in there, a female.

Ruth told them other stories, all of which happened to her personally. She told them she'd worked for some time as a district midwife, going to people's homes to deliver babies. One busy night in about the 1950s, she went to deliver the baby of a woman who'd already had two children, who was home alone. Her husband had gone to take her other children to their grandparents' home for them to babysit for a while, and he hadn't come back yet.

The woman had the baby, and Ruth cleaned up afterwards. There were a couple of buckets of dirty water she needed to tip away. But there wasn't a toilet in the house; it hadn't yet been modernised; the family had to use a communal one halfway down the street. So she took the buckets down there to get rid of the water. When she came back, she realised she'd locked herself out! The door had locked automatically when she shut it. She realised she should have put it on the latch.

So she had to call through the letterbox, explaining that she'd accidentally locked herself out; and a woman who'd had a baby less than an hour earlier had to get up and answer the door. Ruth was thankful they'd brought her bed downstairs for the baby to be born.

She made a mental note to make sure to remember to put a door on the latch if she ever needed to go out to tip dirty water away again. Thankfully most houses had their own toilets by then though.

Another story Ruth told was about when she was delivering another baby at night. She'd just delivered it, and was just waiting for the afterbirth to come out, when the lights went out. There was a friend in the house with the woman who'd just had the baby that time. It was just as well. The new mother said the lights must have gone out because the money in the electricity meter had run out. She needed to put another shilling in it, but she didn't have one. Neither Ruth nor the woman's friend had one either. So the woman asked her friend if she'd go across the road and ask a neighbour for a shilling.

Ruth decided that from then on, she'd always take a torch with her when she went out delivering babies.

The students collected other embarrassing stories as well as those ones. After the programme, quite a few listeners wrote in to tell them how much they'd enjoyed it. The students had enjoyed making it themselves!

Chapter 7

Becky Gets to Interview the Brother of a Famous Pop Star for her Radio Show

Becky struck up a friendship with a girl on her psychology course called Karen. Karen lived close to the university, and lived at home, like Becky. Her parents were church-goers, and Karen went with them every week.

One day, Karen told Becky that there was a man who went to her church called Michael Green, who was the brother of one of the founder members of the pop group Fleetwood Mac, Peter Green. Becky only had a vague idea about who Fleetwood Mac were, having been born a year or so before the start of the new millennium, which was long after the time when they were at their most active. But she was interested to know more. She immediately thought it would be great to interview someone like that on her radio show. She thought the tutors would be bound to be impressed with her, and might even give her higher grades because of it. She thought it sounded as if it would be fun to do anyway.

She asked Karen if she'd mind if she came to church with her one day, and if she could introduce her to Michael there.

Karen agreed. Then Becky checked that it would be alright with her mum, since it would mean spending part of the day with another family. Her mum thought it sounded like a good opportunity.

Becky thought she'd better look on the Internet to learn a bit about Fleetwood Mac before she tried to interview a brother of one of the founder members, so she would have a better idea of what to ask him; and also, she thought it might come across as a bit rude or strange if she were to ask him for an interview, only to have to admit a bit later that actually, she didn't really have much of an idea of who Fleetwood Mac even were.

So she went online to find some information. She discovered that Peter Green had started playing in bands in the 1960s, before he was 20. Then he got what could maybe be called a lucky break, when he was asked to stand in for Eric Clapton, a famous guitarist and pop star, for a few concerts, in a band called John Mayall's Bluesbreakers. He became a full-time member of that for a while when Eric Clapton left soon afterwards, and then he left to start Fleetwood Mac.

Becky read that the band had a lot of chart success, including with songs Peter Green wrote himself, such as an instrumental called *Albatross*, which got to number one in 1969.

Becky read on, and found out that Peter Green left Fleetwood Mac in 1970, because after having been introduced to the drug LSD, he started taking quite a lot of it, and his mental health got worse and worse because of the drug's effects, and he developed schizophrenia. Fleetwood Mac carried on without him, and had a lot more chart success, for years. Peter Green did play on a couple of their songs after that, as well as doing solo projects later on, and playing with a few other musicians.

Becky thought up some questions she thought it would be good to ask Michael Green about his brother Peter, and one Sunday morning, her mum drove her to Karen's house, and then she went with Karen and her family to their church.

After the service, it was the custom there for tea, coffee and biscuits to be served in the church hall to members of the congregation who wanted them. Becky hoped to meet Michael there. She was carrying some recording equipment with her.

Karen hadn't told Michael about Becky, so he had no idea he was about to be asked for an interview.

Karen introduced Becky to Michael while they were having coffee. After a couple of minutes of conversation, Becky told him she was doing a show with some other students on a community radio station as part of a media studies course she was doing at university, and said she wondered if he'd mind if she interviewed him. She took out her recording equipment from a bag she'd been carrying it in, and suggested they go outside where it was quieter.

Michael wasn't sure what to make of it. A little girl, only about ten years old, was telling him she was actually at university, doing a media studies course, and presenting a radio show! He asked her how she'd got to be at university at her age, wondering if someone was playing a trick on him.

He was even more surprised and puzzled when she told him she'd been told she was a genius, who could say some words from the time she was born, and she'd been sent to school when she was only a year old, and had finished when she was ten. Karen told him it was true.

It all sounded strange to Michael. But he didn't see what harm a short interview could do, so he told Becky to wait till he'd finished his coffee, saying that then he'd find a quiet spot with her where she could do the interview.

A few minutes later, he had finished, and they went outside and found somewhere fairly quiet. There were a few people milling around or getting ready to go home, but not many.

Becky was just about to start recording when they heard a dog barking on the other side of a fence. It wouldn't stop! At least for several seconds! Becky felt annoyed, and joked, "If anyone here can speak dog language, tell that dog that if he doesn't shut up, I'm going to take him home with me and ask my mum to put him in a pie!"

She quickly added much more quietly, as if in confidence so the dog wouldn't hear her, "Well, he'll probably be safe, actually, because my mum never makes pies, or does much home cooking at all really, more's the pity. And she probably likes dogs too much to be persuaded to let us eat one anyway; but don't tell the dog that . . . Actually, I don't really fancy eating dogs myself."

The others there were relieved to hear that.

Then Becky felt a bit embarrassed, wondering if she ought to be making jokes like that in front of the brother of a famous pop star. But she thought that as long as what she'd just said didn't become famous too, she'd probably be alright.

Thankfully, the dog did stop barking after Becky made her threat to try and persuade her mum to put him in a pie, just as if he could somehow understand human language. Perhaps he'd just barked so much he'd lost his voice, or got bored of barking, or he'd only ever intended to bark for several seconds anyway, or he'd found something better to do or something.

They waited for a minute or two, but the dog didn't start barking again; so Becky thought it might be alright to stay there and do the interview, instead of trying to find somewhere else to do it.

So she started recording, and introduced Michael.

Michael said, "Hello Becky. It's nice to meet you, and I'm pleased to answer the questions about my famous brother Peter Green of Fleetwood Mac."

Karen had come out with them. She grinned and said, "You don't know what the questions are yet. You might not be so pleased to answer them when you hear them!"

Becky said, "Shush!" Then she asked Michael, "OK, my first question is, do you have any fond, amusing or interesting memories from when you and Peter were children? Can you tell me about a few?"

Michael replied, "Well, here's one: We had some nice family holidays at the seaside, and I once remember Peter on the beach mounting a donkey, and when it started to trot, Peter fell off. Peter was nine years of age then."

Becky wondered why that would be a 'fond' memory, and felt like asking about the state of brotherly love between them, or whether Peter had hurt himself. But she thought he at least couldn't have hurt himself too much, or he'd never have been able to go on to be a pop star; and she thought she'd better not ask Michael questions that might sound a bit rude, such as whether he and his brother were fond of each other, in case he changed his mind about being interviewed.

So she just asked him the next question she'd planned to ask him, which was, "How did Peter and Fleetwood Mac become so famous, when lots of other bands don't? What did they do differently, or what lucky breaks did they get?"

Michael replied, "These questions are things I'd really have to think about to give good answers, because they happened decades ago, so they take a bit of remembering. But I'll give it a go: Peter was playing in a band called John Mayall's Bluesbreakers, and the drummer in it was Mick Fleetwood, and the bass player was John McVie; and when Peter left the band, he took Mick and John with him, and started a new band which he named Fleetwood Mac. It was Peter's exceptional guitar playing and songwriting that made the group successful with their album recordings. It was in the late sixties."

Becky couldn't think of any questions that Michael might be able to answer more easily than the ones she'd planned to ask him right then, so she carried on asking ones where the answers might take some remembering, even though there wasn't much time for Michael to remember anything. She asked, "What are some of the highlights, and some of the lowlights, of Peter's experiences of touring and recording music?"

Michael said, "The band toured the world and became a number one worldwide group. But during these tours, they began to take drugs. This affected Peter's mental health, and it caused him to leave the band in 1970."

Becky thought about asking for details; but Michael had said he'd prefer it if it was a short interview, since he was planning to go home and have his dinner soon. So she asked the next question she'd decided beforehand to ask him: "What has been your own involvement in Peter's career?"

Michael said, "Our older brother gave Peter an acoustic guitar when Peter was about ten and a half years old. I bought a guitar, and Peter and I started playing together. Peter sang and played, and we did this for about four years, and it helped Peter to develop his playing, and knowledge of playing songs on the guitar."

Then Becky said, "I read that he developed schizophrenia, which was thought to have come on because of drugs he took. Has it been in remission for some time? What has helped him most in controlling his symptoms, and what kinds of things has he found trigger them off? Is there any advice he would want to give to sufferers and their families about ways of keeping symptoms at bay, and also to young people getting into drugs, who might be putting themselves at risk of mental illness?"

Michael was a bit taken aback that Becky was asking such personal questions. Becky thought she'd better reassure him that she wasn't just being nosy, and said, "I'm interested in these kinds of things because I'm interested in psychology. I'm doing a psychology course at university as well as my media studies course."

Michael was even more surprised than he'd been before, hearing that a little girl of about ten years old wasn't just doing one university degree, but two! He wondered if he could be dreaming!

But he thought it would be best to just answer the questions, instead of asking her more about it, since she was still recording. He thought about how best to answer, but didn't want to say too much. He said, "Peter doesn't really like to get publicity about the problems he had in the past because of drugs."

Becky said, "Oh don't worry; the radio station I do my shows on is only little; I bet hardly anyone even listens! Probably mostly just our tutors, actually, because our shows go towards our grades, so they have to listen whether they want to or not! Anyone who has the choice might not though . . . well, except my mum, and the mums of the other students on the show, and anyone who tunes in to it by accident, maybe."

Michael chuckled and said, "I expect a few more people listen in than that!"

Then he said, "OK, I'll give you an answer . . . Um, sorry, what was the question again? Or should I say, half a dozen questions; I can't quite remember them all. You'd be better off asking fewer at a time from now on."

Becky made a mental note to edit out his criticism of her asking lots of questions at once before the show went to air. After all, she wouldn't want her tutors deciding they agreed with him! Then she repeated all the questions at once. Michael replied, seriously,

"Yes, Peter went through a bad time in the late sixties with LSD trips, and it had a profound effect on his well-being. But with medication and support from his family, he began to get rehabilitated, and today he's back to good mental health. It's a big problem nowadays – drugs causing mental health problems – and young people have to be careful where they choose to enjoy themselves."

Then Becky moved on to her next question, and asked, "What's Peter doing nowadays?"

Michael told her, "These days, Peter's a keen fisherman, and loves to go fishing in the rivers or sea. He's on a break from touring at the moment, so he finds it relaxing away from the public eye."

Becky had never understood why anyone would want to catch fish for fun. She thought it would be a laugh to ask a silly question like, "Does he catch donkeys too, and maybe cook them for tea, to get revenge for the one he fell off when he was a child?" But she thought she'd better not ask a question like that, especially because Michael's wife had come out and was watching them, and Becky wondered if she might be impatient for them to leave so she and Michael could go and have their dinner (which presumably wouldn't consist of roast donkeys); so she thought she'd just stick to the questions she'd planned to ask.

So instead, she asked a serious question, saying, "What advice would Peter – and you too – give to people who would like to go into the music business?"

Michael, knowing nothing of Becky's thoughts about donkeys, perhaps fortunately for Becky, replied, "There are many avenues to explore, depending on your talent; and if you wish to get work or make recordings, you will need a good entertainments agent and manager. Also there are societies like BASCA – that is the British Academy of Songwriters, Composers and Authors in London you should join, who can help you with improving your talent, and also point you in the right direction to showcase your talent."

That was Becky's last question, and she thanked Michael for being willing to do the interview. She told him when she planned to put it on the air, in case he wanted to listen.

Karen's parents were hoping to get home soon so they could have dinner themselves. So they were pleased when Karen and Becky went up to them and told them they'd finished the interview. But they thought it was good that Becky had done it, and said they'd listen to the programme when it was on.

The media studies tutors were pleased when Becky played it on the radio programme she did with other students. And word got out that the interview was going to be on, and it turned out that quite a few people listened after all. Several students did, and came up to Becky afterwards when they saw her around and congratulated her.

Chapter 8

Good Times Having a Laugh With Friends

Becky had several friends she could chat with about amusing ideas. They would quite often have wacky conversations just for a laugh.

One day, her friend Sharon asked her, "How would you like to sleep on a bed of raw runner beans?"

Becky said, "I expect it would be quite bumpy and hard. I don't think I'd like it much; but imagine if they were still on the beanstalk – you'd have to sleep standing up!"

Sharon said she knew someone who could sleep standing up; he could literally lean over a washing line and fall asleep.

Becky asked, "Hasn't he ever broken anyone's washing line?"

Sharon replied, "Not so far. Well, he doesn't do it very often."

Becky said, "Do you mean he doesn't break them very often, or he doesn't sleep on them very often?"

They laughed, and Sharon said she'd meant he didn't sleep on them often.

Then Becky said, "Wouldn't it be good if people could do all the boring things they have to do like washing up and ironing in their sleep, so they wouldn't even know they were doing them!"

Sharon said that sounded dangerous! Then she told Becky she'd heard of people sleepwalking and doing all kinds of weird things, like stuffing themselves with food in their sleep or trying to chase supposed monsters out of their houses.

Becky said, "If we sleepwalked into lectures, I wonder if the lecturers would notice any difference. Maybe they'd just think we looked just a bit sleepier than usual, or that we must be so bored we were falling asleep, even before their lectures started."

"Imagine if we sleep talked too! Imagine what we might say to the lecturers!" said Sharon.

Becky laughed and said, "Yes! Imagine if someone sleep-walked into a psychology lecture, and then interrupted it and announced, 'I've just read an important journal article that will change the way the world thinks about psychology, and will mean you'll have to stop teaching it too. It's been discovered that every single psychological problem is caused by eating cheese sandwiches. If everyone gives up eating them, no one will have any mental problems any more. All psychologists will have to find new jobs, and so will all psychology professors like you. This whole course will be closed down soon.'

"Imagine if they carried on, 'The important journal article explains everything: It's been found that one way eating cheese sandwiches causes problems is that it makes mothers shout at their children more, and being shouted at a lot gives the children a whole load of mental health difficulties. But cheese sandwiches directly cause mental health problems too. It's not the cheese itself that's the problem, but the chemical interaction between the cheese, the bread and the margarine or butter when they're put together. But different cheeses have different effects: When mothers-to-be eat sandwiches with hard cheeses in them, it predisposes their young children to problems like depression. Cream cheeses cause anxiety; that processed sliced stuff wrapped in cellophane gives people anger and jealousy problems – especially when they can't undo the wrapping; and that granulated stuff in tubs they sprinkle on pasta and things causes schizophrenia.

" 'Now they know things are all that simple, we don't need psychology departments in universities any more. The university chancellor's coming soon to tell you he's closing this one, and all the lecturers will need to find new jobs. Cheese sandwiches are just going to be banned, and then everyone will be happy and never have mental problems again. So you may as well stop teaching us all this outdated stuff now.' "

Sharon laughed, but then said with a grin, "Oh what a shame it would be if cheese sandwiches were banned! I love them!"

Becky replied, "So do I. But if I said they'd discovered they were the cause of all mental problems in a lecture, and then talked about all those different kinds of cheese, I wonder if they'd believe me. They'd be daft if they did. I mean, for a start, no one even puts that grainy stuff in a tub they sprinkle on pasta and things in sandwiches! Imagine eating pasta sandwiches!"

"That's an interesting thought," Sharon said. "Some people might eat them though, you never know. But imagine if everyone did believe you, and all the students walked out!"

They giggled.

Then Becky said, "Or imagine someone sleepwalked into a history lecture and announced, 'I've just heard on the news that the government have decreed that history is a pointless subject that only causes problems, because learning about what countries did to each other in the past just stirs up ethnic hostilities, and we don't want that to happen. So from now on, any history teacher will lose their job unless they teach about the future instead. And they'll have to make their teaching sound good. You're teaching about things that happened 200 years ago. You need to stop now and teach about things you predict might happen in 200 years' time or so, based on your knowledge of where scientific progress and other things in the world are heading.' "

Sharon said, "It would be funny if the lecturer believed it and tried to do that.

"Or imagine if someone sleepwalked into a geography class at school and declared, 'It's just been announced on the news that the capitals of France and Brazil have swapped names. They've signed a pact of friendship and declared they're twin cities, and as a sign of their new bond, they've taken on each other's names, and they say it's permanent. So the capital of Brazil is now Paris, and the capital of France is now Brasilia. All the textbooks that have the old names of their capitals will have to be rewritten. Schools like this one will have to get rid of all the old ones.' I wonder what the teacher would say."

Becky said, "Imagine if the governments of France and Brazil decided they wanted their capitals themselves to swap places, for real, perhaps during the summer when the children were on holiday, and the governments thought it would be a nice holiday treat for them. Imagine if it was scientifically possible, and they had the technology to do it. Imagine if they dug them right out of the earth and towed them behind huge ships for thousands of miles."

Sharon said, "They'd have to get them out of their countries first! How would they do that? They couldn't tow them right across the land, because for one thing, there'd be too many people and things in the way. They'd have to lift them miles and miles up into the air somehow, and ferry them to the sea in the sky. And how far would they have to dig down to make sure the capitals didn't just fall to bits when they were moved?"

Becky said, "I don't know. Maybe they'd have to dig down miles and miles. And maybe they'd somehow get lots of powerful rockets underneath them and blast them up into the air, and send them hurtling into the sea."

They laughed, and Sharon said, "I wouldn't fancy living on one when it happened! But the capitals would be different shapes and sizes, so each one wouldn't fit in the place where the other one was!"

Becky replied, "Maybe they'd have to chop bits off each one to make it the same shape and size as the hole the other one came from, and then hurtle the chopped-off bits into the sea on massive rockets to make new islands."

Sharon laughed and said, "Wow, it would be even worse living on the bits that got chopped off than it would be living on the main bits that got towed across the sea! And how would they get the cities back in the land again when they got there? They couldn't just hurtle them around on rockets again and hope they landed in the right places; they'd have to be very precise about where they put them."

Becky said, "Maybe when they were in the sea, the governments would realise they hadn't quite planned for that bit, and that the technology hadn't quite been invented yet, and the cities would have to drift around in the sea for years till they did."

Sharon said, "I don't know if I'd like to live on one while that was going on! And how would they stop people falling off the edges? I suppose they'd have to build big fences all around them to stop people falling off when the wind blew and the waves got high and they rocked and things. And they'd have to put big fences around the places in the countries where the cities used to be to stop people falling in the massive holes left there."

Becky said, "Imagine dropping a pebble down one of the holes! I bet you wouldn't hear it hit the bottom!"

Sharon said, "Maybe you'd have to drop a great big boulder down there to hear it. Mind you, you still might not. Maybe if someone pushed loads of things at once down there they might. Hey, imagine if the hole was so deep it reached down to the bit near the centre of the earth where it's molten and it's . . . I don't know – I think they reckon it's a few thousand degrees centigrade or something. They could drop all the rubbish in landfill sites down there, and it would be incinerated, so that would be a great way to get rid of it all!"

Becky said, "Imagine if they'd accidentally made the hole so deep it reached almost to the other side of the world, and not all the rubbish burned up, but some of it just kept on going till it got cooler again and then landed on the bottom of the hole. The pressure from all the rubbish might mean what was left of the earth in the hole gave way, and all the rubbish busted out the other side. And to the people who saw it, it would look as if it was going upwards, not down. And imagine it was going so fast it busted out of the earth and hurtled up into the sky, and they never saw it come down anywhere. The people in the country where it came out might not know why it had happened, and invent a new law of physics that said that sometimes gravity reverses itself, so in some places things fall upwards, not downwards."

Sharon said, "Imagine if the rubbish flew up with so much momentum it went really far, and it hit the moon, and it was so hot it burned big parts of it off! If people didn't know it had happened, imagine if spaceships that went up to the moon reported that it was a different shape from the shape earlier astronauts had said it was!"

Becky replied, "They might think the earlier astronauts and astronomers had made a mistake about the shape of it because they didn't have such sophisticated equipment to look at it with in those days."

Sharon said, "Or imagine if a lot of the rubbish landed on the moon, but no one realised it had done it. When astronauts landed on the moon and found it, they might think it was evidence of life on the moon, and go traipsing around it trying to find the civilisation that had left it there."

Becky said, "Or maybe they'd think it must have been left by an ancient civilisation that must have lived there when the moon was easier to live on, and scientists might develop theories about how it used to be easy to live on, but then something bad must have happened and it lost its atmosphere."

Sharon replied, "Until they looked at the rubbish and found things like 'Made in China' and 'Made in Bangladesh' printed on the bottom of a lot of the things. Or they'd see a lot of things written in French, and they might think, 'Wow, French is older than we thought! There must have been French people living here millions of years ago with an advanced civilisation, long long before Earth's got to this stage! Maybe humans first came to Earth because French people from the moon came here in spaceships and colonised the place, but then lost a lot of their knowledge and skills to make things they used to make on the moon, so they ended up having to go through the Stone Age and all the other ages we've had!'"

Becky said, "Hey imagine if in the old days when people were first naming planets and their moons and the stars, for some superstitious reason they thought they were all sinister, so they gave them all scary horrible names, like naming them after diseases and other bad things. So in the future, every time NASA announces a mission to explore somewhere in space, think about how it would sound! Imagine if they excitedly announced on the news one day, 'We're sending a mission to explore the planet Smallpox Heights!' Imagine if Scientists all over the media were excitedly talking about how much they were looking forward to it!"

Sharon said, "Yeah! Or imagine if they excitedly announced, 'We're sending a mission to explore Death-Giving Hell Hole.'"

Becky said, "Or they excitedly announced, 'We're sending a mission to explore Doom Bringing Mountain.'"

Sharon said, "Or, 'We're sending a mission to explore Thornweed Stinkmud Gardens.'"

Becky said, "Or, 'We're sending a mission to explore Cough-giving Poison Gutter.'"

Sharon said, "Or, 'We're sending a mission to explore Depression-Causing Vertigo Cliffs.'"

Becky said, "'We're sending a mission to explore Wreaking Dead Fish Dump.'"

Sharon said, "'We're sending a mission to explore Dusty Dreary Smoghole.'"

Becky said, "'We're sending a mission to explore Drizzly Dirt Pit.'"

Sharon said, "'We're sending a mission to explore Hope-Draining Hollow.'"

Becky said, "'We're sending a mission to explore Deadly Bug Drainage Dump.'"

Sharon said, "'We're sending a mission to explore Life-Squelching Toxic Mould Spore Alley.'"

Becky said, "'We're sending a mission to explore Sweat-Causing Slog Mountain.'"

Sharon said, "'We're sending a mission to explore Night-mares Come True.'"

Becky said, "'We're sending a mission to explore Intolerable Boredom Island.'"

One of their friends, Lorna, overheard them talking and joked, "So you've heard of my old school then? You sound as if you're giving very accurate descriptions of it!"

Becky grinned and said, "Only if your old school was hurled up into space somehow, and it's now orbiting the sun and been mistaken for another planet or star and been given a name."

Lorna smiled and said, "Now there's an enjoyable thought!"

The friends nattered on like that for the next hour till it was late, having a laugh and enjoying themselves thinking up new entertaining ideas.

———

On another evening, Becky was with her friends again, and a student called Luke said to her, "I know someone who can whistle on two notes at the same time. I don't know how he does it. I'd never have guessed it was possible till I met him."

Becky said, "Imagine if people could sing on two notes at the same time."

Luke then told her he'd known a girl who'd had an old tape recorder, and she thought it had got dusty or something, but for whatever reason, it wouldn't erase things any more. Instead, it became possible to record things over the top of each other. Most of the time it might have been a pain not to be able to erase stuff, but the girl had the idea of singing in harmony all by herself, by recording herself singing a line of a song, then recording in the same place with a descant, and then doing the same thing with a different one, and she ended up doing that about six times, so when she played it back it sounded as if there were a group of people singing in harmony when really it was just her.

Becky said, "Hey imagine if some people could speak with several different voices at the same time, and if they were annoyed, instead of raising their voice, they would speak with more and more of their voices the more annoyed they were. And imagine if they could create a real surround sound effect, so to the person they were talking to it would sound as if there were annoyed voices coming from behind them and to their sides as well as from where the person was."

Luke replied, "That would be spooky if they were talking to someone who didn't know some people had the ability to do that!"

Becky said, "Imagine if sound could be sucked up into the air by the wind or evaporate into the air like water vapour, and it would come down somewhere else, like the way water droplets that rise up from the sea can come down somewhere completely different as rain. Imagine if the sounds came down with the rain, so anyone who went out in it might hear random bits of people's conversations from America, Australia and all around the world, maybe one straight after the other. So someone who went out in the rain one day might hear a stream of little bits of conversation all around them that went:

" 'My brother blew up the science lab at school today.' 'All it takes is two teaspoons of bicarbonate of soda.' 'I wish my son could do that.' 'Well no matter how much he'd like to, he'll never manage it because cats can't fly.' 'What you could do with is a great big dog!' 'I bought ten this morning for only £2; they were on special offer.' 'If only you could get them to fix your radiators!' 'I haven't got any in the house now; my brother came to see me yesterday and ate four big ones just like that!' 'My favourite place to go for food like that is a carvery.' "

Luke grinned. But then he said, "And if it wasn't just voices but all kinds of sounds people could hear, now that could be scary! You might be walking through a field in the rain when you heard the sound of a car right behind you! Or you might hear the sound of waves of the sea coming from your back garden! People probably wouldn't dare go out in the rain!"

"Yikes!" replied Becky. "Still, it wouldn't be so bad once you knew it was going to happen and got used to it. You might even go out in the rain specially to see if you could hear interesting things. You might hear the sound of an accordion playing where you'd expected to hear leaves on a tree rustling in the wind. You might hear the noise of squelching through mud to the rhythm of your walking, so it sounded like yours even though you were walking on concrete. You might hear the sounds of a football match coming from a flower bed."

Luke said, "Imagine if sounds could get trapped in things and come out later. So for instance, in a factory where sardines got put in tins, some of the noise of what was happening in the place would get enclosed in some of the tins, so when people opened them, they heard the sounds of talking or machinery or doors closing and things."

Becky responded, "Spooky stuff! But then, maybe after a while people would look forward to hearing things and wonder what they might hear, and be disappointed if they opened a tin and didn't hear anything. But they'd probably still jump if sounds came from unexpected places. Imagine if the sound of someone flushing a chain got stuck in a loo when someone put the lid down immediately after they flushed it, and the next person to use it sat down and heard the chain flushing straightaway, while they were sitting there. Mind you, it would be worse if it somehow came from just above them; they'd feel as if they might be about to get things pouring down on them!"

Luke laughed and said, "Oh yuck! But it would be such a scary world, and it might be hard to get things done sometimes. I mean, imagine if someone said to a friend, 'Let's go and get something to eat.', but it was drowned out because just at that moment, a voice that sounded quite like theirs said louder than theirs, 'I've got to go now; I've got to take my dog for a walk.' The other person might say bye and turn and walk away, and the person who spoke might think they were rude, and not talk to them for hours, if they didn't realise their voice had been confused with the other one, because they didn't hear what it said because they were talking at the same time."

They both decided that living in the kind of world they were living in might be better than they'd thought, considering what it could be like if it was different!

——

On another evening, Becky's friend Shirley said to her, "Isn't the news gloomy sometimes! I don't know why they think we need to know most of the stuff they tell us! Hey imagine if someone managed to sneakily swap a newsreader's script with a fake one just before they read the news one day, and the newsreader didn't realise at first. I wonder how long it would take before they did! Imagine if they didn't realise for a while and read stories out loud on the radio in a very serious voice like:

" 'Thousands of mice demonstrated outside the Houses of Parliament today, demanding equal rights for rodents. A spokesmouse shouted through a miniature megaphone that they would keep on demonstrating till mice were allowed to become MPs, and till it was made the law that by the year

2050, fifty per cent of all management positions in businesses would have to be held by rats.

"'Two squirrels got married at Wembley Stadium today, in a grand ceremony attended by 100 thousand spectators! People have been partying loudly all over London ever since, and the celebrations are expected to go on till the early hours of the morning.

"'Two teenage swans have broken the record for making the longest sausage in the world. It stretches right across the Atlantic Ocean from America to Europe.

"'A duck has given birth to a litter of puppies in Richmond Park. Scientists have described this as an extremely rare event, and the Queen came to look at them in awe and wonder, before she picked up several puppies to cuddle.

"'After it was discovered that Brazil nuts are unusually radioactive for a food product, the American government has announced that America is decommissioning all its nuclear weapons, claiming that in this new age of environmental awareness, it's good to have a green alternative. So if America goes to war with any country, and defeating them isn't easy, as a last resort, America will drop tons of Brazil nuts on them from the skies, instead of nuking them as they might have done in the old days.'

"I wonder how long into that news report the newsreader would realise it just had to be a fake and stop reading!"

Shirley and Becky spent a while joking about how funny it would be if someone often managed to sneak one fake story into news bulletins, taking turns to suggest funny fake stories.

On another evening, Becky and some of her friends started playing a game that made them laugh a lot. It started when her friend Mandy said,

"Imagine if we were employers and we had to interview people for jobs, and we were fed up of asking ordinary interview questions like, 'What are your strengths and weaknesses?' and, 'What special skills can you bring to this job?' and 'Why do you want this job?' because we were convinced people knew a lot of interviewers ask questions like that, so they were researching what the best answers were to give beforehand and just giving those, regardless of whether they were true, and anyway we were bored of asking those questions, so we decided to start asking really unexpected questions just for fun, to see what happened, and to see who coped best with them.

"Imagine if one of you was interviewing someone for the job of computer programmer, and you asked, 'If you went on a quiz programme on television, and you were asked, "Would you prefer to answer questions about nineteenth-century pig farming or plastic surgery in ancient Rome?", which would you choose?' That would confuse them, wouldn't it! They'd wonder what kind of answer you were looking for, and why on earth you thought pig farming and ancient surgery were relevant to computer programming! I wonder what they'd say!"

Becky and her friends giggled. Then Luke said, "How about if one of us asked an interviewee, 'Now tell me: What's the biggest amount of food you've ever stuffed into your stomach in one go?' "

They laughed, and Becky said, "Or we could ask them what the weirdest combination of food they've ever eaten is.

Imagine if one of us asked, 'Have you ever eaten chicken with breakfast cereal – I mean plonking bits of chicken right in the cereal with sugar and milk? Or how about dunking fish fingers in orange squash, or mixing ice cream and peanut butter? How adventurous do you get when you're trying out food combinations?' They might worry that if they said they didn't eat weird food combinations, we'd think they weren't adventurous, and that would make us think they weren't as well-suited for the job as we'd like them to be. So imagine if they made up lots of weird food combinations, like grated cheese mixed with chocolate, and they told us they'd eaten that, and we asked them if they liked it, and they pretended to love it!"

Mandy grinned and said, "They'd get a nasty surprise if you had some cheese and chocolate right there in the room, and you gave them some, and told them they could feel free to mix it up and eat it right there in front of you."

Becky said, "Or imagine if you asked them if they liked eating rabbit food, and told them everyone in the company loved rabbit food so they'd really fit in if they did too, and if they said they did like eating it when they didn't really, just in the hope of getting your approval, you produced a bowlful, and said they could feel free to eat it right there in the interview!"

One of the friends, Gary, said, "Imagine if one of us asked them, 'Have you ever used a word instead of the one you meant to use without realising, and wondered why the person you were speaking to didn't understand you, like keeping on saying sea when you meant tea, so you asked them several times if they'd like a cup of sea? Or you said the word dread when you meant bread, so you asked them if they'd like some dread, when you were really just trying to be nice and offering them bread? I love to hear entertaining stories about that kind of thing, so I'm hoping you can tell me one.' I wonder if they'd make one up, thinking that if they pleased you, you'd be more likely to give them the job, even though it made them look daft."

Sharon said, "Imagine if one of us asked them, 'How would you like it if language was somehow passed down in the genes, so people who had some immigrants as ancestors had the ability to speak the languages they spoke, but they wouldn't realise it till they suddenly heard someone speaking one of them, and then they'd suddenly remember it, but when they did, they'd forget their native language all the while they were listening to the person speaking the other language? Do you think it would be a good thing or a bad thing if people were made like that, and would you like to be like it?' I wonder if they'd worry about what kind of answer you were hoping for, and whether they might give the wrong one."

Becky said, "Wouldn't it be fun if one of us asked them, 'Have you ever accidentally put something that was meant to go on your dinner on your pudding, or something that was meant to go on your pudding on your dinner, like mixing curry with rice pudding, or putting custard on roast potatoes?' "

One of the friends, Jane, said, "Imagine if you were interviewing someone for a job as a psychotherapist, and every single question you asked was about how good an engineer they thought they'd make. That would confuse them, wouldn't it! They'd wonder if they'd come to the wrong interview!"

The others laughed.

Becky and her friends joked around like that for some time.

Then Sharon said, "I heard this programme on the radio a while ago about why forecasts like weather forecasts and government economic forecasts are often wrong; and I expected it to start off with someone talking seriously, considering it was a serious programme. I was all eager to hear what they were about to say . . . But the first thing I heard was this strange-sounding rattly noise. It went on for several seconds, and then it turned out to be some snooker balls rattling around or something, and then the presenter started going on about forecasting how well he'd do in a snooker game. I wondered why it started with something as irrelevant as snooker balls just rattling around.

"Imagine how it would have ended if things were on there in order from the most important thing to the least, so all the sound effects came at the end all together, and the presenter somehow expected people to just know why they were on there!

"Before the talking started, when this rattly noise came on where I'd expected to hear a voice, I started imagining it going on for a bit, and then being able to distinguish words in it, that said, 'Don't complain about this noise; I bet a lot of you are thinking about doing that! But it's just my voice; I can't help it sounding like this!' "

The others laughed.

Then Jane asked, "It said forecasts are often wrong then? Did the programme ask people why they even bother making them then? And did it explain why they're often wrong, or was the presenter too busy playing snooker to bother telling anyone?"

Shirley said sarcastically with a grin, "That would have made good radio, wouldn't it, just the sound of snooker balls rattling around for half an hour! Somehow I think the makers of that programme would have got the sack pretty quickly if it was like that!"

They giggled.

Sharon said, "They gave a few reasons on the programme as to why forecasts can be wrong. One thing they said was that when people like government economists make forecasts, if they know what a lot of other supposed experts are saying, they can be scared to say something that contradicts them a bit, in case they're wrong and they lose their reputations because of that, so they'll say something that fits in with them . . . and then I suppose they end up losing their reputations anyway if they all turn out to be wrong!

"But another reason they gave was that forecasts about the kinds of health services that'll be needed in a few decades' time can be wrong, partly because new technologies might be invented during that time that cure things that used to be big problems, and also because people can be worried by forecasts and decide to change things to try to stop them coming true, for instance if there's a forecast that a few million people will be dying prematurely from smoking-related illnesses in a few decades, and lots of smokers are worried by that, and it motivates them to give up smoking, so not nearly as many people end up dying as would have done if the forecast hadn't been made.

"That's good, but it does mean that if the government uses the forecasts to make plans about which parts of the health service to put most money into in the future, they can end up putting the money into parts of it where it isn't needed as much as it is in other places that are beginning to need it a lot more than they used to, like the parts where they treat all the old people who have chronic diseases they're just living with for years because they're not dying of things the way they used to before the technologies were invented to cure them of some life-threatening things.

"And forecasts about inflation can end up wrong too because things change. One reason why is because, say if the forecasters say it'll go up by two per cent the next year, lots of employees might go to their bosses and say, 'They're forecasting that the cost of living's going to go up by two per cent next year, so I'd like a two per cent wage increase to cover the costs.'

"If the bosses agree – well, at least the bosses of companies that sell things – then if they want to still make the same amount of profit they're making, they'll have to get the money they're spending on the wage rises back somehow instead of paying the extra wages out of their profits, so they'll put the cost of their products up a bit. But if lots of them do that, it'll mean the cost of living goes up more than expected for everyone, because so many things they normally buy get more expensive, so it ends up going up by more than two per cent.

"Still, you'd have thought any forecaster who knew what they were talking about would be able to predict that would happen and take it into account when they were making their forecast.

"The programme talked about weather forecasting too, saying it's got better over the years, and that now they use things like satellite images of what's going on to help them make the forecasts."

Mandy grinned and said, "And yet they still manage to get them wrong sometimes! Actually, it's funny: Have you noticed that weather forecasters on television often say things like, 'This has been the sunniest day since records began', or, 'That was the worst storm since records began', or, 'We've had the most rain today since records began', or, 'The temperature over the past week has been the highest since records began'! They seem to be breaking records so often, you wonder how it could possibly be happening. You know, one day they'll say a record's been broken, and the next week they'll say another one has, and then a few days later they'll tell you another one's been broken!

"I read a joke on the Internet about how what probably really goes on is that they somehow lose their records every few weeks so they have to begin them again, and then they forget they ever had the old ones, so the records they're referring to when they say, 'since records began' are ones that only started a few weeks earlier."

They giggled.

They carried on having fun and talking about things they were interested in for a while.

Chapter 9

Becky and Her Friends Spend an Evening Chatting About the Paranormal

Sometimes Becky and her friends helped each other out, or supported each other when they got a bit upset about things. Sometimes they could cheer each other up and end up having interesting conversations despite having started the evening feeling down.

The Friends Talk About Sleep Paralysis

Becky and her usual crowd got together one evening to cook a meal and chat, and partway through the discussion, they put some pies in the oven.

Before they started cooking, they sat down for a while, and one of them, Craig, told the group he was being scared at night by strange things – he wasn't sure if they were horrid dreams or ghosts, or something else. He said he would drift off to sleep, only to be woken up in a panic not long afterwards, feeling as if a weight was on his chest trying to crush him and stop him breathing. One of the scariest things was that he couldn't move while it was happening.

One night he'd managed to lift his head with a great effort, only to see a huge dog in the room with its mouth covered in blood. Another night he saw a little plant on his windowsill suddenly grow very fast and stretch out towards his throat, as if it wanted to wind itself around him and strangle him or something. He'd also heard cackling, and thought he saw human-like figures in his room. He was scared about what they were doing and who they were.

Sometimes he'd leave clothes in piles on the floor if he couldn't be bothered to hang them up when he took them off before he went to bed, and when he spotted them when he wasn't fully awake, they seemed to have transformed themselves into dead bodies in the night. He wondered if he had demons in his room, or whether the experiences were some horrible omens of his death, sent by some kind of supernatural power.

A few of the friends thought they might be grateful to have the pies as comfort food later at the rate the discussion was going. But one of them, Lauren, laughed and said to Craig, "You've been watching too many horror films! They've been giving you nightmares! Try not to watch them too near bedtime!"

Craig didn't laugh though. He said, looking worried, "You know I don't like horror films."

Becky managed to reassure him by saying, "I've heard about this kind of thing. It's just got natural causes. I read that scientists think it's to do with something going on in the brain. It's called sleep paralysis. When people dream, the muscles stop working, probably to stop people acting out their dreams and getting themselves into danger. Most people will wake up not knowing their muscles were paralysed while they were dreaming, because they were asleep when it happened. But some people start waking up when the paralysis hasn't worn off. So they can be half asleep and half awake, realising they can't move, but still dreaming. And because beginning to wake up paralysed is scary, it can turn the dreams scary.

"Some people can get sleep paralysis if they're especially stressed or worried when they go to bed, or overtired or over-worked."

Another Rebecca, whom the friends called Becky2, said, "Oh I wonder if that's where reports of alien abductions come from . . . you know, when people think there are aliens in their room who take them away and tie them down or something, and do horrible things to them like experiments and opera-tions to try to implant baby aliens in them, or whatever people think they do. Maybe people used to think it was demons doing that to them, but now they think it's aliens, because they've heard of it happening to other people who said it was aliens."

The Topic of Psychic Surgery Comes Up

Another friend, Monica, said, "That reminds me a bit of psychic surgery. What's that all about? There was something on the telly about a man who said he could do operations on people without breaking their skin. Could that really be possible?"

Adam replied, "Oh that's a fraud; I've heard about that. They do things like holding little bags of chicken liver and blood concealed in the palm of one hand, and then they make it look as if they're putting their hand inside the person by rolling some of their flesh over their hand, and then they take their hands away and show the chicken liver and blood on their hand, as if it's a tumour or something they've just taken out of the patient."

"Yuck!" several friends said in unison.

Angela asked, "What happens afterwards when the patient complains that they've still got what they had before?"

Adam said, "I don't really know. I expect they use some excuse. But I think a lot of the time, they do those fake operations on people who haven't really got things they need removing, but things like indigestion, which would go away by itself sooner or later anyway. When it does, some people might think they're better because of what the psychic surgery did. So they can keep on believing in it."

The Friends Talk About the Claims That People Can Have Surgery Under Hypnosis With No Anaesthetic, and Other Things They've Heard About Hypnosis

Lorna said to the others, "What do you think of these reports of people having surgery while they're hypnotised without feeling pain? The idea's always sounded a bit strange to me.

I don't understand how it could happen. There's no way I'd want to try it myself! Does anyone know much about how true it is?"

Dawn replied, "I doubt it works. At least with severe pain. I actually read that there've even been reports on the BBC and other media outlets about it happening, but that they haven't given the full facts, for some reason or other. Maybe it's partly that a lot of journalists don't know enough about the subject to be able to tell when something's unlikely, and ask more questions that might expose problems with a story. And I suppose it could partly be that they'd rather not do that anyway, because it would ruin a good story if there was found to be nothing in it. I don't know.

"But one report said there was a woman having an operation on her throat, which couldn't be done under general anaesthetic, because she needed to be awake during it so she could talk sometimes so the surgeon could tell he hadn't just accidentally done something catastrophic to her vocal cords; so she was just hypnotised during it, and she didn't feel any pain, and even sang while it was going on! But it turned out that for whatever reason, the report didn't mention that this woman had had a local anaesthetic where the operation was going on, so she probably wouldn't have felt any pain because of that.

"The hypnosis was probably done just to help calm any anxiety she had, since it can help relieve that, because hypnosis is like deep relaxation, or like the kind of feeling people get when they're 'in the zone', as some people say – concentrating so hard on something they're oblivious to things going on around them, like if someone was playing a video game, and got so engrossed in it that people were getting on with their lives around them without them really noticing.

"I read that hypnosis can help with the kind of pain that can come on because of anxiety, like when people get tension headaches, or if muscles in other parts of them get so tense it hurts, or if they get really bad butterflies in their stomach or something. It can reduce or stop that kind of pain and discomfort because it can relax people, so their tension eases off, and because it can distract them from it, since pain can seem worse if people are focusing on it all the time so it's all they're thinking about, just like what can happen if people start feeling worried, and then they start worrying about why they're so worried about what they're worrying about, and focusing on their worry, so they're noticing it and thinking about it a lot, and that makes it feel worse, while they might have forgotten about what was worrying them for a while if they'd just got absorbed in something else when it first started.

"But as for hypnosis helping with anxiety during operations, I read that other kinds of distraction can help with that just as much. I actually heard about someone who played a video game while doctors were doing some procedure on him, that they had to do quite often, so he knew what to expect so he wasn't worrying about what might happen next. He got really absorbed in the video game, so he didn't notice the pain anywhere near as much as he normally did, because he was so distracted from it. Maybe some brain chemicals that got released because he was enjoying himself helped with that as well, like maybe dopamine and adrenaline or something – I don't know much about this stuff, but I think things like that can help. I've actually heard that soldiers who get wounded in battle can sometimes not notice or feel the pain for a while, because they're so full of adrenaline and distracted by trying to stay alive that the pain signals don't register in their brains for a while or something.

"But I read that media reports of hypnosis during surgery are often sensationalised, and leave out certain details, like that people have actually taken sedatives and painkillers too, and they've been given local anaesthetics; so people who read the reports get the impression that the hypnosis was stopping the person having the operation feeling pain, when really it was only relaxing them to calm them down, and it was standard medical procedures that were eliminating the pain.

"And I've read that some people who make money from hypnotising people have made claims about how it can really relieve pain, without mentioning the importance of those other things."

Lorna said, "That's bad! Do you know any more about hypnosis?"

Dawn said, "A little bit. Not that much. One thing I know is that when therapists hypnotise people, it's different from when stage hypnotists do it, where they tell people to do all kinds of daft things for fun . . . Or at least it should be! People still have a choice about whether to obey people when they're hypnotised. People who go up for stage hypnosis probably do daft things under it mostly because they want to entertain the audience, not just because they're hypnotised. The kind of people who volunteer to go up might be the kind of people who secretly love the idea of behaving in daft ways for fun, and think it would be nice to have an excuse to . . . Not like certain people here, who don't seem to need an excuse to behave in daft ways for a laugh! . . . Well, that's most of us really.

"But other reasons people do what they do under stage hypnosis might be that they want to please the audience, and that they'd feel awkward refusing to do what they're told, partly because it would disappoint everyone's expectations. So the audience can think they're under the control of the hypnotist when they're not really."

Becky said, "Hey wouldn't it be fun if we did a stage hypnotism show for an audience here at the university, where one of us told people to do all kinds of daft things for a laugh! My grandpa told me that years ago he watched a funny stage hypnotism show on television, where this hypnotist got three grown men up from the audience, and he told one of them that when he commanded him to, he was to start shouting in alarm, 'The Russians are coming! The Russians are coming!' And he told him he had to keep on shouting it till he commanded him to stop. (I think the Cold War was still going on in those days.)

"He told another man that when he heard the first man say the word 'Russians', he was to start shouting, 'Shut up, ya fool! Shut up, ya fool!', over and over again.

"And he told the third man that when he heard the second man start shouting that, he was to start whining, 'Mummy, I want to go wee wee! Mummy, I want to go wee wee!'

"So he had these three grown men all saying those things for a while. It would have been a laugh to have been there listening!"

The others grinned. One, Ben, said, "Wow, imagine if people said all kinds of things in a stage hypnotism show we did because we told them to! We could maybe tell someone to

128

insist on saying something like, 'It's raining in here; the rain's coming upwards from the floor instead of falling down!' And we could maybe tell another person to argue with them, saying things like, 'Don't be silly! I've eaten all the rain in the world! There can't possibly be any more left!' And then we could tell a third person to argue with both of them, saying things like, 'All the rain got sucked up to the moon years ago, you idiots! It never rains any more! If you think it does, it must be because you're dribbling without realising it and your dribble's going all over your clothes, you disgusting imbeciles!'

"Or imagine if we told someone to shout in alarm over and over again, 'My mother's growing dandelions out of her head!' And we told someone else that when they heard the word 'head', they were to start pretending to cry, and yell, 'I can't find my electric socks! I can't find my electric socks!' And we told a third person that when they heard the word 'socks', they were to start shouting, 'There are ninety-seven wriggling squirrels in my shoes! There are ninety-seven wriggling squirrels in my shoes!'

"Or imagine if we asked one person to start pretending to be upset, and to yell, 'I've got a raisin up my nose! I've got a raisin up my nose!' And we told another person that when they heard the word 'nose', they were to start shouting, 'Pull it out with a pair of pliers! Pull it out with a pair of pliers!' And we told another one that when they heard the word 'pliers', they were to start shouting, 'I want to eat some pliers for dinner! I want to eat some pliers for dinner!' And imagine if we had a fourth person up there, and we told them that when they heard the word 'dinner', they were to start shouting, 'You can't do that, you stupid idiot moron! Pliers can walk and talk and think, almost as if they're human! It just wouldn't be fair!' "

They all laughed at the ideas.

But when the laughter died down, Dawn continued seriously, "Anyway though, I was going to say that when therapists use hypnosis, it's different from stage hypnotism, and it can help with things like giving up smoking. It works better on some people than on others. It might work because people are relaxed and really concentrating on what the therapist says, so they're more likely to be able to really get into imagining what it's like to experience what the therapist tells them to; a therapist might tell them to imagine that they're smelling cigarette smoke and it smells really revolting, so it puts them off it, and to really imagine how they're poisoning their body by it, thinking about how they need their body to live. The person who's hypnotised might concentrate on those messages a lot more because they're hypnotised than they would normally, when their mind will usually be full of other thoughts and they're not so relaxed.

"The therapist might teach them how to get into the relaxed state where they're concentrating on only those things, so they can hypnotise themselves from then on; and they can advise them to get themselves into that state and think about those things whenever the desire to smoke comes over them from then on, whenever they've got a free moment then.

"Apparently it doesn't always work, and when it does, it works better for some people than for others; and there are more effective therapies out there for smoking, and other things hypnosis gets used for; but it might be worth people giving it a go if they've tried other things and they haven't worked, or they could try it in combination with other things."

Lauren grinned and remarked, "I read a headline in an article that said, 'Hypnosis to Quit Smoking and Aids'. I thought, 'I don't think quitting AIDS is something hypnosis can help with, actually!'"

The others sniggered.

Then Miriam said, "I've heard something about hypnosis being risky in the wrong hands though, because people can develop false memories under it."

Dawn said, "Yeah. I found out about that too. I read that some unscrupulous or misguided therapists have caused that kind of thing to happen. They can do it by hypnotising people who go to them for help with depression or anxiety or other problems affecting their mental health, who really want help to feel better because problems like that are a real burden to them, so they're more likely to be willing to make a quick decision to trust someone who seems to be an authority figure who claims they can cure them than they would be if their problems weren't bad enough to bother them much, and to allow themselves to get engrossed in what the therapist tells them to do, because they assume it's designed to help them. and then the therapist can say they want to investigate the deep-rooted cause of their mental health difficulties, and ask them questions about whether certain bad things happened to them in childhood, such as being sexually abused, telling them that their memories might have been repressed, but that they might recover them if they imagine in great detail what might have happened, and then ask themselves if it did.

"They can advise them to imagine being abused, as well as such details as who might have committed the abuse, what time of day it could have been when the abuse happened, where it might have happened, and all kinds of things like that. The therapist can ask questions that suggest that more and more of the things they imagine might be true, encouraging them to imagine more and more things, such as by putting into their minds the idea that the abuse was possibly violent, and asking them to see if their imaginations come up with violent details, saying it'll be a way of finding out if it was. Then they can tell their clients to go home and try to imagine more things that happened, claiming that imagination is a good guide to what really happened.

"And they can tell them that if they dream about being abused, their dreams are likely to be telling them something significant. And because the clients trust their therapists, and assume they must know a whole lot more about that kind of thing than they do, since they must have studied it, and they're professionals, they can believe them. And some so-called therapists even give their clients drugs to help their imaginations along.

"So some people can end up believing they were abused for years by their parents when they weren't really, or believing other bad things happened to them when they didn't really, even believing very dramatic things such as that they were in a Satanic cult where human sacrifice was practised and that they witnessed friends being murdered, or that they've got multiple personalities because of the way their brain coped with trauma in their past.

"Then over time, because their therapists are telling them that what their imaginations are coming up with is a good guide to what really happened, they can become more and more convinced that what they're imagining really did happen. There have been court cases where therapists have been sued for inducing false memories like that in their clients, who went on to accuse family members of severe abuse when it didn't happen really, which led to a lot of bad feeling between them."

Gary said, "Blimey this is bad! I think I might have just lost my appetite for any food we might have later on . . . although considering how much I like food, maybe it'll come back by then."

One of the Friends Tells the Others What They Know About People Saying They Remember Past Lives Under Hypnosis

Lorna asked, "What about past life regression under hypnosis, and asking people to remember details of their very early childhoods under hypnosis that they wouldn't normally remember? I'm not talking about the technique you've just described, Dawn, but just about asking people to go back in their minds to when they were babies, without putting ideas in their minds first. What do scientists think about the accuracy of that?"

Dawn said, "I've read something about that too. I read that really early memories of childhood, like when people think they're remembering things that happened to them before they were a year old, or thereabouts, can't be accurate, because the part of the brain that stores memories hasn't developed properly before then. So they must be products of people's imaginations.

"And I read that people's memories of past lives aren't real, but a lot of them have been proven afterwards to have been imagined by people, based on a mixture of things like fantasies they've had in the past, things they've heard on the radio or in plays or on television or in old news reports or stories they've heard, novels they've read, what other people have told them about their childhoods and the childhoods of their grandparents, and other things like that. People's minds can use those things to dream up stories under hypnosis that they can believe are true.

"For instance, there was a famous case of a man who hypnotised a woman in America in the 1950s, who then said she'd gone back to a life she lived over a century before in Ireland. She said she was called Bridey Murphy. She started speaking with an Irish accent, and sang Irish songs and told stories from Ireland. She said she'd married a barrister, and gave quite a few other details about the life she said she'd lived.

"But journalists investigated the story, and they found that it was likely the product of vivid fantasising during hypnosis, because they found out that the woman had had a neighbour as a child who'd come to America from Ireland, whose name was Bridey, and her maiden name had been Murphy; and there had been other people descended from Irish immigrants around her who could have told her lots of things about Ireland that she remembered. And the journalists actually went to Ireland to see if they could find records of someone called Bridey Murphy who'd been born and died when the woman said she'd been born and died, and married to a man with the name she'd said her husband was called; but they couldn't find any, or any records of other family members she said she'd had. Not that that would mean they'd definitely never existed. But the woman herself apparently didn't truly believe her supposed past life had been real.

"I think the kind of people who are most susceptible to being hypnotised might be people with good imaginations. Maybe some of them are used to fantasising about what it must have been like to live in the olden days. But I think the therapists who encourage people to remember past lives often ask them questions that give them ideas that can inspire them to imagine more details, such as asking them all about where they are when they say they're sensing being in a different place and time, which people can feel as if they are under hypnosis because they're imagining things so vividly; and they can ask them what's going on, how they're feeling, and so on, so they're prompted to imagine things more and more vividly with more and more detail; and the therapists can give them suggestions that encourage them to take their fantasies in different directions, like asking them if they travelled around, when they hadn't been thinking of that till then.

"But there are some people who think remembering past lives must be impossible anyway, because memories are stored in the brain; and when the brain deteriorates, like when people have dementia, or when people are injured and get brain damage in the part of the brain that stores memories, you can tell their memories are deteriorating or no longer exist. So when they die and the brain dies, it's reasonable to think that all their memories die."

The Friends Discuss the Idea of Karma

Lauren said, "I wonder if a lot of people who believe in that doctrine of karma that religions like Buddhism and Hinduism teach think people with dementia must have got it as a punishment for bad things they've done. If they do, it sounds a bit daft to me, because in the end, people with dementia won't even be able to remember what they're supposed to have done wrong in life, so they won't have a clue about what they're supposedly being punished for! And it's even worse when people who believe in karma think suffering in this life is a punishment for bad things people did in past lives, that they won't even have a chance of remembering! If karma did that, it would be a bit like punishing a puppy for chewing something up a few days earlier, when it probably won't even remember doing it, so it won't have a clue what it's being punished for, or that the punishment's meant to teach them not to do it again, or even that it's a punishment, instead of just some random act of cruelty!"

Then she started making fun of the idea of karma, saying, "Karma sounds like a weird belief to me! For one thing, what kind of sophisticated cosmic organisation must there be for it to be good enough to arrange for every single person to get the karma they deserve? I mean, surely it must be massive! Do people who believe in karma imagine there are billions of spirits on the karma case, each one of them assigned to take charge of the fate of someone on Earth, and trained to calculate exactly what people's bad and good deeds deserve, and given the task of monitoring a person 24 hours a day to see what they're getting up to, and to mark each bad and good thing they do down, so they can either do the calculations at the end of the person's life, or continuously adjust them as they're going along?

"So might one of them think, 'Oh, he's just walked on by instead of helping an old lady across the road; that means the cancer he's going to get in his next life for the bad things he's already done is going to be that little bit worse, and we're going to make sure it takes longer for him to see a doctor so he gets diagnosed later than he would have done if he'd helped her'? But then if the man does help the next old lady he sees, does karma reverse that decision to reward him?

"Or if the calculations aren't anywhere near as precise as that, surely that makes karma even less fair. I mean, if someone does quite a few bad things in their life but a lot of them just get overlooked, how can they really get what they supposedly deserve?

"And if there aren't masses of spirits all beavering away spying on everyone and calculating what they deserve for the things they do, how does karma get worked out? How could whatever causes karma even ever get to find out exactly who's living in the world at the moment, and know everything they're doing, let alone working out what they deserve in their next life, as well as making sure they get everything they deserve in this one?

"I mean, it sounds like an industrial-scale task! Maybe the karma gods are masters of industrial organisation! Maybe they've invented karma machines or cosmic karma computers that they've had since mankind began, that can somehow monitor and collect data on thousands of people at once, and make thousands or millions of calculations at the same time about what their karma's going to be!

"Imagine if you died, and the next thing you knew, you were in a massive room full of really advanced technology, and the karma gods were at one end of it supervising it all, and you suddenly realised everyone's fate's determined by computers, after they had the algorithms they used programmed into them by the karma gods at the time when humans first walked the earth! Imagine if the karma gods told you they'd had to upgrade their systems lots of times over the centuries, because the population of earth kept growing too large for the computers they had at first to cope!

"But if there aren't billions of spirits madly calculating what everyone's fate's going to be in their next lives, and there are no computers to help the karma gods, how could karma even happen? What could cause it? Maybe the karma gods are so powerful they can do it all on their own, although it must give them a headache, all that spying and calculation! Maybe they're gods who've been enslaved to do the work by more powerful gods, because what powerful god would ever want to do such laborious work? Or maybe the gods all take turns at it, so none of them get worn out by it! Maybe there are handover times where the gods who've just finished working on it update the gods who are about to take over on what they've done. Or could it all be done by robots, who were programmed by the gods thousands of years ago, and just left to get on with it while the gods went off and did more enjoyable things?"

Mandy said, "Yeah, I think karma sounds like a daft idea too, as well as an unfair one! For one thing, why do the karma forces have to wait till people's next lives before pun-ishing them, instead of punishing them in their current lives? Punishing them in the lives where they did the bad things would seem a whole lot fairer! I mean, in their next lives, they'll be completely different people, who won't know a thing about the bad things they supposedly did in their past lives, and might not even want to do things like that!

I mean, just imagine if someone was a psychopath who did horrible things, but in their next life they were a really good person who loved helping other people, and felt sickened and depressed when they heard about nasty things happening to people, and couldn't even remember what they did in their past life! How would it be fair for them to be punished for it? So much for karma being fair!

"And what about little children who suffer horribly before they can even talk, let alone understand that their suffering's supposedly happening because they did something terrible in a past life! How is it fair that they're made to suffer for things they don't know anything about, and couldn't even dream of doing in their current lives, because they don't even have a clue that such things go on, let alone knowing how to do them?

"Even if people really can remember past lives under hypnosis, it doesn't make any difference if they're completely different people now!

"And if these spiritual forces that supposedly determine everyone's karma are so powerful they can arrange it so people get to have horrible lives because they did bad things in a past life, how can it be that they aren't powerful enough to do the fairer thing and make people suffer in the life where they're actually doing the bad things? Or if they sometimes do, why can't they do that all the time?

"And if they're that powerful, why can't they actually stop bad things from happening? If they care enough about bad things to make sure people are punished for doing them, and they know exactly when they're doing them and what they're doing, how come they're not caring enough to stop bad things in the first place?

"And it's even worse, because if people think bad things that happen to them must just be their karma, surely a lot of them aren't going to be motivated to try to change their lives for the better, which they often might be able to do if they didn't have that belief!

"And maybe a lot of people who live nice lives in countries where people believe in karma aren't motivated to help people who are suffering, because they think they're just getting their karma. Or maybe a lot of those people do help them, because they believe it'll get them some good karma in the future. But I wonder if a lot of them worry that if they do help them, it might be against the will of the karma gods, because it reduces the amount of bad karma they want those people to get, so they might take revenge by giving them some bad karma instead of the good karma they're hoping for.

"I actually read a book by someone who was trained as a guru in India, after his dad became an advanced one; but then he got disillusioned with Hinduism and gave it up, and he said he thought belief in karma was responsible for a lot of the poverty in India, because people think it's just poor people's fate, including the poor people themselves, who might not try to get out of poverty if they think poverty's just their destiny. And if all the politicians in the government believe in karma, they might not be motivated to provide good health services in poor areas or a good welfare system, because they might think poor people are just getting their just deserts when they're ill or going hungry.

"And I wonder if the idea of karma ever gets used by criminals to quieten any qualms of conscience they might have about what they're doing, allowing them to shrug off responsibility for it, because they can justify it and even sneer at their victims by saying they must have bad karma if they're becoming crime victims. Maybe it could be used as an excuse by bullying parents as well, who might say things like, 'I'm not to blame for what's happening to my children; it's obviously just their karma.'

"Of course, if the parents really believe in karma, hopefully they won't do that, because they'll be worried they'll suffer themselves for the bullying in some future life. But maybe they won't worry about it too much if they can justify their bullying as rightful punishment."

Adam said, "Yeah. I don't like the idea of karma at all! I mean, for one thing, how does it make sure people get the kind and amount of suffering it wants them to have? Surely it must have to manipulate them into situations where they're going to get it, like making them walk down a particular street late one night where they're going to become a crime victim or something. But that would have to mean that as well as that, it uses criminals to inflict the suffering it wants people to get. But if it uses criminals to inflict suffering on other people, so as to give them their just deserts, how can it be fair that it then goes on to punish the criminals it's been using when they were just doing what it made them do? Unless they get let off future punishment, in which case, how is that fair, since they might have enjoyed doing what they did, and are fully intent on doing it again just as soon as they've got the opportunity?

"I heard that the Hindu religion doesn't teach that karma actually makes people inflict suffering on others, but that everyone's got free will to behave the way they want to. But at the same time, it seems that it teaches that crime victims became victims because they're getting their karma. You wouldn't have thought both those things could be true at once! I mean, say a couple of men are planning a robbery: Surely karma will have to control them to make sure they rob someone who deserves some bad karma, instead of someone who's lived lots of good lives and doesn't deserve it!

"That's if the explanation for why some people become crime victims is always that it was their karma. If it isn't, then how can people possibly know who's a crime victim because of their karma and who's one because of something else, or that anyone at all is one because of their karma?

"And I wonder if putting things down to karma could prevent people from thinking of alternative explanations for why crimes and other things happen, such as that criminals aren't being given tough enough sentences so they're often soon let out of prison and free to commit more crimes. If that's the case, then belief in karma could stand in the way of progress, because using it to explain why bad things happen might prevent people from looking for more likely explanations and doing something about them.

"And how could karma cause people to suffer because of anything other people do if it can't control people's behaviour so as to make them cause the suffering? I wonder if people somehow believe it does control it and doesn't control it at the same time. Karma sounds like a contradictory belief to me."

Shirley said, "I don't think people's beliefs can be very extreme, because sometimes you hear on the news that a horrible crime's been committed in India, and that loads of people have come out to protest that there weren't enough safeguards to prevent it happening, or that the criminals haven't been punished severely enough, or something like that. If they all believed that karma causes all suffering, you'd have thought they'd just accept the crime as the victim's karma and not try to get something done to change things."

The friends pondered on that for a little while.

A Slight Bit of Humour Breaks Out

Then Becky said, "This subject's in danger of giving me brain-ache! Shall we stop for a while and have a drink?"

The others thought that was a good idea.

While they were having refreshments, one of them, Danny, told the others about a humorous conversation he'd had on an Internet forum. He said,

"There's this daft man on a forum I like to go on, who does things like boast about things he's probably never done in his life really. The other day he said he's so famous in his part of the world that everyone's heard his name by the time they know how to tell their left hand from their right.

"I joked, 'That's nothing! I've made such a name for myself, my name's programmed into everyone's genes before they're born. They know it from birth. They can tell others all about me as soon as they can talk, before they've got a clue about which hand is their right and which is their left. If anyone doesn't know it, it means they're some kind of mutant.'

"A friend of the boaster told me I've got a big ego, although he said he wasn't complaining. I joked,

" 'Funnily enough, only this morning I was boasting about my big ego! It gives me complete confidence that I can totally vanquish anyone foolish enough to stand up and argue against me on this forum! People on another forum try it once or twice, and then shake in terror as I approach! Sometimes I just send my ego out to chase them away while I sit comfortably at home. When they see it coming, they think it's a steam roller and dash for cover!' "

The Friends Discuss Karma Some More

Lorna joked, "Wow, what a spooky world we seem to be living in, with egos without bodies, and some strange spiritual force of karma manipulating everyone from far, far away, by remote control!"

The friends smiled. But then Craig said, "I was going to say something about karma before we stopped for a drink. Sorry to turn this conversation serious again, but I've been wondering if anyone who believes in it really thinks some suffering can happen without it being karma, like if they think people can be crime victims without it being their karma. The thing is that if they do believe that, how could they ever be sure any one thing was karma at all?

"If some people think suffering that's deliberately caused by others isn't caused by karma, because karma can't make people do bad things, then which kinds of suffering are supposedly caused by karma and which kinds of suffering aren't, according to their beliefs? I don't know much about what people believe about karma at all; but I've never heard of anyone saying some kinds of suffering are caused by karma and some aren't ... Mind you, I've hardly heard a thing about it at all really.

"But here's another thing: If some suffering's supposedly extra, because karma isn't causing it, then how is it fair that karma causes as much suffering as it does, when a lot of people are going to suffer a lot of things anyway? Or does it somehow know how much suffering people are going to have independently of it in their lives, so it reduces the amount it would have given people who are going to have a lot, to make up for it? Yeah, those karma gods must have to work hard calculating all that! Or does it cause them the same amount of suffering no matter what, which would make it unfair?

"And what if karma's loaded all the suffering on a person it thinks they deserve for one lifetime, and then they suffer because other bad things happen to them that aren't their karma, like if they get attacked by criminals? Does it just look on in horror, helpless to do anything except calculate the just deserts of the criminals? Not that I know how it could do that, since it's supposedly some kind of impersonal inanimate thing!"

Monica said, "Are the karma gods just inanimate things then, like robot gods? It all sounds a bit confusing! Anyway, I've got a few questions for the karma gods, if they can take time out of their busy karma-calculating schedules to answer . . . Mind you, it would be spooky if they did, and we suddenly realised they're real after all!

"But I wonder: If karma isn't deliberately using some people to inflict suffering on other people, how can it make anyone do anything that helps to bring on the repayment it wants to give people for what they did in past lives? And yeah, how can crime victims be victims because they're getting their karma, if karma isn't making criminals commit crimes against the people who deserve it? Or is it really just suffering by natural causes that's caused by karma? And how does it cause that? Do people think karma causes cyclones, or that it directs disasters like that to places where there are a whole stonking mass of people who are just ripe for some bad karma, at a time when somehow there are no people who've lived lots of decent lives and don't deserve it in the area?

"And do they believe doctors are fighting karma when they try to cure people? Or if someone gets cured, do they just think their karma isn't as bad as they thought it might be when they first got ill?

"And if karma doesn't manipulate criminals into giving people the bad karma they deserve, could it just be constantly looking out for ways to harm people that actually are within its power, changing its plans if it finds it can't do it one way, and being relieved if it happens another way that isn't under its control, because it can mark that down as part of their karma, which takes some of the pressure off it to find other ways of harming them; so if someone, say, gets attacked by a group of people, it thinks, 'Oh good, now I don't have to keep looking for ways to make them suffer any more. I thought I might have to pick up a bit of slippery mud and put it down in front of where they're walking to make them slip on it and break their arm. Thank goodness I don't have to bother making the effort to do that any more; people have no idea how hard it is for inanimate spiritual forces that haven't got hands and would have to travel billions of miles down to earth to do things like that!' "

Lauren said, "Yeah! And if the belief is that everyone's got free will so karma doesn't determine what they do, how can it control people who are just due for some juicy karma enough to make sure they're in the right place at the right time to get the suffering it wants them to have? And how can it control things enough to make sure worse things don't happen to them than it calculates they deserve? I mean, say someone's in an earthquake, but it doesn't think they deserve to die young, but just to suffer a bit, how can it make sure they're not, say, hit on the head by a falling slab of concrete and killed, but they get just the amount of suffering it thinks they deserve?

"Or say there's a ferry disaster in India or something, and hundreds of people die. Lots of people there who hear about it might think it was their karma. But karma must have had to do quite a bit of coordination to make sure everyone it wanted to die on the ferry was there! How would it have got them all there? It would have to have tampered with lots of people's minds to get them to decide they wanted to go on that ferry, and to make sure anyone who didn't deserve to die didn't get on it. And karma must have to manipulate people like that all the time to get them into positions where they can receive the suffering it wants them to have, or to avoid the suffering people in a certain place are going to have if they don't deserve to suffer with them! So much for the doctrine of karma teaching that people have free will to do what they want! Yeah, it sounds like a contradictory belief to me!

"That's unless karma's so good at foretelling the future it can just cause people to be born in the places where it knows they'll end up getting all the suffering it thinks they deserve, because it knows all about how the lives of people there are going to turn out before they're even born. Or perhaps it just makes some people get born in places where they're almost bound to do badly in life, such as being born into poor families in a poor country with a high crime rate, and it feels confident that things will work out for them the way it wants them to, like that someone will be in a family that won't be able to afford to give them a good education, so they'll have no chance of going to university and getting a highly paid job so they can climb out of poverty.

"But then if at the age of thirty, the person gets caught in a blizzard and freezes to death, a lot of people will think that must have been their karma. But how would karma know that was going to happen, even before they were born? If it did, then karma sounds creepy to me! But if it didn't, maybe it would be disappointed that the person had escaped the rest of the life of poverty and misery it had intended them to get."

Angela said, "I wonder if a family that believed in karma and that didn't like wasting food might eat something for dinner that was just beginning to go off, and all get food poisoning, and think, 'Oh no, it must be time for us to get a bit of karma; but it's funny how we're all getting the same kind of karma, and at the same time', instead of thinking, 'We'd better not eat food that's starting to go bad again.'"

Miriam said with a slight smile, "Can this conversation get any more depressing? . . . Well yes, actually it can, because I'm just about to make it worse! Sorry about that, folks. I'm just wondering: How does karma treat people who do bad things but they thought they had a good reason to do them, such as people in really miserable marriages who escape from them for a little while every so often by having affairs, or women who eventually murder their abusive husbands? Can karma supposedly read people's thoughts, so it can understand their motives, so they don't get such bad karma if they didn't have bad motives, or does it just judge by what it sees happening, with whatever spirit-eyes it has?

"I heard something about people who believe in karma believing that the better a person's life is, the more likely they are to be able to escape having to be reborn as someone else, and to get to go somewhere better instead. But that doesn't sound like a fair system, since the worse situations people are born into, the more likely they'll often be to end up doing bad things that'll supposedly mean they just get stuck being born into bad situations again and again, such as stealing to get food for their families, or murdering an abuser next door to protect their children, or whatever.

"Or would karma judge murdering abusers and stealing to provide food for the family as good things, and reward a person who did things like that for it in their next life instead of punishing them? But then, what if someone murders an abuser next door to protect their kids from him, but it means the children of the murdered abuser end up going hungry for a long time, because he's no longer around to work to provide food for them, and their mother can't get a job because she has to spend all her time looking after them? What if the person who murdered the abuser knew that would probably happen, but murdered him anyway to stop even worse things happening, so they're partly responsible for what happened to his children? I mean, things often don't just have either good or bad consequences; a lot of actions have a mixture of both! So how would karma judge that?

"I suppose belief in karma could be used for good, such as if governments tell their people they'd better not commit crimes or there could be a punishment waiting for them in their next life. I don't know if that would ever work. But it would probably be more effective to expand the size of police forces, and then to tell people they're putting a lot of money into making policing more effective so they'd better not commit crime or they might well find themselves being punished in this life, by being put in prison!

"I don't know if I'm misunderstanding the doctrine of karma here; but it seems like a stupid illogical harmful belief to me!"

Becky said, "I heard about a way that a certain kind of belief in karma was used to help people though. Well, people who believed in the ordinary kind of karma before, and it was getting them down.

"There's a therapist in America who started working with a lot of immigrants from Cambodia who'd gone to America to escape some terrible things that were happening in their country in the 1970s, when a psychopathic extremist regime came to power with a communist ideology that gave them the idea that successful, educated people should be cut down to size and treated as the enemy. They went to war against their people, and about a quarter of the population ended up being killed. Besides a lot of poor people who were just trying to live their lives, that included most educated people, like teachers and doctors, and other kinds of people who'd been working to do good for society before, who were deliberately targeted.

"Some people managed to emigrate to other countries. But years later, they were still suffering symptoms of trauma because of their war experiences.

"A lot of people from Cambodia went to therapy in America because of the anxiety all the trauma they'd suffered was causing. Some of them had seen close relatives killed in front of them.

"The therapists they went to at first didn't know how to treat them. They tried using the traditional old treatment for post-traumatic stress disorder, which was to get them to talk in great detail about their terrible experiences, with the idea that doing that would relieve their symptoms because airing their memories would help get them out of the system. But the Cambodians didn't like that kind of treatment, because they thought uncovering old memories would just make them feel really upset about them all over again, which it probably would have done. So that kind of therapy didn't work on them.

"At first, psychiatrists thought a lot of them must have mental illnesses like Schizophrenia, because they said they were seeing ghosts and other supernatural things at night, so they put them all on anti-psychotic drugs. But they didn't get better. This new therapist thought it was odd that the percentage of Cambodians who'd come for help who were on anti-psychotics was way way higher than the percentage of other people, as if rates of schizophrenia among Cambodians were much much higher than the percentage in the general population. He started an investigation, and it turned out that most of them really had that sleep paralysis that Craig's got. When the therapist investigated why so many of them had it, it turned out that a lot of them were really stressed because of their traumatic memories, and because of their difficulties adjusting to living in a new country where they didn't speak the language; and they only slept for a couple of hours a night because of all the stress. Both stress and sleep deprivation can bring on this sleep paralysis.

"Most of the Cambodian clients were taken off anti-psychotic drugs. They were a bit disturbed to discover they'd been put on such powerful drugs by mistake. The new therapist started helping them with tasks that would make their lives easier, such as assisting them to fill in forms to get financial help, and going to appointments with them, to help them make themselves understood and to explain to them what was being said to them and the way things worked.

"That did a lot to lower their stress levels. But a lot of them were still feeling miserable a lot of the time. One reason for that was that a lot of them felt hopeless, because they thought the terrible things that had happened to them and their relatives in Cambodia must have been caused by bad karma they had because of terrible things they must have done in a previous life, and they thought any bad fortune they were still experiencing, such as divorce and heartbreak over it, must be a continuation of bad karma, and that there was nothing they could do about it. The feeling of being doomed could make them anxious and panicky. They were Buddhists. I think Buddhism's the predominant religion in Cambodia. Buddhists believe in karma as well as Hindus.

"The therapist went to a Buddhist temple and did a lot of research into Buddhism and karma, to see if he could find something that would help them; and he discovered there's a branch of Buddhism that has a philosophy that teaches that it's possible for people to change their bad karma into good karma sometimes, manipulating the direction it goes in by changing their actions and thought patterns. It turned out to be a bit like cognitive behavioural therapy, which aims to make people happier and less anxious and depressed by teaching them techniques they can use to try to put things they're feeling hopeless about in a less negative perspective in their minds where it's possible, and to focus on how they can solve problems instead of making themselves more and more miserable by brooding on how bad things are.

"So the therapist started teaching his Cambodian clients that they could improve their karma by doing that, instead of having to be continual victims of it. He merged Buddhist ideas with cognitive behavioural therapy. And their mental health improved."

One of the friends, Julie, said, "That's interesting. I think it's possible for the more well-known idea of karma to help people in certain situations as well. I read about a journalist who travelled to the countries that had been hit by the massive tsunami in 2004 that killed loads of people in countries like Thailand and Indonesia. He interviewed people to ask them whether their religious beliefs were giving them any comfort, or an explanation as to why it had been allowed to happen. Some mothers in majority Buddhist countries who'd had young children who'd been killed said they were comforted by their belief that it must have been their children's karma, for bad things they'd done in previous lives. That must have been better for them than thinking of the tsunami as some horrific random happening that could strike out of the blue and kill people for no reason.

"If they'd been scientifically educated, I don't suppose they'd have received that kind of comfort, although they might have been more likely to analyse the real reasons why it had happened and campaign for things to change, for instance for early warning systems to be put in place to give people more chance of escaping future tsunamis, and for some government policies to change.

"Apparently, there had been a lot of deforestation in coastal areas in some of those countries to make room for houses and other things; but the forests had actually protected inland areas to some extent from tsunamis and cyclones, because they formed a barrier that slowed them down and took some of the energy out of them, so they weren't so bad when they got inland. Cutting down a lot of the trees meant the inland areas of those countries weren't so well protected. So it seems that one thing their governments could have done to prevent disasters from being so bad in future would have been to forbid any more deforestation there, and to have forests of trees planted around the coasts, as well as forbidding houses from being built in coastal areas, so fewer people would be living in areas that were at a high risk of experiencing natural disasters from then on. I don't know if they did that.

"But still, I read that a lot of people were inspired by their belief in karma to fund-raise for projects to help the disaster victims, believing it would either improve their own karma, or improve the karma of people who'd died so they'd have better lives next time around. Then again, it's possible they would have still wanted to raise a lot of money for disaster relief if they hadn't had a belief in karma, so it's difficult to know how much of a difference the belief really made."

Shirley said, "I've heard about belief in karma being used for good. I can't guarantee this story's true, but I heard someone from Singapore once say there was someone who worked in his office who got migraines a lot. One day he went to a Hindu priest to see if he could give him any advice about how to get rid of them. I don't know why he went to a priest about them, but maybe he'd tried other things and they hadn't worked. The priest told him his migraines were being caused by bad karma that he was suffering because of bad things he'd done in a previous life, and he said the way to get rid of them would be to dedicate his life from then on to doing good. The man gave up his office job and spent his days from then on doing work to help people, and he didn't have a single migraine after that.

"I don't know what would have really stopped his migraines. Maybe they were brought on by stress at work before, or some kind of food he only ate at work, or something toxic about the environment there that his body was especially sensitive to, or something else like that. The man telling us the story thought there must be something to this karma belief if something as dramatic as his migraines completely stopping happened when he followed the priest's advice. It was a good outcome anyway, whatever the cause. But I suppose it's a good thing his migraines weren't being caused by some kind of illness he really needed medical treatment for, or the advice might have dissuaded him from trying to get doctors to look into it."

The Friends Get Light-Hearted and Start Joking

The friends thought that was interesting. But Ben smiled and said, "I'm wondering why some of you have spent so long thinking about this karma stuff! I mean, some of you must have pondered this subject for a while before you came here tonight to have come up with so many questions about it! Was it just more interesting than thinking about what you ought to say in your essays?"

Danny answered, "Lots and lots of things are more interesting than doing essays! That's one reason why I spend time on Internet forums. I was on one the other day when I had a conversation about cows. Hindus think they're sacred, don't they? I don't know if that means they worship them.

"But anyway, I was talking to a farmer who'd had experience of rearing cows. He said, 'It's interesting to watch the "pecking order" at work at milking time; each cow takes her place in line, with the most senior or highest-ranking cow going first. If the farmer tries to change the milking order, the cows get into a scuffle and might not submit to being milked.'

"I half-joked, 'Wow, so cows have hierarchies? What determines a cow's position in the hierarchy? Are cows really power-crazed megalomaniacs vying to rule over the herd or to have a decent position in the pecking order? Or do they just have really good manners, and like to queue nicely, so they don't like it if the farmer wants to make some of them jump the queue?'

"Someone else said, 'It's the inflection of the MOOOOO-OOOOOOO that determines the rank of the cow. But then there are Moooooos for "I need to be fed", Mooooooos for "I need to be milked", and Mooooooooooos for "Better get out of my face or else!"'

"I replied, 'Aha! So it's the cows who've learned to muster up the most aggressive mooos who get to the top of the hierarchy? That makes sense. Or the cows who can manage to sound as if they need to be fed or milked the most urgently can go near the front, because perhaps the rest of the cows are courteous or caring? It would be interesting if they could talk so we knew what they were saying. Then again, it might be boring a lot of the time, since they don't have interesting lives, so their conversations might be quite dull a lot of the time, like perhaps spending a good half an hour discussing the taste of grass and whether it's nicer with dew on it. I knew some people who used to have conversations like that about cups of tea.'"

Shirley joked, "You mean about whether tea's nicer with dew in it?"

Adam quipped, "I'd prefer it with grass in it . . . at least if it was the cannabis kind."

Becky joked, "Wow, just imagine if cows ate a lot of cannabis plants! Maybe anyone who drank their milk every day would feel so laid-back they wouldn't want to bother to work; and if everyone in the country was drinking cannabis milk because all the cows in the country somehow got to eat cannabis plants, maybe no one would bother working, and the place would grind to a halt! Imagine everyone drinking cups of coffee before they started work, expecting them to wake them up, and instead they ended up feeling so laid-back they couldn't be bothered to do anything! Imagine a boss coming in and yelling at his workers, if he hadn't had any milk that day. He might say, 'Hurry up. We've all got a deadline to meet!' And then imagine if a well-meaning person in the office said, 'Calm down. I'll get you a nice milky cup of tea to help you.' And they did, and the boss ended up feeling so laid-back he said, 'Let's not worry about the deadline!' "

Shirley grinned and said, "He might need to drink about ten gallons of milk before it had that effect . . . if that would even be possible in one go! I expect he'd explode all over the floor before he could ever finish it all! Yikes! Watch out for the exploding boss! But then, the workers would probably have to have drunk that much as well if they were going to be really laid-back, so maybe everyone in the office would explode, one by one, perhaps. I wouldn't want to be anywhere near that office during the great milk explosion!

"But maybe everyone in the country would want to get the cannabis effects, so everyone would drink that much milk at once, so everyone in the country would explode! . . . Or maybe we'd all just have really really bad stomach aches, so bad it was impossible to feel laid-back! Then no one would ever try that again! But the country would still grind to a halt for a while, as almost everyone in it was off sick!"

Lauren said, "If everyone in the country exploded and died, karma would have a whole lot of work to do, wouldn't it, deciding where to make everyone be born next so as to make sure everyone was in a place where they'd get the amount of suffering they deserved! Perhaps it would be overloaded, and the whole karmic system would come to a crashing halt!"

Becky said, "That could be a relief to a whole lot of souls that didn't fancy coming back here! Imagine if someone who'd had a hard life was dying, and they thought that at least when they did they'd finally get to rest; but as soon as they died, their soul was put into a baby who was just being born, and it remembered where it had just come from for a little while, so some of its first cries were caused by its distress at finding itself back here to live life all over again!"

Mandy said, "Yikes! Yeah, you'd have thought the forces of reincarnation, just supposing they exist, could have the grace to at least allow people to have a bit of a rest before they're sent back here, especially after the bad karma they've just inflicted on them! That's if they're the ones that do it. I suppose they might just watch the show while other forces do it, although they'd have to at least be in league with them to make sure people were born in the places where they were going to get the karma the karmic forces wanted to inflict on them."

Miriam joked, "I agree about how it would be nice of them to give people a break from the world for a bit. It would only be considerate of them to do that, except for people who'd behaved like savages. Those ones would deserve to get reborn over and over again as blades of grass that kept being walked on or chewed up by cows, or something worse. Then again, I don't know if grass minds that kind of thing happening to it, or even has any consciousness so it would know it was happening . . . I hope it doesn't, actually, otherwise just think of how much grass must have suffered over the centuries.

"But as for people who'd been decent, it would be nice if the forces of reincarnation could even try to find it in themselves to be abnormally nice just for a little while out of sympathy, and lay on health spas for souls to help them recover from the karma they made them suffer on Earth, where the souls could get a massage and some soothing time in a sauna, and some good food!"

Lorna said, "Being reincarnated could sometimes be good though. I mean, just imagine if we came back in a couple of hundred years' time, and discovered all this amazing impressive technology that had been invented since we died. And imagine if all diseases had been cured, and there was no more war or poverty in the world, because somehow good people had got into power all over the world, and they'd all started governing their countries well, and got together to solve the world's problems. We might enjoy being back here then."

Ben said, "I've got a suspicion the world will be destroyed in a nuclear war long before that could ever happen!"

"Misery guts! Still, you never know," said Lorna.

The Friends Talk About Little Children Who Have Claimed to be Other People in Previous Lives, and False Memories

Angela said, "I've heard about little children claiming to remember past lives, thinking they used to be people they can't have known much about at all; and when the details of their claims are investigated, they turn out to match those of people who died not long before who lived fairly nearby, although not near enough for their families to have known them. Has anyone heard about that?"

Dawn said, "I have. I heard there was a psychiatrist in the 1950s called Ian Stevenson who was interested in that kind of stuff, believing in reincarnation and other paranormal-type things, and he travelled to lots of different places in the world, collecting stories about little children whose parents were sure they were remembering past lives as people who'd died nearby in those countries not long before. I wanted to find out more about that, so I read more about him on the Internet.

"The thing is that I think most of the children lived in cultures where it's common to believe in reincarnation, so that could have had something to do with it. For instance, maybe some of them started thinking they were reincarnations of those other people when they said things to their parents that people from other cultures would interpret differently from the way some people in their cultures might, and then their parents started telling them they wondered if they were reincarnations of them; for instance, if any of the children saw a photo of a child who died some time before, without having been told who they were, and said, 'That's me!', it's possible that some parents who believed in reincarnation would start wondering if they meant they were that child in a past life, when parents who didn't would just tell them they'd made a mistake, thinking they must be assuming they were the one the picture was taken of when it was really someone else.

"I actually heard about a woman in Israel who gave birth to a son, and just a couple of hours afterwards, she heard that her brother had been killed in a war Israel was having at the time. The woman named her son after her brother. When the boy was growing up, he would often look at a picture of her brother and say, 'That's me in the picture, right?'

"I don't know how the family reacted to that. Maybe they didn't deny it, because they were a bit spooked and wondered if it was possible that he was really a reincarnation of the brother.

"I don't know if the boy thought it was him because he assumed that since he had the same name as his mum's brother who was killed, he must be the same person, reincarnated. But he would even say things like, 'A terrorist killed me. When I grow up, I'm going to kill all the terrorists!'

"But his mum's brother might really have been killed after he was born. I don't know when people who believe in reincarnation think souls enter new bodies – at the moment they're born, at conception, or what.

"But anyway, about these children the psychiatrist collected stories about, I'm thinking it's possible that some of their parents might have encouraged them to start believing they used to be other people without realising they were doing it, by doing things like wondering if other things they said could mean they were the reincarnations of certain people, and unwittingly making comments that put the idea that they were into the children's minds.

"For example, if a child's scared of water, for no reason their reincarnation-believing parents can think of, the parents might start wondering within earshot of the child whether they could be the reincarnation of someone they've heard about who recently died of drowning; and that might spark off the child's imagination; and the parents might discuss what they know about the person within earshot of the child so they pick up some information about them; and then the more things the child says that sound as if they're hinting that they might have been the person, the more the parents might become convinced they were; and the more the parents become convinced they were, the more the child might become convinced they were too, because they're sure their parents must know what they're talking about. And the more they imagine being the person, suffering things they suffered, the more they might start to feel emotions when they're talking about being them, which might make what they say seem more convincing.

"The psychiatrist said that a lot of the children displayed strong emotions when they were talking about bad things that they said happened to them in a previous life, and also they behaved in ways that made it seem as if they could have been them. For instance, some children who thought they were people of the opposite sex in a past life wanted to wear clothes the people of the opposite sex wore, and some wanted to play games they might have played; and some children in countries like India that have a caste system believed they'd been people from a higher caste in a previous life, and behaved snobbishly towards their lower-caste parents.

"But a lot of children really like role-playing, pretending to be other people; so it's possible that the more convinced they became that they were certain other people in previous lives, the more they wanted to act out being them.

"Also, there would be an incentive for someone in a low-caste family to persuade a little child of theirs they were someone of a higher caste, in the hope that the family they supposedly came from might accept that they really were them, and treat them to things that gave their family a higher quality of life than they would have otherwise because of their low caste, which would have stopped them being so successful in life, for reasons such as that low-paid jobs might be the only ones people in their caste are allowed to get.

"And there were children who believed they'd been shot in a past life who got scared when they heard gunshots or other loud noises. But I think a lot of children are scared of loud noises. And the more they started imagining being killed by being shot, the more such things would likely have scared them.

"Another thing is that if a little child starts telling their parents they can remember being someone else in a past life, they might be just doing it for fun at first, or they might be being fanciful; but if the parents think they're being serious and are pleased and excited about it, and praise the child and give them special attention because of it, the child will see it pleases the parents, and love all the special attention they're getting, so they'll likely want to keep making the claims and imagine more and more things, to get more of their parents' approval, and to keep the special attention going so they get more nice feelings from it, especially if they're also getting it from neighbours and relatives and friends of their parents. It's just human nature to want more of that kind of thing.

"That wouldn't explain how they would have known details about people who've died who they hadn't even met;

but news about things like murders and tragedies would have been likely to spread from village to village, brought by people like travelling salesmen, and maybe other people who travelled around a bit; so it's quite likely their parents would have got to hear about them, and discussed them while the children were around, which might have got the children's imaginations going.

"Some of these little children were thought to have birthmarks in the same places where the people they said they thought they'd reincarnated from had been wounded, such as from bullet wounds they got when they were killed; and their families and the psychiatrist took that as evidence that they were them. But it might have just meant that the parents had heard the stories about the people who got killed, and when they saw that their children had birthmarks in the same places as the wounds those people got when they were killed, as far as they knew, then because of their belief in reincarnation, they started wondering out loud whether their children could be reincarnations of them, and if their birthmarks were signs of it. And that could have started the children vividly imagining they used to be them.

"Or the parents might have even assumed from the start that their birthmarks must be signs that they'd been wounded in the places where they had them in a previous life, and then done some investigation to find out who'd died with wounds in those places, and then started suggesting to the children that they might be reincarnated from them, which could have set off the children's imaginations.

"It's possible that the children came to genuinely believe they were reincarnations of other people who'd definitely existed, even if some of them hadn't really believed it at first.

Some psychologists think that even when people think back over their own lives, especially if they use their imaginations to picture the details of things that happened, the more their real memories can gradually become distorted by what they imagine happened, or even by what they want to believe happened, because memories fade over time, and people can use their imaginations to help them try to bring to mind what's missing in them; and then as an event's remembered again and again over the years, it gets harder for people to distinguish what's real memory and what's the product of what they've imagined when they've tried to recall it.

"Also, the more a person vividly imagines a thing they think might have happened in their past, the more familiar it'll seem to them; and the more familiar a thing seems, the more likely a person is to come to mistake it for a real memory. Something like that anyway.

"Well, I don't know if that happens to everyone, or whether some people are a lot more susceptible to it than others, because they're more suggestible or something; and I don't know how often it really happens. I don't really know that much about this stuff."

Miriam said, "I think I know what you mean, because I've heard a couple of stories where things like that happened.

"One was told by a man called Ben, who said that when he was about ten years old, his teacher made his class do this horrible activity where they had to play some kind of short card game over and over again, where pairs of kids played against each other; and the kids were given points according to how well they did, and the ones who won it the most were put in a winners' team, where they'd still play against others in the class, but they had control over some of the rules of the game, and could get together to confer with each other between games about whether to change them if they liked.

"Ben was put in the winners' team. They decided it would be nice to change the rules to make it more likely they'd win the rest of the games. One rule they changed was to allot themselves an extra card each to make it more likely they'd win, since each card was worth a certain number of points, and the people with the highest number of points at the end of a game would win. They decided they deserved it, because before they did that, they repealed a few rules that no one liked, so they thought they could justify rewarding themselves because they'd done everyone a good turn. At least, that's what they told themselves about their motives.

"You might not understand what on earth that has to do with people's memories getting distorted over time; but I'll come to that in the end.

"After a while, someone else in the class started winning so many games it looked as if he was going to get onto the winners' team, and one of them was going to be demoted out of it despite them having an advantage over the rest of the class, since there always had to be the same number of people on the winners' team. So most of them decided it would be a good idea to change the rules so they could award the person who had the lowest score on the winners' team a hundred extra points, to prevent him from having to lose his place on the team.

"Earlier that day, a boy who'd been Ben's friend up till then had said he didn't want to play with him any more because his team was doing unfair things and he was annoyed about it. Ben was upset about that, so when the rest of his winners' team decided it would be great to award one of them extra points, he argued with them at first, saying it wouldn't be fair on the others in the class.

"The rest of the team disagreed, saying it would be great, and that it wouldn't be fair on the team if he refused to agree to them doing it. A rule that they couldn't change was that everyone had to agree to a rule change or it couldn't happen, so they thought it was important that he agreed with them. They protested that they all needed to stick together and protect the team.

"The discussion was going on in front of the whole class, and the whole class got angry and started shouting about how unfair the new rule change would be; and then they got up and started coming towards the team. Ben must have worried about what was about to happen. And torn between allowing himself to be persuaded he needed to stick up for his team and agree to the rule change, and siding with the class and continuing to say it was unfair and refusing to go along with them, he didn't know what to do.

"He knew the right thing to do would be to refuse to go along with the team, but he thought it would be nice to stick with them, and it felt great to have the power to change the rules so they could get the upper hand over the others.

"Ben said he can't remember what he actually did now, because he's told the story lots of times since, and sometimes, to make himself look like a nice person, he's told it with the ending that he refused to go along with the team and stuck up for the class; but sometimes he's told it with the ending that he gave in and decided to stick with what the team wanted. So over time, things have got confused in his memory, and he can't remember which ending was the real one now.

"He said he's been told that people tell stories to look good, and to make themselves feel good about themselves. I don't know how often that's really the case. But maybe if you deliberately tell a story in an inaccurate way enough times, as your memory of what really happened fades, you start to think you remember that that's what really happened.

"In any case, the teacher intervened to stop the chaos and ended the game after that, saying it had been designed to teach them how people can be corrupted when they're given unlimited power over others. If most of the pupils who'd been complaining about the unfairness had been the ones on the winners' team themselves, it's likely they'd have behaved as unfairly to the rest of the class as the real winners did.

"I suppose it's possible that neither of the endings Ben thinks might have happened really did, and that what really happened was that the teacher stopped the game before he made any decision at all, before someone got hurt.

"I heard another story involving hazy memories, about a woman who trained to be a teacher, and she was assigned to teach in this horrible school in a rough neighbourhood, where it was hard to control the kids and there was a lot of fighting. She didn't like the idea of working there, especially because she hadn't been trained to deal with kids like that, so she didn't know what to do for the best. But she started going to an evening class about teaching children after school finished for the day that she hoped would help. It didn't. It turned out to be all about teaching well-behaved kids who always did what they were told.

"One day, she'd had a really stressful day, because all the kids had started fighting and the police had had to be called. She really didn't fancy going to her evening class. But she did.

But she got really fed up of the lesson where they were being shown a video of these well-behaved kids just getting down to learning with no problem; and because she was feeling so stressed, she eventually jumped up and declared that the class was stupid and no good, and swore quite a bit.

"She said she seems to remember herself going on to explain sensibly why it didn't have anything to do with teaching the kinds of kids she was teaching, but she suspects that what she really did was just swear some more and proclaim that the class was stupid again. Then she walked out and never went back. Maybe she's thought so often about the way she'd like to have behaved that her imaginings about what she'd like to have said have got confused a bit with her real memories. That's what she thinks might have happened."

Dawn said, "That's interesting. So psychologists must have a point when they talk about memories getting distorted over time.

"I've heard that psychologists have even done experiments where they've been able to quickly implant false memories in people, to prove it really is easy to do. One technique that's been used is where a psychologist tells some people they might very well have got upset when they were little because they got lost one day when they were out shopping with their parents, after checking first with their parents that that didn't really happen. They can make up some details about what supposedly happened, saying the parents have told them about it, and then tell the people they're experimenting on that if they can't remember it themselves, they should imagine it happening vividly and then think a lot about whether it really did happen over the next week or so, trying to recall details of it. A lot of people have ended up really believing it happened after that . . . Well, unless they just told the psychologists they did, because they thought not being able to remember it would make them look stupid or something.

"Of course, it's also possible that they were remembering something like it accurately, but their parents had forgotten all about it, so they told the psychologists before the experiment that it hadn't happened.

"But if the people the psychologists were experimenting on really did believe it when it hadn't happened, it proves that false memories really can be generated that easily, so maybe something similar was often happening with the children whose families the psychiatrist Ian Stevenson interviewed about their supposed past lives in the 1950s. Maybe the more the children imagined having them, the more details they thought they remembered, especially if they dreamed about them too, and their parents believed their dreams might well be actual memories, or meant to convey significant information from the spirit world, so the children believed they were special and important to remember.

"And in cultures where most people believe in reincarnation and the spirit world, if a little child has an imaginary playmate, some parents might wonder if the imaginary person's someone from the spirit world, and ask questions about who they are; and the more questions they ask, the more the child will be encouraged to make up details, maybe sometimes taking inspiration from real-life things they've heard about.

"The psychiatrist Ian Stevenson interviewed the parents and family members of the children whose stories he wanted to hear about as well as them, to find out more about what the children had said. The only children he interviewed about their own reincarnation stories were the little ones, because he thought little children would have been less likely to have picked up the information they were telling him about past lives from stories they'd heard or read.

"But like I said, they could in reality still have overheard them when the parents picked up stories about people who'd been killed a while before in nearby villages from people who travelled around a bit and heard and passed on the stories, or from other people who'd found out about them from people like that, who then met their parents and told them about them while they were chatting in the market place or in pubs or wherever people tended to meet together. Or the parents might have found out about them from local newspapers, if there were such things around in those days where they lived and they'd been taught how to read, and discussed them around their children.

"And it's possible that some parents told the psychiatrist that their children had said things they actually hadn't said, perhaps sometimes because they thought it would improve their life prospects if they had great stories to go in his book that might make them famous.

"And in most of the cases, the children were claiming that they used to be members of their own families who'd died a while earlier, so the personal details of those would have been known to the parents; and it was the parents who gave the psychiatrist most of the information, partly because a lot of the children were too shy to talk to him in person.

"Quite a large percentage of the children said they'd died violent deaths in their previous lives. That might help explain how they got to know the details of the names of the people they said they thought they were, and the places where they lived, since news of a violent death would be much more likely to be spread around than news of someone who'd died peacefully at home."

Monica said for fun, "I heard a comment once by someone who said it's funny how a lot of people who claim to have discovered they were reincarnated claim to have been a famous person in a previous life, like Henry VIII, rather than just an ordinary person. I think lots of people might claim to have been Henry VIII. If they all were, just how many Henry VIIIs must there have been around? Maybe there were secretly dozens of them, who took turns at ruling, with each one ruling for a month at a time while the others had a rest. Imagine what big fights they might have got into if one of them ordered a policy change the others disagreed with, or if one wanted to sleep with a wife that was officially his but had been married by another one of the Henry VIIIs. Maybe that was the reason there was only one Henry VIII left in the end, because their fights were so deadly all the others were killed."

The friends giggled.

Then Dawn smiled and said, "I suppose you never know! Anyway, to finish the story about these children, the psychiatrist did think it was quite possible that their accounts were the result of imagination and other such things, so with every case, he investigated it to see if he could come up with possible natural explanations for it, and to check whether the person a child said they thought they were had really existed, and had died in the way the child said they did; but he was often fairly convinced that the stories were genuine cases of reincarnation, although he did say he could never be absolutely sure, and that he was aware that there were alternative explanations for what he was finding. It seems he really wanted to believe it though.

"Another thing he took to be evidence of reincarnation, according to what I read, was where children were especially gifted; he thought they must have developed their advanced talents in a previous life if they were advanced for their age group, and at a very young age too. But maybe their parents just started teaching them early; and apart from that, some kinds of intelligence are genetic; and even where the parents aren't gifted, the genes can still exist, and people in previous generations of the family can have had the ability to pick up certain types of skills more easily than other people could.

"Another problem with the psychiatrist's research could have been that the people he used as interpreters might have been telling him the children said things they didn't really say; some were found to be fraudulent, but for some reason, the psychiatrist was convinced they weren't being dishonest with him personally.

"And I read that one thing that casts some doubt on the existence of reincarnation in general is that people's claims about their past lives fit with the expectations that people in their particular cultures have; for instance, people in cultures where humans would never be expected to come back as people of the opposite sex aren't known to ever report that they have, while people in cultures where it's believed that it's possible to do that often report that they have; and people from cultures where it's believed that humans can't be rein-carnated from animals never say they have been, while people in cultures where it's believed that they can have often said they did. That gives the impression that the ones who claim to have been reincarnated imagine things based on their beliefs about the way things are."

One of the Friends Tells the Others About a Joke He Made

Danny said, "I had an argument on a forum with a man who claimed to be a Buddhist. They believe in reincarnation, or at least a lot of them do. Anyway, this man was annoying me, and I made a joke for a laugh. I linked to a post someone made that mocked the idea of reincarnation, and said he should go and dispute what the man who'd written it said in a duel. I really meant an argument on the forum. I told him,

"'Go on, go and fight! Fight to the death – yours, preferably. But you won't mind dying in the duel, because since you believe in reincarnation, you're bound to think you'll just bounce right back and come to life again. Is reincarnation a bit like being a jack-in-the-box, where no matter how many times you're pushed down, you just spring back up? You won't mind that then.'

"I said, 'Actually, I suppose it must be like a video game, where you can get killed, sometimes perhaps any number of times, but then you can just respawn yourself and go back to the beginning and start again. So you'll have to go back to being a baby. I suppose it'll be a shame that you won't be able to go straight back to fighting the duel you just lost, but at least you'll be alive again, and you might have it to look forward to when you've mastered enough levels of life to get to a place where you can start fighting it again.'"

One Friend Tells the Others About a Story About a Space Alien Working for the American Government in the 1950s

The friends smiled. Then Miriam said, "I wonder if anyone's ever claimed to have been a space alien in a past life! Probably!"

Becky grinned and said, "Yeah! Maybe they'd say they were supposed to have been reincarnated back on the planet they lived on before, but there must have been a mix-up in the planetary soul reallocation department and they got sent to the wrong place or something."

The friends chuckled.

Then Lauren said, "You hear some weird stories about space aliens, and government cover-ups of alien landings on Earth and things! I've heard about some stories of alien landings that turned out to be fake.

"I heard a story not long ago about a man who travelled around as a Christian evangelist – who was also maybe a UFO evangelist or something – who claimed that in the late 1950s, a friendly alien from Venus called Valiant Thor zoomed down to Earth and met him, telling him the aliens had had their eyes on earthlings ever since they'd invented nuclear weapons, and they'd come to ask governments to be peaceful instead of blowing the Earth into oblivion one day, and to share alien technologies with us – although it seems they somehow didn't manage to do that, for some reason.

"But the man said he introduced the alien and his companion aliens to the American government, where the alien Valiant Thor advised them at the Pentagon for three years. Goodness knows what he was supposed to have advised them on; it seems they didn't take any notice, if it was to do with being more peaceful. But after that, the alien supposedly dematerialised one day, and went to live in the woods somewhere in America, where no one will ever find him, because there's a special force field around his residence that repels anyone who comes near or something.

"It's no wonder he wanted to settle there instead of going home, since Venus is actually thought to be uninhabitable, because the temperature there is over four hundred and fifty degrees Centigrade, which is apparently hot enough to melt lead, and there's no evidence of water there. Goodness knows how the alien was supposedly born and raised there in the first place . . . I suppose if you can dematerialise at will, maybe that's how to survive on Venus – maybe the whole place is chock-full of dematerialised aliens who don't know of each other's existence because they're all invisible to each other. Maybe they just risk materialising for a few minutes in the hope they can survive for that long when they get lonely or want to find a mate, hoping other aliens will have done the same thing at the same time so they can talk to them or mate with them or whatever; and maybe the politician aliens there all risk materialising for a few minutes every time they need to have a meeting, and just have a lot of very short ones instead of any long ones.

"Not joking for a minute though, it seems some people took this man's claims seriously, and it seems there was actually a film made about them, and he wrote a book about them; and there have been TV shows about aliens and things that have suggested that the events really did happen. But the man who said he'd met the alien was most likely just a conman, trying to sell books he'd written about UFOs.

"I heard that his story actually sounds a lot like the plot of a science-fiction film that had been released at the beginning of the 1950s. It seems that's where he must have got the ideas from.

"And I heard that he made claims that he was a high-ranking official who had security clearance at the Pentagon; but he actually didn't, and he never worked for the American government at all. And he claimed to be an assistant director of an important organisation that turned out not to even exist! And he claimed to have gone to a university that doesn't exist either, and to have got a PhD from another one that doesn't actually do PhDs!

"Only a couple of people claimed to have seen the alien he declared he'd met, but one of them seems to have been a fraudster who claimed to be the nephew of a certain American admiral, but almost certainly wasn't, and made some really weird claims, like that the admiral had entrusted him with diaries about his contact with aliens when he was a boy, and did all kinds of other strange things. His supposed nephew was probably hoping all his claims would help to sell books about that kind of thing that he'd written.

"But the other person was actually who she claimed to be, the great-granddaughter of an American president who was in the White House when this alien supposedly materialised on Earth. She claimed to be sure the American government was covering up evidence of alien visitations. But she actually seems to have been a bit nutty, or mentally ill, or to have had some kind of slight brain injury or something, because she would make all kinds of weird claims, like that aliens tried to recruit her to join a colony on Mars, and that she was working to 'open natural stargates', and assist in the 'grounding of the

Mother Arc energies into the earth core', and all kinds of things like that.

"As for this supposed evangelist though, he made his claims about the friendly alien in 1967; but between the time when he supposedly met him and then, he wrote two books and made a couple of films about UFOs, but didn't mention the alien once! The only logical explanation seems to be that he hadn't made up the story then!"

Lorna joked, "Some people do make up wacky things! Wow, if dematerialised aliens do exist though, we could be sitting on some right now! Maybe each one of us is sitting on an invisible alien without knowing it! Mind you, they might have said 'ouch' or something when we sat down if they existed and were sitting here first."

They all grinned.

Then Angela said, "I wonder if people who get sleep paralysis where they think they're seeing aliens would feel any better during episodes of it if they read books about friendly aliens, and started thinking any aliens that zoomed out of space and for some reason picked their bedroom to land in out of all the places in the world they could go would probably be friendly ones."

The student who'd brought up his sleep paralysis problems at the start of the conversation, Craig, said, "I don't know about that! What you think in your dreams isn't really within your control, and the feeling of paralysis is going to make whatever you see seem scary!"

The Friends Talk About Some Reasons Why Some People Sense Things That Aren't Really There

Then Craig asked Becky if she'd finished saying what she'd wanted to say about sleep paralysis before, or whether she had more she could tell him. She replied:

"Well, I've heard that apart from being more likely to happen to people when they're stressed, it happens to some people much more often than others. I've read that some scientists think it might have something to do with the temporal lobes, which are parts of the brain near the ears. I don't really understand it because I haven't read all that much about it, but they reckon that in some people, those parts of the brain are more active than in others, and sometimes they can get overactive, and then people can think they're having out-of-body or psychic experiences. Experiments have been done where people's temporal lobes were stimulated with electrodes or magnets put near them, and then some of them felt as if someone was near them when no one was really, or they felt as if they were flying or floating, or even being touched."

"Wow!" said a couple of the group.

"What on earth are the temporal lobes really for?" asked Angela. "They can't be there just to give people weird experiences. What do they do normally?"

"I think they help interpret what people see and hear," Ben responded. "I don't know why it seems some people's make up things to see and hear too."

Julie said, "Oh I've heard about that kind of thing. I heard there was one man who invented this helmet thing, and did experiments on people where they put it on, and he used something to make magnetic fields go through it to stimulate those parts of the brain, and some people felt as if they were sensing God, or someone with them. He thought it was really one side of the brain sensing the other, and mistaking it for something outside."

Adam said with a smile, "Maybe there are some people who could feel as if they sensed God, who when they were told they were sensing their own brain, would say they were one and the same."

The friends grinned. Then Julie said, "I heard about a castle that had the reputation for being haunted, especially a particular bed that had strange magnetic fields flowing around it. I can't remember why they were there, but it was because of some totally natural thing. But people who slept in the bed often thought ghosts had been in the room in the night, maybe because they got weird sensations or impressions of things because of the way the magnetic fields were affecting their brains. I think an experiment was done where volunteers slept in the bed to see what happened."

"What did happen?" asked Lorna.

Julie said, "I can't remember now."

"Oh, a fat lot of good you are!" said Lauren, grinning, and they all laughed.

The Friends Discuss Ghost Sightings and Other Strange-Seeming Things

Mandy said, "I went to a talk by someone who used to believe in ghosts but doesn't any more, and now goes around telling people they don't exist. She said she met a woman who was convinced she had ghosts in her house because a cupboard in her kitchen kept opening by itself. The woman who gave the talk reckoned it was probably just that someone had put it up crookedly so the door was tilted a bit so it was falling open sometimes."

Miriam grinned and said, "Or maybe it was just the woman's kids getting things out and forgetting to close the door afterwards . . . Or opening it and then telling her it just flew open by itself, thinking it was a good joke."

Julie said, "Or maybe it was *her* getting something out the cupboard and then forgetting to close it, not realising she sometimes forgot to, so she was often surprised when she noticed it was open."

Becky2 said, "I came across a website with stories on it that were written by someone who goes out ghost hunting. She told a funny story about a day when a group of them went out to do that, and she was at the front, walking through this cave, and suddenly she felt something touch her leg. She thought it must be a ghost, and screamed. That scared everyone else, and they all screamed too. And they were all startled, so some of them jumped and dropped the things they were carrying. Then they all ran off, leaving her behind. Then she suddenly realised that the thing that had touched her leg was only the loose strap of her rucksack. She was embarrassed, and didn't know whether to admit to the others what had really happened, or if she should just keep things mysterious."

The friends giggled, and Mandy said, "The speaker doing the talk I went to about belief in ghosts said she was once with a group of ghost hunters in a pub that was supposed to be haunted. They were upstairs looking around, when suddenly from the floor below they heard a loud crash, with glass smashing. They were all scared, thinking it must be the ghost that haunted the pub. They went downstairs feeling nervous, only to find the landlord laughing his head off. He'd dropped some things on purpose to scare them!"

"I don't understand why he'd want to waste some of his glasses just so he could see them all scared and have a laugh about it!" said Becky, looking puzzled.

"I dunno," said Becky2. "Maybe it's something that's more likely to be done by the male of the species!"

"Oy!" said a couple of the young men in the room, grinning good-naturedly.

Ben said, "I don't suppose anyone can really tell whether ghosts exist or not, but I heard that natural things can happen that make people think they're seeing ghosts. One is that when there are sounds that are too low-frequency for people to hear, then for some reason, they can see strange images, and think they must be ghosts, because there doesn't seem to be any other explanation for them.

"There was a man working in a university laboratory who thought he saw this grey thing coming for him one night. It was between him and the door, so he thought the only thing he could do was to turn and face it down. When he did, it disappeared.

"But the next night while he was working again, it came back in a different form. Then he noticed something he was working on was vibrating in one part of the room, but it didn't vibrate if he put it in other parts. He wondered what was causing it. After a while he turned off an extractor fan, and the thing he was working with stopped vibrating. He suddenly felt a lot better than he had while the fan was on, without being sure why, and the spooky form wasn't there any more. He realised the fan must have been making really low-frequency sounds that he couldn't hear, but that were causing weird effects.

"They say at certain low frequencies, sound makes the eyeballs resonate, and that causes optical illusions like the things he saw. So that might be one reason some people think they're seeing ghosts. And I heard it can cause strong emotions too, like anxiety or chills or sorrow."

Lorna said, "I think I'd feel anxiety and chills and sorrow if my eyeballs started vibrating, or whatever you said they do!"

The friends chuckled.

Becky said with a worried look, "Wow, I've just thought! If we can't hear some sounds, that must mean there might be sounds around us that are really loud but we still can't hear them because they're too low-pitched! Couldn't that mean our ears are being damaged without us knowing, since loud noise can damage hearing?"

Miriam said, "Well I wouldn't worry if I were you; if it *can* happen, I don't suppose it happens very often, or there would be a lot more people going around with damaged hearing that no one knew how they'd got; or a whole neighbourhood of people might have their hearing damaged at the same time, from babies to old people. I don't know, but I've never heard of that happening."

Becky2 said, "I'm surprised babies don't damage their *own* hearing with the way they yell – it's so loud!"

Angela said, "Imagine if really low-pitched loud sounds went on in the earth before earthquakes. People's eyeballs might be resonating all over the place, and there might be sightings of things people thought were ghosts, and myths might grow about how ghosts would come and warn people earthquakes were about to happen."

Adam said, "Or maybe myths would get spread about how ghosts *cause* them, since lots of people might notice they appeared just before them."

Lorna said, "Actually, I think earthquakes *do* make very low-frequency sounds before people realise they're on the way. I've heard that research is being done into whether animals can sense some earthquakes coming, which they might partly do by picking up low-pitched sounds that we can't hear. There are stories of animals running away or behaving in an agitated way before some earthquakes happened, although it's hard to know whether that was the cause, or whether something else was. Sometimes there are little earthquakes before a big one that people can feel but they don't do any damage, so a lot of animals might have been bothered by those rather than sensing something bigger on the way.

"Or sometimes it could be that people's pets get agitated for other reasons, not all of them known to their owners, so it wouldn't necessarily be the impending earthquake causing it; and most of their episodes of agitation might be quickly forgotten by their owners, but the time when they got agitated before the earthquake might stick in the mind a lot more because it seemed so significant, so they might think their pets must have been able to sense it coming, rather than it being just one of their regular episodes of agitation.

"I think there are people who are planning to set up a system where people can send reports in when their pets are agitated or when they notice other animals are, and if there are a lot more reports before earthquakes, they'll know there must be something in the stories about animals being able to sense them coming."

Angela said, "It'll be good if animals really can sense them, since if there's enough time for animals to escape, surely humans could escape too if they were given enough warning. Has anyone tried to invent a warning system that can detect what scientists think animals could be detecting, which could set off an alarm when it detects it? Maybe then countries prone to earthquakes could have earthquake sirens. Do you know if any countries have tried to develop any kind of early warning system for earthquakes? Then again, I suppose they'd have to do their best to make sure animals really can sense them coming before they went to all the time and expense of doing that, unless they've developed another way of detecting them coming. Do you know if they have?"

No one knew much about the subject, but Ben said, "I don't think scientists have managed to develop a reliable method of predicting earthquakes yet. There are earthquake early warning systems, but they can't warn of earthquakes before they happen, but just detect the earth moving in the very first stages of one. So people can be alerted to it, but they'll only have seconds to react before it fully hits, such as by jumping up and running outside in case their house falls on them."

Angela said, "That's a pity. I think I'll look on the Internet tomorrow to see if I can find out whether any scientists are trying to develop technology to help them actually predict them."

Some of the others said they might do that too.

Then Miriam said, "Anyway, about ghosts and things like that again, I was on an Internet forum not long ago, and a man posted a message saying that for years, he'd been worried he had demons in his house, because things of his would sometimes go missing in his home, and he was sure he hadn't just forgotten where he'd put them, because he always used to have a really good memory. And once when he and his brother were moving house, boxes with things they'd packed in them would seem to suddenly launch themselves at them, as if they were being pushed by an unseen force. And he said he would write phone numbers and things in a notebook, and then come back some time later and find there was nothing on the page he'd written them on.

"And he said that when he moved house, he and his girl-friend looked upstairs one day and sensed a spooky ominous presence that felt malicious.

"Some people suggested natural explanations for what had happened, like that he'd always been a bit more forgetful than he thought he'd been, because most of the times when he'd forgotten where things were before hadn't stuck in his mind; it was only when he got panicked by thinking demons were moving them that the incidents seemed significant so he remembered them. They said stress stops the memory functioning so well and makes people's thinking less clear, so the stress he was feeling might have been making him more likely to put things down and forget where they were, and then when he couldn't find them because he thought he'd put them somewhere where he hadn't really and was worried when they weren't there, he got panicked some more.

"They said stress makes people forget the positive things that are happening and just focus on the bad things too, so if he put fifteen things down one day and found almost all of them where he expected to, but just one thing wasn't where he expected it to be, he'd get panicked about the one thing, instead of reassuring himself that at least most things were where he thought he'd put them.

"One person said she'd had lots of boxes fall on her when she was moving house, but she'd always put it down to either a box tilting gradually as things were moved around it till it fell over, or a box underneath it being moved a bit so it unbalanced it, or the vibrations from the washing machine's spin cycle or from a lorry going past outside, or the cat bumping it. She said she wondered if because the man was so stressed at the time, he'd immediately got scared and started suspecting it was demons, instead of setting his mind to thinking of possible other explanations.

"Someone asked him if it was possible that people had sometimes played what they thought were jokes on him, thinking it was funny to tell him things had moved or boxes had fallen over when they hadn't really.

"They said boxes that had been badly stacked could easily fall over if someone just slightly brushed past them; and if a box wasn't full, its contents could tip over to the other side if the box was moved just a bit, and the force of that could knock it over.

"One of them gave him advice about his problem with phone numbers and things seeming to disappear from his notebook, suggesting that when he wrote in it in future, to prevent the possibility that he might be just writing on pages and then forgetting exactly which ones he'd written on and later thinking he'd written on different ones than he had so he would be scared when the ones he went to write on turned out to be blank, he made himself a rule that he could only ever write on a new page when the previous one was full.

"They suggested an alternative thing he could do was to write on a single piece of card that he could keep in his wallet in the exact same place all the time, so he'd always know where it was and couldn't mistake it for another one. If something was written on a card, and it was the only thing of its kind in his wallet, he'd know that if the words disappeared from that, there truly was something to worry about. But if they didn't, he might be reassured.

"Someone said that as for the feelings of hate he'd thought he sensed when he'd moved house, it could have been something to do with the acoustics; they would have become different once everything had been packed up, perhaps more echoey, and that could have given the place a spooky feel. And since he and his girlfriend had already thought there were malicious spirits in the house, imagination could have done the rest.

"The man felt better after that, and told them that something had happened since they reassured him that he'd have really worried about before, but instead he'd done a test to see if he really had anything to worry about. He said parts of the catches on the windows in his house would keep falling off, and one had fallen off and slipped out of his hand when he'd tried to grab it. There was a pipe underneath, and he'd expected it to hit that with a clang, but it hadn't. He didn't hear it hit the floor at all. He looked for it, but couldn't find it. Before, he'd have started getting scared that a spirit had snatched it from his hand and stolen it. But instead, he decided to be more scientific about things and do a test, to see if he could drop another one deliberately that landed without going clang on the pipe but disappeared out of sight.

"He managed it on his second go. It dropped with a little thud on the floor. He realised the reason he hadn't heard the first one drop was probably because he was moving around at the time, and the noise it made was a lot quieter than the noise he was making, so he'd drowned it out. He found a screw from it on the bedroom floor a couple of days later.

"He also said he hadn't been able to find his torch at first when he'd wanted it to look for the bit from the window on the floor, and at first he'd started getting stressed again, thinking a spirit must have moved it; but then he searched for it, and found it very near the place where he thought he'd put it down.

"He felt reassured after that, and said he'd be more scientific about things from then on."

The Conversation Turns Humorous

Danny said, "The other day there was a programme on telly about the most haunted pubs in the country. Someone joked to me that they thought it was funny that out of all the things ghosts could be doing, like exploring the universe, they would go back to where they died and relive their misery, just doing things like walking around the same old bit of a room."

Luke said, "Yeah, just think! If people really do have souls, and ghosts really exist, and when you die it's as if your soul's set free to go wherever it likes, you'd have thought it would want to take the opportunity to go to all kinds of interesting places.

"Hey just imagine! You could go and travel on trains all over the place without paying; you could stand right behind a ticket inspector all day, and when he was fining people for not buying a ticket, or telling them they'd receive a fine in the post, or whatever happens, you could be saying to yourself,

'Bwahahahaha! I've been right behind you all day, not paying for a thing, and you haven't caught me once!' "

The friends giggled, and Julie said, "Just imagine what you could do if you could do anything you wanted! You could go and sit in Parliament, and if a government was about to bring in a law you didn't like, you could walk up and down in front of them till they were all scared and ran away."

Shirley chuckled and said, "Yeah, just imagine what it would say on the news! 'Every one of the Conservative MPs ran out of the House of Commons today. When a reporter asked why, they all said they'd seen a ghost.' "

Gary said, "Imagine if a ghost kept scaring them! They might decide to meet somewhere else in the hope of avoiding ghosts. But imagine if the ghost followed them, and in the end they were too scared to meet at all. Imagine if it said on the news, 'Parliament was dissolved today, because all the MPs were scared they were being stalked by a ghost!' "

Mandy said, "Mind you, if it was common to see ghosts, people probably wouldn't be scared of them any more. They might even try to hire them to do things for them, like going to explore other planets and reporting back. All that money they're spending making robots they're sending to explore Mars, or whatever they use to explore it; they could get ghosts to explore it and tell them what it's like for free!"

Luke grinned and said, "The ghosts might play jokes on them though. Imagine if NASA asked one to go and explore planets beyond our solar system, and the ghost secretly waited a little while, just hanging around on Earth, and then went back to them with a few rabbits in a box, and said they'd found a planet where rabbits talked and ruled the place, and there were human-like creatures, but they just ran around eating grass all day, except some who the rabbits kept as pets who lived in hutches and got fed bowls of grain and apples. The ghost might say they'd brought some of the rabbits back with them who'd agreed to talk to people at NASA, but their vocal cords might have got damaged as they came into Earth's atmosphere, because they hadn't spoken since. NASA might get scientists in to examine them to try to work out what must have gone wrong.

"Or the ghost might say the rabbits had been so awed by the trip down to Earth they'd stayed quiet all the way, and it seemed they'd forgotten how to talk rabbit language during that time, but maybe they could be taught English. NASA scientists might try to teach them, only for the ghost to laugh later and say they'd only been kidding."

Lorna said, "Wow, I bet NASA wouldn't take any chances after that; they'd probably tell the ghosts they'd have to give human observers piggybacks to the other planets from then on, so a human could make sure they were doing what they were supposed to."

Becky said, "Wow, imagine riding on the back of a ghost! But they still wouldn't necessarily do what they were told. Imagine if NASA spent millions of dollars designing and making special radiation shields the humans could wear to protect them from the radiation in space, only for ghosts to take them to a pub in Lincolnshire or somewhere instead, and start just pushing a door open every so often, going, 'Ooooooooooooooooooooooh', and moving a few glasses around. When the person on their back asked them why, they might say, 'Well after roaming the world and other planets, I've realised that this is the only thing I want to be doing with my life; there's no place like home!' "

Angela asked, "Why do people say ghosts make that ooooooooooooooh noise?"

No one knew.

The Friends Talk More About the Causes of Belief in Ghosts

Then Dawn said, "I've heard that ghost hunters go around to pubs and caves and places to see if they can see ghosts, and they sometimes hear things that they interpret as ghost voices, when really they're other things entirely. I mean, say if you were in a big cave by the sea and you heard seagulls squawking – or whatever the sound they make's called – faintly in the distance, then if you were all psyched up to expect to hear a ghost voice, you might think it was one. You might even think you distinguished words in the sound, if it was far away. Or if a recording was made while ghost hunters were in a particular place, and then it was played back later, there might be a bit of noise from some kind of static or some other type of interference on it, and people listening hard might think they could faintly distinguish voices in it.

"It reminds me of when I went to visit an aunt and uncle of mine for a few days, and the walls were thin so I could hear them snoring and making funny grunting noises in their sleep at night. Sometimes I thought I heard my name being mentioned, or one of them saying something like, 'Oh no'; but then a second later, I realised it was just one of their funny grunting noises.

"I've heard that that kind of thing's called pareidolia. It's where the brain tries to make sense of things by trying to recognise patterns in them it can put together to make something understandable. It's not just when it hears things that it does that; it's the reason some people do things such as thinking they're seeing pictures of Jesus in bits of toast as well, when really they're just interesting patterns.

"I heard about one person who thought she saw the face of Mary the mother of Jesus in a bit of toast, and she kept it for years because she thought it was so special, and then sold it for nearly 20 thousand pounds!"

The friends grinned.

The Topics of Astrology and Homeopathy Briefly Come Up, Though Much of the Conversation Consists of Humorous Teasing

Then Lorna said, "I reckon thinking ghosts and spirits cause things without having any good evidence they do is a bit like the way people believe the stars cause things to happen to people, like good luck or bad luck. Why do people think that? How could the stars cause things like that?"

Becky said, "I don't know. But I read an article about how some people believe different personalities have a lot to do with different star signs, but some people reckon it's really to do with the sun. They were saying babies born in the winter might grow up grumpy, because they spend their first months in a world with not much sunshine, and when it's quite dark all day, people can feel quite gloomy. I don't know why they'd think that would affect them for the rest of their lives though."

The friends smiled, and some of them pointed to those who'd been born in the winter, playfully teasing them.

Danny joked with a grin, "Hey Monica, Miriam, Adam, and you others who were born in the winter: Does that grumpiness theory apply to you then? I've never noticed it, but maybe you try to hide it. Yeah, I bet you just pretend to be cheerful when you're around us, and then go back home and grumpily complain all the time till you meet us again! Do you grumpily talk to yourselves for hours when you're alone, hoping no one will hear you through the walls and discover the secret of how grumpy you really are?

"Or do you have days when your grumpiness subsides a bit, so sometimes people can meet you and you seem quite normal, and that's why we haven't discovered your grumpy sides yet? We've just been lucky enough to only be with you on your OK days?"

Monica said, "We're not really grumpy! I bet there's nothing at all in the idea that the weather makes a difference!"

Ben joked with a grin, "Well we've decided to believe it anyway, just for fun. And now we're curious about just how grumpy you can get! Do you intimidate our tutors by bursting into their offices and having great grump-fests every time they mark your essays too low for your liking? And do you feel relieved when you leave us and get back to your rooms because you're then free to let your grumpy sides out, say by having fun going on Internet forums so you can go into full grump mode, complaining about everything you can think of and arguing with people?"

Miriam grinned and joked, "That sounds more like Danny's game!"

Danny said, "I don't get grumpy on forums! I argue, yeah, but I just do it for fun!"

Julie grinned and said, "But it sounds as if Ben was just suggesting it's possible to get grumpy on forums for fun. You can't get out of it that easily!"

Danny said, "Well OK, there was that one time . . . but maybe I won't tell you about that."

Becky2 coaxed, "Oh go on!"

Danny said, "Well OK, I don't like admitting to it, but there was that one time when I was arguing with people who annoyed me more and more the longer the argument went on, and I decided to de-stress in the end by arguing with someone else, more aggressively than was fair to them, as a way to take out my frustrations."

Dawn smiled and joked, "Is that called homeopathic arguing? You know, the cure for the disease is . . . just a touch more of the disease?"

Angela asked, "What? Is that really how homeopathy works?"

Dawn replied, "Well, not quite, really. But homeopathy's based on a theory that diluting a substance that's making someone ill down and down and down till the levels of it are undetectable and then giving it to them will cure them. I read a comment by a doctor who said that if scientists discovered that actually worked, they'd have to change their understanding of the laws of nature.

"But quite a few controlled trials have been done of homeopathy, where some patients were given homeopathic treatment and some were given a placebo; and it was discovered that homeopathy was no more effective than the placebo. Some people in both groups got better. But since no more of the ones given homeopathy got better than the patients in the placebo group, it was concluded that the ones who recovered probably would have done anyway by then, or else they might have done other things that helped while they were in the trials.

"But a lot of people still benefit by going to homeopaths. That's often because if they've got a condition that's being caused or made worse by stress, such as muscle tension that's so bad it's causing a lot of pain, then spending an hour in the company of a caring homeopath who's willing to focus entirely on them and their needs and talk over their problems with them can de-stress them, so their pain will go away till they're really stressed again. A sensitive caring friend could do the same for them, although part of what de-stresses homeopathic patients might be the medicine they're given that gives them hope that they'll recover soon. No homeopathic medicine has been proven to be effective by scientists though. And some has got active ingredients that aren't technically homeopathic, for good or ill."

The friends thought that was interesting, and pondered it for a few seconds, until Danny said mischievously, "Maybe that means seeing a homeopath could cure grumpiness then, unless it's hardwired into people who are born in the winter so nothing will work."

Monica felt a touch of irritation and said, "Not that again! Haven't you got any jokes about other subjects?"

Danny smiled and joked, "Not at the moment, Grumpy! See, what you said just proves people born in the winter are grumpy!"

Shirley joked, "It's no good, Monica; he isn't going to give it a rest. I think all of us born in the winter had better just admit he's right. Let's get it over with.

"I'll start. OK, I'll confess: I'm so grumpy, I go on Internet forums with the intention to argue with people when I go to my room, but I never can, because once I start spreading my misery on a forum, everyone's so put off the place by it that they all leave! I haven't been able to have an argument on a forum for years because of that!

"I often cheer up a bit in the summer, and earlier this year I managed to get hundreds of Facebook friends, all attracted by what appeared to be my cheerful personality. But now the weather's getting colder, my real personality's come out, and just recently they all unfriended me! Now I've got no one to talk to there at all; but that's making me even grumpier!"

Julie said in mock shock, "Wow, you lost hundreds of Facebook friends? That must be near-record-breaking grumpiness!"

Lorna said, "That's nothing! I'm so grumpy, I used to win awards at school for clearing playgrounds in seconds just by walking out there and spreading my grumpy vibes around! No one wanted to be anywhere near me when I did that. Teachers used to thank me for getting kids back into lessons way way faster than they ever could, because all the kids thought going back to lessons was way preferable to having to put up with being anywhere near me and my grumpiness! Maybe some of them even worried they'd catch it."

Adam said, "I got an award at school for managing to keep quiet for long enough to actually complete an exam, since most of the time I couldn't go for more than five minutes without complaining grumpily about something, even when the teachers had ordered us all to be quiet and work."

The friends laughed.

Then Julie smiled and asked, "Is there a star sign where the people under it are said by astrologers to be especially grumpy?"

Becky2 grinned and joked, "Yeah, yours."

Adam said, "It would be funny if there really was one. Just imagine if someone was reading about what kind of personality people with their star sign were supposed to have, and they read, 'You are an especially grumpy person. You make people's lives a misery everywhere you go with your constant complaining and bad moods. Astrologers determined thousands of years ago that people with your star sign do the world a favour when they spend their lives alone indoors."

The friends giggled.

Then Angela said seriously, "Do you think there might really be something in astrology though? I can't speak for anyone else, of course, but I've read what the personality of people with my own star sign's supposed to be like, and for me personally, it's impressively accurate! . . . And no, it didn't say I'm grumpy!"

She smiled as she said that, and continued, "If it's not the stars that made me like that, do you think there could be anything at all in this claim that the weather makes a difference? Mind you, I don't know what weather conditions could have caused my kind of personality, or most other people's. What kind of weather would make newborn babies turn into people who were dreamy, like people who are Pisces are supposed to be, or generous, like I think people who are Sagittarius are supposed to be? And what about babies who spend the first weeks of their lives in hospital so they don't experience any weather? I wonder if there's a theory somewhere that they'll grow up with a special condition called hospital personality. I wonder what that would be like . . . Then again, I suppose it's partly the light levels that count, not just the weather.

"But if it's the stars that supposedly make the difference instead, how could just a few minutes of difference between when the stars are in one sign and when they're in the next one make such a dramatic difference on people's personalities that they can have completely different ones? Or if the transition between one sign and another's a bit more gradual than that, what kinds of personalities will people have if they're born during the time when the stars are moving from one sign to another one where people are supposed to have the opposite kind of personalities, like from a sign where they're supposed to be short-tempered and mean to one where they're supposed to be kind and easy-going? Why do astrologers seem to classify them as being either one thing or another?

"Has any astrologer ever tried to explain that? It sounds a bit dubious to me, thinking about it."

Ben said, "I'm pretty sure neither the weather nor the stars have anything to do with causing people to have the personalities they've got. It's probably mostly just life experiences and genes that do that.

"Also, don't forget that everyone born when you were would have to have the same kind of personality if what astrologers say about the personalities of people born under your star sign really is correct. It's not proof that astrology's accurate if it's just you and a minority of others who've got them.

"I don't know what strange things might be going on around us, or in space or whatever, but I've read a few articles about astrology by people who don't believe in it.

"One said some astrologers reckon the effects of the stars are caused by the pull of the gravity around certain planets on the baby being born at the time of their birth, or something like that; but apart from the mystery of how on earth that could have anything to do with people's personalities, it said that all things have a field of gravity around them that pulls things towards them, although most are so faint they don't really have any effect, especially if the object a field of gravity's surrounding's far away from other objects; even if the object's huge, the pull of its gravity will get less powerful the further away it is; so the gravitational pull of the doctor delivering a baby is much stronger than that of the planets, even though a doctor would probably be trillions of times smaller! So if any gravity at all was going to influence anything as major as personality, the doctor's would be more likely to do it, although of course it doesn't."

The Friends Start Making Jokes Again

Lorna said, "What's this gravitational pull thing? Are you saying it isn't just planets that can have gravity around them, but everyone has a bit, so it's as if we've all got something on us that's trying to pull things and other people towards us a bit? Yikes! So we can be walking away from someone because we don't like them, but our little gravitational pull will be trying to pull them towards us?"

Shirley, who'd never heard of gravitational pull either, joked, "Yes, and their gravity will be trying to pull you towards them while you're trying to walk away, so it'll be as if your and their gravitational fields are having a tug of war with you both; and they'll both be pulling the air in between you towards them too, so it gets pulled in opposite directions, till if you walk fast enough, it'll be pulled apart, and other air will rush in to fill the gap, so it'll be as if you're both making wind."

Sharon grinned and said, "Yeah, and if you're both running really fast, the air will be pulled apart so fast that the air that rushes in will be going really fast, and then there'll be a hurricane, right there in this room, or wherever you are."

They giggled. Then Angela said, "But does gravity really pull things? So when you fall down, you're not really just falling, but it's like the Earth's actually pulling you down? That's spooky! Or if you drop a glass or something, it's as if the Earth's saying, 'Come into my arms, my darling glass; let me smash you against my hard surface!'?"

Craig said, "I don't think it's the Earth that's pulling anything. And I think gravity might only pull things because of the force of the rotation of the Earth making something suck them in . . . Oh no, it can't be that, can it, since other planets rotate too and they haven't got gravity . . . Or have they? I didn't think they did have, because people in space float instead of being able to stay where they are, unless they've got heavy boots on or something, don't they. I thought that was because there isn't any gravity up there. Is there a bit after all then? It's a bit confusing."

He asked Ben, "What *is* this thing about gravitational pull and gravity fields and stuff then?"

Ben said, "I don't know either actually; it's just what the article I read said."

Luke wondered out loud, "How strong would a field of gravity be around a person? How would anyone even know it's there if it's not strong enough to effectively pull things towards it?"

Mandy said playfully with a grin, "Ah, but maybe it can. Really light things. Maybe if someone just sat still for a week, they'd find a load of dust on their head by the end of it, because their gravity had been pulling bits of dust towards them all that time. That would be a bit yucky!"

Julie laughed and said, "If someone tried to sit still for a whole week, they'd have a lot more to worry about than dust! Just think how hungry and thirsty they'd get!"

"Yeah," said Gary. "And just think how desperate for the loo they'd be by the end of one *day*, let alone a week!"

Mandy said, "Yeah, alright. But just imagine if someone put a time-lapse camera in a room so it would make things that happened slowly look speeded up, and it had some kind of microscope on it that made everything look much bigger, and they left it there for a week, and then people saw what looked like monster grains of dust spookily floating towards the massive furniture and landing on it all by themselves, as if they were alive! Maybe gravity's what makes dust land on things. I don't know how else it gets there."

"It might just blow in the windows," said Miriam. "Mind you, it would look spooky anyway if you had special equipment that enabled you to see it flying through the air towards things, or flying towards you if you were sitting there some of the time!"

"The dust is coming! Take cover!" said Julie in the tone of voice someone in a horror film might use, flinging her hands over her head.

They chuckled. Then Lorna said, "If gravity really does pull things towards it, that must mean it's a bit like a magnet. You know if you turn magnets around they can push each other away instead of zooming together? I wonder if gravity could ever change for some reason and start pushing things away."

"Wow, imagine that!" said Luke with a playful grin. "Imagine if the Earth somehow got knocked into a slightly different orbit, and it meant gravity did the opposite of what it does now, so it started pushing everyone off the Earth, so suddenly everyone on Earth and everything that was loose on the ground hurtled into space! Or just into the sky. And then imagine if Earth went back into its original orbit and pulled everyone back down again."

"Splat!" said Adam.

But Luke said, "No, just imagine if before everyone got to the ground, Earth went into its other orbit again, and everyone shot off into space again, and then it went back to its original orbit and they all came down near the ground again; and then it went into its other orbit and they all hurtled back into space again, and then it went back to its proper orbit and they came down again, and Earth kept alternating between the two orbits, and everyone kept hurtling up and down, up and down, up and down, up and down, up and down into space and back to near the ground again for years and years!"

The friends laughed. Then Sharon said, "Actually, don't things burn up when they come back into the atmosphere, or something like that? And if we were all in space, gravity wouldn't be able to get us to pull us back down, unless somehow it turned mega-powerful!

"Mind you, imagine if gravity pushed people and things up so quickly it pushed all the air in the atmosphere up into space with us all, so oxygen was still all around us and we could breathe it for ages. And imagine if it didn't pull us back down again. We'd all be bouncing around up there wondering what to do. Scientists might try to bounce around till they found each other so they could discuss how to make things that would help people survive in space."

Becky said with a grin, "Hey imagine if there was a man with something wrong with him that meant his field of gravity was much more powerful than it should be, so all kinds of little things would zoom towards him every time he went near them. If he sat at a desk, pens would start rolling towards him by themselves as if by magic! If he opened a cupboard in the kitchen, packets of soup and things would suddenly jump out at him. If he put his hand in a tissue box to get a tissue out to blow his nose, the entire lot of them would jump out of the box into his hand!"

Becky2 said, "It would have been difficult when he was little. Imagine he was in a toddlers' group. All the other kids' toys would come sailing towards him, and the other kids would think he was trying to nick them."

Gary chuckled and said, "They'd do that even when he was an adult. Imagine him sitting there when toy cars wheeled themselves towards him."

Angela said, "Wow, people would think there were ghosts in the room, wouldn't they, especially if they didn't know him so they didn't realise he always had the problem of things coming towards him! They might get a priest in to exorcise the room."

Miriam said, "And if they knew it kept happening to him everywhere he went, they might think ghosts followed him around everywhere. You know some people believe in guardian angels? They might think he had guardian ghosts!"

Becky laughed and said, "But aren't guardian angels supposed to care about the people they're guarding, or protecting, or whatever they're thought to do? You'd have thought ghosts that were guardians would do that too. But if things kept jumping out at the man, people wouldn't think they were very friendly ghosts, would they!"

Shirley giggled and said, "No. Just imagine if he was trying to eat dinner at the home of someone he was trying to impress. All the peas and beans and other little things on the plate might zoom off it onto his lap. And just imagine if they were all covered in gravy! If the people in the house didn't know about his problem, they'd think he was a really messy eater!"

Luke said, "Yeah. Just imagine if he thought he'd try leaning his face down to the plate to try to eat what was on it before it could go in his lap. It might jump off the plate and hit him in the face! A potato might bop him on the nose, and meat might wrap itself around his chin! Beans might jump into his mouth. Gravy would splatter all around his face! Imagine what they'd think about him then!"

"He'd probably go in there and ask if he could eat his dinner from a big bucket, hoping that then the food wouldn't zoom into his lap, or get on his face so easily," said Shirley, laughing. "If he tried to use a knife and fork in it though, he might still not be able to keep the fork steady enough in his hand to stop it zooming towards his face and splattering the food all over it. Or bits of food might zoom up and splatter all over his hands and wrists while he had them in the bucket."

Lauren giggled and said, "If he asked for a bucket, they might think, 'Do you think you're a pig?'"

Mandy said, "He'd probably go in there wearing a bib, and they'd think, 'Why is a grown man still wearing a bib! Does he think he's still a baby? Perhaps he'll be asking if he can sit in a highchair next!'"

Becky said, "Yeah, and they'd think that all the more if he went into another room and their baby's toys came rolling towards him, and the people came into the room after the toys had stopped all around his feet so they didn't realise they'd come by themselves, so they thought he'd got them to play with!"

Sharon said, "And just imagine what it would be like at a party! Imagine if the man sat down and someone put some peanuts or crisps near him on the table. When they weren't looking, they might all fly out of the bowl they were in and hurtle onto his lap, and when they looked and saw them all there, they'd think, 'You pig, wanting them all yourself! And all at once too!'"

Becky said, "And I wonder what they'd think if they put a glass of wine near him, and that spilled itself on his lap too! They'd say, 'OK, I can understand you heaping all the nibbly things onto your lap, but why you want the wine on there instead of in your mouth, I don't know!'"

Gary laughed and said, "The poor man would go everywhere wearing waterproof trousers, and probably a waterproof top too, as if he was about to go on a sailing trip or something!"

Shirley said, "Gosh, imagine if when he did go out, all the water in puddles whizzed out and landed all over his legs! And just imagine that when he went past trees, they would all bend their branches towards him because his gravity was pulling them down! He'd have to keep dodging out the way so any fruit and things on them didn't bop him on the head!"

Danny grinned and said, "Yeah, and just imagine if his gravity was so powerful that when he went to the seaside, the tide would start coming in faster because his gravity was pulling it in!"

Angela said more seriously, "I've never understood this thing about how the tides are controlled by the moon's gravity. I mean, for one thing, the moon's really far away. For another, I didn't think there was much gravity there, so I don't know how it could affect things on Earth. And for another thing, if Earth's gravity's so much stronger than the moon's, shouldn't it be pulling the seawater *down* instead, so the moon can't make it do the stuff it does?"

No one knew the answer to that, but Danny said playfully, "Hey, just imagine if the Earth somehow lost its gravity. Maybe instead of the waves just rising up a bit and then coming down again, they'd rise up right into the sky!"

Sharon joked, "Hey, imagine if the moon's gravity one day got much stronger, and it pulled all the seawater in all the seas on Earth right up into the sky, and then they all sploshed down onto the moon!"

"Wow, imagine that!" said Gary. "Imagine there were no seas left on Earth, and people could try walking from Britain to America and across other places where oceans had been, to see how long it took them. And imagine if railways and roads were built where the oceans had been, and towns and cities got to be there!"

"All that extra space would help sort out any over-population problem the world gets to have, wouldn't it!" said Monica. "Actually, couldn't they do that now, by digging a hole in the seabed that went down miles and miles and miles, so all the water would eventually drain away through it into the earth's core, if there's room in it? That might be good. If the earth's core cooled down, would that mean there would be no more volcanoes? Aren't they something to do with all the heat down there getting too much for the rocks to cope with or something?"

No one seemed to know. Then Danny said, "Hey, imagine if there was such a huge volcano it flung the lava up so high that a lot of it landed on the moon!"

"To go with all the seawater that had sploshed up there, you mean?" said Sharon.

Gary said, "Wow, just imagine if all the seas did get sucked up onto the moon so there were none left here. Imagine if governments wanted to send more people to the moon. Spaceships would have to be more like ordinary ships. They might have to touch down into feet and feet of water! Imagine astronauts chugging around the moon in a motorboat. I wonder if the moon would look any different from down here if it was covered in water?"

"It would be covered in old seaweed and rotting fish too, if the things in the sea were sucked up onto the moon with the sea," said Sharon. "Hey imagine if over the centuries, people forgot the seas used to be on Earth, and then one day there was a mission to the moon, and the astronauts took samples of the things on it and brought them back to Earth, and scientists reported, 'We're excited to tell you that a lot of water's been found on the moon! We've tested it and it seems remarkably similar to water on Earth, only it's much saltier. We hope to send another scientific mission there to try to work out why the moon's so salty. And excitingly, we've found lots of fish fossils, which proves there must once have been life on the moon. We think this must mean that millions of years ago, Earth and the moon were joined together, part of the same planet, and a massive meteor must have crashed into it and broken it in two.'"

"I wonder if there are some things in the seas that could even survive on the moon," said Julie.

The Friends Have another Discussion of Astrology

Angela said seriously, "One thing I'm wondering is, if the moon's gravity's really much less powerful than ours and yet it can still haul the sea about or whatever it does, how can we be sure the gravity of stars isn't doing something strange on Earth too?"

Ben said, "Well I suppose it might be, but it's very unlikely to have anything to do with people's personalities. I don't see how the two could be connected; it sounds surreal, like saying, 'My television went to my freezer and got me out some fish cakes to eat for tea.' I mean, people's personalities probably have a lot to do with their experiences and the way they were brought up and their genes. But I don't see how the gravity of inanimate objects could have anything to do with them.

"Anyway, that's not the only reason I don't believe in astrology. There are other reasons too.

"One thing one of the articles I read about it said was that a couple of people wrote a book where they looked up the published predictions that well-known astrologers and their organisations had made for five years. Out of over three thousand specific predictions about people, including politicians, film stars and other famous people, only one in ten was accurate! The article said a lot of people could probably do better than that by just reading the news and guessing, based on what those people had already done that would lead to consequences!

"And studies have been done to find out if married couples with star signs that are supposed to be incompatible divorce more than those with supposedly compatible star signs, and they found no difference.

"And there was an experiment where astrologers were given the places, times and dates of the births of quite a few people, and results of questionnaires that those people had each been given about what their personalities were like, but the astrologers were given them anonymously and separately so they had to match them up and say whose was whose, and they got them nearly all wrong.

"And astrologers don't always agree with each other about predictions and things. So it seems it's best not to rely on astrology."

Miriam said, "I think it's bad when you hear about politicians using astrology, or their wives using it. I heard about a president in America in the 1980s whose wife had her own private astrologer. I mean, can you imagine if a government leader wondered whether to go to war or something, and he thought the best thing to do to help him make a decision about whether to was to ask an astrologer if the omens were good, rather than sitting down and examining the pros and cons, and trying to think of strategies to avoid war, and thinking through the pros and cons of each strategy like a sensible person?"

Adam said, "Come on! Politicians are quite capable of not doing sensible things like that even if they *don't* use astrology!"

There were a few smiles at that. But then the friends began to feel a bit gloomy. That was until Dawn said, "Hey, remember there are a couple of pies cooking in the oven. They should be ready soon."

"About ten minutes, I think," said Angela. That cheered them up a bit.

One of the Friends Tells the Others About a Study of People Born to Parents Who Believe in the Chinese Astrological System

Lauren said, "I wonder if real believers in astrology might sometimes influence their children to get to have the personalities their star signs say they're going to have by getting them interested in the kinds of things their star signs say they're going to like doing. So, you know, someone who has a child who's a Pisces, so their star sign says they'll be a bit dreamy and arty, might get them involved in the theatre or something from an early age, so they might end up interested in that, and then their parents and other people will think their star sign predicted what they'd be like accurately.

"I heard about something like that happening in China, where they have a different zodiac system. I think they think people's personalities will have a lot to do with what year they were born in, and the years are named after animals. Every so often, the Year of the Dragon comes around; and people born that year are said to go on to achieve especially great things; so lots of couples actually plan to have a baby in that year, and wait till that year comes around if it's not that far away before they have them. Quite a lot more people get married in the two years before one of those years comes around than they do in other years, hoping to have their first child in that year. So a lot more kids are born that year than in other years. That's what I've heard. Doctors working on maternity wards know they're going to be busier in those years than in other years.

"I heard about one boy who was born in that year whose parents expected him to do great things with his life, who knew from a very early age that they were expecting him to be a university professor or something, who would go and study in a university in America. They made special efforts to make sure he got a good education and learned English, so he'd do well when he went to America; and he did end up going to university there.

"He studied economics; and he met an economics professor he looked up to, and they decided to do some research together. The man from China was curious about whether children born in the Year of the Dragon really do go on to achieve more than children born in other years. By then, he believed that people's belief in the significance of zodiac signs was just superstition; and he had a theory that children born in the Year of the Dragon would actually do worse than children born in other years, because class sizes in schools would be bigger because there were more children, so each child wouldn't get as much attention from teachers as children born in other years, and there might be shortages of learning materials in their schools because there weren't enough to go around.

"But he found out that children born in that year actually got higher grades than children born in other years. At first, he thought it was probably because teachers had a bias towards giving them higher grades, maybe because they expected their work to be good, so they were less critical of it than they were of other children's. But he checked their university grades, where their papers were marked by computers somehow; and he found out that they still got higher grades than other students.

"So then he decided to find out if the reason was that their self-esteem was higher than other kids' self-esteem, so they believed in themselves more, so they made more effort to work, because they were sure they'd succeed. But he found out that they didn't have higher self-esteem than other children.

"So then he wondered if they expected to achieve more in life, thinking of themselves as more intelligent than other children, so they made more effort to study and succeed than other children for that reason. But he found out that they didn't have any higher expectations of themselves and their intelligence than other kids did of theirs. And he found out that they weren't more ambitious to get into good careers than other children.

"Eventually, he discovered that what was going on was that the parents of those children would often encourage them to work hard, checking on their progress with teachers more, and helping them more in various other ways than parents of other children often would, even letting them off doing housework so they could study more – he said that's what his own parents did with him – and they helped those children with more money later in life too.

"So he realised that the real reason they did better in life than other children did on average was because their parents expected them to do better, so they gave them advantages that would help them succeed better, and encouraged them to study more.

"So the parents' belief that their children were going to succeed well in life was like a self-fulfilling prophecy – you know, that's where people feel sure something's going to happen, so they do certain things, and those things actually make it a lot more likely to happen.

"It can work the other way around too, say if some school-teachers think the kids they're teaching are a bit stupid and probably won't achieve much in life, so they don't bother to put much effort into teaching them, and that makes it more likely that the kids won't do very well, so they'll end up with bad grades; and then they might not succeed much in life because of that.

"But maybe that Year of the Dragon study shows that if all parents encouraged and helped their children to succeed in life more, a lot more children would go on to achieve more in life."

A Couple of People Tell Stories About Serious Effects That Believing in Astrology has Had on People

The students were thoughtful for several seconds. Then Angela got the pie out of the oven, and they carried on talking as they were eating.

Monica said, "I read a news story about how thousands and thousands of people in India ran away from a town one day because some astrologers had predicted there was going to be a disaster there that day; but nothing happened."

Danny suggested, "What if that was because the person who would have caused the disaster didn't realise it was him who'd have caused it, and ran away with the rest, so he didn't?"

Angela replied, "Does it work like that, or would a disaster have happened no matter what?"

Monica said, "I don't know. I don't even know if astrologers would agree on that one. But I think the disaster was predicted to be some kind of huge storm or some other natural disaster.

But then, a lot of astrologers said it wasn't going to happen . . . or said *afterwards* that it hadn't been going to happen. I can't quite remember which of those it was. Or maybe some said one thing and some said the other."

Lorna said, "Wow, astrology must be popular in India if thousands of people in one town believed in it enough to all run away!"

Angela said, "I once heard about a woman who read her horoscope in the paper, and one day it said she ought to beware of some risk or other. She didn't really believe it, but that day she had an accident, and took horoscopes really seriously from then on, and didn't dare go out for a while."

"Even on the days when her horoscope said it was going to be a good day?" quipped Adam. But then he said, "That's bad though. But I bet the accident was a coincidence. I read an article about how coincidences that seem amazing are actually far more likely to happen than people realise. When you think about how many hours there must be in a year, and the huge variety of things that might happen to people in all that time, there's a fairly high probability that at least a few times in their lives, coincidences will happen to them that seem amazing, just by chance."

The Friends Discuss Strange Coincidences and Premonitions, and the Prophecies of People Like Nostradamus, as Well as Joking Some More

Becky said, "Oh yeah, I remember going on holiday with my mum somewhere right up the other end of the country, and one of the first people we met was from a few roads away from where we live!"

Miriam said, "I've had an experience like that."

Monica said, "So have I!"

Then Julie said she had. Then Becky2 did. In fact, there was a chorus of people saying "So have I" all around the room, as one friend after another said it. They all burst out laughing at that.

Then Danny said, "I read a book by a man I'd never heard of once about his wartime experiences, only to find out a week after I'd finished it that he was about to be interviewed on the telly about them! I still think that was a weird coincidence! And not long ago, I read about a weather forecaster with a strange name I'd never heard of who once made a rude gesture while he was doing a weather forecast on telly, and then just a couple of days later I put the radio on, and heard that that very man was going to be interviewed soon, although about something completely different. I'd never heard of him before. So that was odd too."

Ben said, "I think that's sometimes to do with noticing things you wouldn't have paid attention to before because you've just come to think they're significant in some way. You might have heard the weather forecaster's name before but forgotten soon afterwards, because the name didn't have any meaning for you, and only started to have meaning after something about him stuck in your mind. So you might have thought hearing something else about him soon afterwards was more of a coincidence than it really was. It's called the psychological focusing effect. Mind you, strange coincidences do happen sometimes."

Sharon said, "Wow, a weather forecaster made a rude gesture on air? I wonder if it was because he was fed up of people criticising him for getting the weather forecasts wrong so often. Or I wonder if he just made it by mistake! Mind you, I expect stranger things have happened.

"I heard a funny thing the other day about something one BBC weather forecaster did! I'm not quite sure how it happened, but she pressed some button she shouldn't have, and it confused the computer, and then instead of sensible-sounding temperatures appearing on the weather map, it said it was going to be ninety-nine degrees Celsius in quite a few towns, which is virtually boiling point! Imagine all the water in fish and duck ponds turning into steam and suddenly disappearing!"

"Restaurants would be pleased," said Mandy. "Instead of cooking stuff, they could just send their chefs out to the park to get ready-cooked duck . . . only, if the temperature was about boiling point, all us humans would be cooked too, I suppose!"

Miriam said, "Imagine if carnivorous aliens came down at that moment! They'd have a feast, wouldn't they!"

"Till they got cooked too!" said Gary with a chuckle.

Sharon said, "One of the funny things in the weather forecast that went wrong was that the weather forecaster was actually telling viewers it would probably snow at the time! Another thing the computer did when it went wrong was to replace the names of about six towns with the words 'Town Name', so it looked as if whoever names towns in this country had run out of ideas for what to call new ones, so they just named six of them 'Town Name'."

The friends laughed.

Then Luke said, "Do you know, I heard that when people first started doing weather forecasts about 150 years ago, they were reported in the papers, and some of them called them prophecies, for whatever reason. I think it was because they thought there was some uncertainty about whether they were reliable.

"Imagine if Old Testament prophets forecast what the weather was going to be like nowadays, so they said things like, 'In 2721 years from now, on a month and date that will then be called the 21st of February, in a land as yet barely populated which will then be called Great Britain, the temperature will rise to ninety-nine degrees Celsius, on a temperature scale that is as yet unheard of, but it basically means that all the water in all the duck and fish ponds . . . oh, you probably won't have heard of those, will you, because I'm not sure they've been invented yet . . . or have they? Anyway, all the ponds, and the rivers, and maybe even the sea, will start boiling, and everyone in the country may as well roll themselves in pastry to make pies, because they'll all be turned into steak!' "

Some of the friends laughed, and some said, "Ugh!"

Then Angela said curiously, "Seriously though, do you think it's possible to foretell the future? What do you think about premonitions? I've heard people say they've had dreams about disasters and things happening in certain places, and then they've gone and happened!"

Adam chuckled and said, "Hopefully they didn't actually cause them, just so they could claim they dreamt about them and then they happened! But if that means accurate supernatural prophecies can really happen, it's a good thing no Old Testament prophet really did say that stuff about people in this country being cooked on a certain date by freak hot weather, isn't it, or we'd all have to watch out! Or emigrate!"

The friends sniggered.

Then Angela asked the others, "What do you think about Nostradamus? I've heard that he predicted the rise of Hitler, and even the terrorist attack on the World Trade Center in 2001!"

Ben said, "I've read about that. It seems he didn't really do those things. I read that his predictions are so vague that it's impossible to be sure what they're predicting at all, and the claims about things he's prophesied coming true have all been made with the benefit of hindsight, where certain things he wrote have been interpreted in ways that have made them fit certain events. But they could really fit all kinds of events, because they're so unclear that they need to be made sense of by being interpreted in various ways, with some people taking them to mean one thing, and others thinking they must mean another. None of them say anything straightforwardly. They seem to be written in a kind of code, that could be interpreted to mean all kinds of things that have a lot of significance in the world.

"And also, some of his supposed prophecies probably weren't even made by him, since apparently there are some that didn't appear in print till decades or even much longer after his death, like one that supposedly seemed to cryptically predict the death of a French king, who died between the time Nostradamus died and the time the supposed prediction first appeared in print. So it's hard to know whether he wrote it, or whether it was made up by someone else after the king died.

"And there have been recent hoaxes where some verses of his have been altered slightly and spread around the Internet to make them fit major events more, such as one or two that seemed as if they could be about the attack on the World

Trade Center in 2001. Lines were put together from different passages of the famous book he wrote; and the other bits that were originally in those passages that would have made them seem irrelevant didn't get a mention by the people who did that when the concocted passages were spread around the Internet.

"And there was actually a supposed passage that was made up altogether by someone who wanted to illustrate that it's really easy to make up vague-sounding poetry and then fit it to all kinds of different events; but it was spread around by other people as if it was a real prediction Nostradamus made. Then quite a few people added bits to it, like one bit that seemed to say World War III would begin soon after something bad that happened in 2001; and it got spread around a lot with the added bits, with people claiming that Nostradamus himself had written them.

"But even with the things that Nostradamus actually did write, not only are his original writings vague, but he was writing in a kind of old French that isn't used today, so it's more difficult to understand, and easy to mistranslate. So a lot of the translations don't even say exactly what he originally wrote.

"And there's more room for mistranslation because a lot of them are based on copies of his work written some time after his death, that might themselves have been inaccurate. And some translations deliberately make some alterations, to make the verses sound more as if they refer to certain past events.

"That's what I've read anyway.

"And I read that Nostradamus didn't really prophesy the rise of Hitler, but he used the word Hister, which is the Latin name for part of the river Danube, I think.

"And it seems that quite a bit of what he wrote was plagiarised or partly plagiarised from earlier books by different people.

"I read that a lot of things about Nostradamus were made up by people in the nineteenth century, who wanted to sensationalise his predictions to sell tabloids.

"I've heard about that happening with other people too, such as a woman who's said to have lived about five hundred years ago called Mother Shipton, who's said to have made prophecies too. I read that in 1881, a lot of people were scared the world was about to end, because there was a lot of publicity about a supposed prediction she made about the world ending that year. But then a bookseller admitted to making it up, to help sell a book he'd written about her!"

Angela said, "That's bad! What about the kind of premonitions that ordinary people sometimes have though? Like I said, I've heard people say they dreamt about some disaster happening, only for it to actually happen soon afterwards! And not all of them are disasters they could have caused themselves."

Dawn said, "I don't know all the reasons why premonitions and things like that can come true, but I think some of them might just be coincidences. Also, I think sometimes people can subconsciously pick up clues that a certain bad thing might happen before they dream about it. Worries in the back of the mind about the clues are what brings the dream on. For instance, a relative of theirs might be ill with something serious and they've started to look a bit worse, or they've become a bit concerned about an accident happening in a certain place because it's a dangerous stretch of road. They might not consciously think much about things like that, but they might still be a bit anxious about them, and dream about something bad happening because of that. Then if it happens, they might think the dream was a premonition.

"Or someone might dream about some vague outline of a bad thing happening, read about a disaster in the news the next day that has similarities, and over time, feel more and more sure that the details of it were in their dream. Just as I was saying earlier, people's memories can become more inaccurate over time without them realising.

"But often it could just be coincidence; when you think of all the people around and all the time they spend dreaming, sooner or later someone's bound to dream about something that goes on to happen."

The Friends Talk More About Scary Dreams and Sleep Paralysis

Becky2 said, "I used to have scary dreams when I was little sometimes – not premonitions, but dreams I had often that I worried might come true one day. I sometimes dreamt I was in the middle of a road trying to get to the other side, but I felt paralysed and couldn't move, no matter how hard I tried, and there was a car coming! Thankfully the dreams only lasted a few seconds, so nothing worse happened in them."

Julie said, "I used to dream I was waking up and looking at the time. I was convinced I was awake, and I thought something horrible must have happened to my alarm clock, because instead of telling me the proper time, it would tell me times like 25:78. Or there would be letters on it where numbers should be, saying things like, 'You're late!' or, 'You've slept a whole extra day!' Scary!"

Then Craig piped up, "Hey Becky! Now we're back to talking about dreams again, you told me what you've read about what they reckon causes this sleep paralysis you think I've probably got; but did you read anything about what can cure it? Even if I know what's causing it, it'll still be scary. I'd like to be able to get rid of it."

"Oh sorry," said Becky. "It was ages ago when we stopped talking about it, wasn't it. The articles I read did say a few things. One or two said people can sometimes help themselves wake up properly when they've got it if they're awake enough that they can remember it's just their brain and body doing weird things, and then think that although they can't move most of themselves, their eyes might still move, so trying to concentrate all their attention on trying to blink repeatedly might help. Or they can try to move another little part of themselves before they try moving the rest, since if they can move that, it'll get easier to move the rest, and they'll start waking up more.

"So you could try moving just your little finger or something to start with, concentrating all your effort on that one thing. That'll help distract your attention from the scary half-awake dreams as well."

She carried on, "The articles said some doctors think people are less likely to get sleep paralysis if they've had a good long sleep, so they advise going to bed at a decent time, and doing things to help sleep come on and carry on for as long as it needs to, like making sure the bed's comfortable, that the room's not too cold or too hot, and that you don't drink alcohol near bedtime; booze might help you get to sleep, but it's been found it can make people wake up earlier than normal, so they don't end up with as much sleep as they really need.

"And it's best if people don't smoke or drink coffee, especially in the few hours before they go to bed, since they're both stimulants that can make it harder to get to sleep. It's also recommended that people exercise during the day to tire themselves out a bit, although not too near bedtime, or it'll keep them awake because of all the adrenaline flowing around their systems afterwards.

"Actually, one thing I heard is that sleep paralysis is less likely to come on if you're not sleeping on your back. So if you often do, it might be worth trying to find another comfortable position.

"Another thing I reckon you can try is doing things when you get in bed that fill your mind with things that make you feel happy and peaceful, like if you know of a book you find soothing and absorbing that you can read, so it occupies your mind instead of worries about what might happen, which might come on if you're not thinking of anything else, and they might prime your brain to bring on the scary dreams later without you realising. Whatever you go to sleep thinking about might sometimes be what you end up dreaming about. So if it's something nice that gives you a warm happy feeling, or something you're keen to think about, you might end up dreaming about that, and not wake up till you can wake up properly, without still being paralysed because your body's still trying to protect you from acting out your dreams.

"Anyway, have a look on the Internet from time to time as well, because new treatments might come along that work really well sooner or later."

Lastly, Becky said, "One article I read, an NHS one, said that for people who can't get rid of sleep paralysis, antidepressants can help, not because people who get it are depressed, but because they can reduce the amount of dreaming sleep people get."

Craig thanked Becky, and said he'd try what she suggested.

A few weeks later, he told her it was working and he felt much better. Becky was pleased.

Chapter 10

Bad Times at the Psychology Department Christmas Party and in the Days Afterwards

B ecky's first Christmas at university wasn't entirely a happy one; she learned to avoid parties where the drink flowed freely for some time after that, though for years to come, she entertained others by telling them about some of what happened at the psychology department Christmas party.

It was arranged by a few of the tutors. They invited other psychology tutors, plus those from departments where similar subjects were taught – sociology, social work and philosophy. They announced that any students from those departments who wanted to come could, and they could bring a couple of friends each. So students from several other departments came too, plus several people from outside. The tutors hired out one of the university bars for the evening.

Most of Becky's friends had other things to do, so they didn't want to go. But she was still keen to find out what it would be like. So her mum gave her special permission to stay up late in the bar with the others, and said she'd collect her and bring her home at around 11 o'clock.

It was the kind of party where everyone was supposed to bring something for people to eat and drink to start with, and then people would get whatever else they wanted from the bar, so Becky's mum gave her a couple of packets of cakes and a carton of fruit juice to share.

For the first hour or so, nothing too eventful happened. When Becky first went in, she couldn't see anyone she was friends with, so she sat next to a small group of students she recognised from her department who she didn't know that well. At first, they talked about what they thought of the work the tutors gave them to do, what they were planning over Christmas, what they wanted to do when they left university, and other things like that; and though it couldn't be described as great fun or getting into the party spirit, Becky thought it was quite nice, especially since she was sitting with a big plate of food, and when she'd finished, it was piled high with more by her indulgent fellow psychology students. She didn't really like the music, and thought it was a bit loud, but she put up with it, which was easier to do because she was enjoying the food.

The Students Tell a Few Funny Stories

Some of the conversation did become amusing after a while though. The first time was when one of the group, Amy, said, "Someone sent me an email the other day with some funny stories about things children have said. I think they were originally posted on Internet forums by their parents and other relatives. One mum said she said to her three-year-old boy one evening, 'I hope you like your pizza. Mummy made it from scratch.' She said a look of horror came over the boy's face, and he asked, 'Whose scratches did you use?' I can understand how it might have sounded scary to someone who'd never heard the saying!

"And one mum said she sent her little son to his room for a while one day and told him off because he was being too aggressive with his toy guns and swords and things. Ten minutes later she went to his room to see if he'd calmed down, and found him quietly playing with his Lego. She thought it was good that he was doing something calm and creative instead of pretending to be going around destroying things. She thought he must have listened to what she'd said when she told him off, and told him she was proud of him for listening and calming down. She asked him what he was building. The boy said he was making an ultimate Lego weapon so he could destroy her.

". . . Actually I'm not sure if it was the mum or the dad who said that happened to them."

The group at the table giggled. Then one of them, Pippa, said, "My family are Catholics, and my parents have got a crucifix hanging above their bed. I remember when my brother was about two, he went into their room one morning and said, 'I can see Jesus on the Weetabix.' Whether he was confusing the word Weetabix with crucifix, or whether he somehow thought crucifixes have a strong resemblance to a breakfast cereal, I don't know. Nor does he, because he can't remember saying it now.

"And I remember once when he was about three, our parents took us for a walk in a park on a Sunday evening, and near the entrance there was an ice cream van. My brother went up to it and sternly told the man selling ice creams that he shouldn't be there on a Sunday; he should be in church. Anyway, we went around the park, and when we came back, the ice cream van was still there. It turned out that my brother had had a big change of attitude, because he said to my parents, 'Can I have an ice cream?' "

Becky said, "My auntie Diana told me that when she was little, they had bunkbeds, and she slept in the bottom one, and my auntie Joan, who's Diana and my mum's older sister, had the top one. My mum slept in the same room in a separate bed. My grandma told my auntie Diana that one day not long after my mum learned to talk, when she was about three, she was watching my grandma washing up, and Grandma pulled the plug out when she'd finished, and my mum said, 'Water going down the top bunk.'

"Why she thought the sink was the top bunk for a minute, I don't know. Or maybe she just confused the words plug and bunk, or sink and bunk, since they sound a bit similar. I don't know why she said it was the top one though. Or maybe she didn't, but my grandma remembered what she said slightly wrong."

Amy said, "Another story in the email I got said a mum said her little daughter once accidentally stepped on a crayon and broke it, and said, 'Oh no Mummy, I just assaulted the crayon.' "

One Student Talks About Something Sad That Happened to Her, and Becky Gives Her Some Advice

Most of the group at the table laughed. They might have carried on telling cute and amusing stories for a while, but instead the party descended into gloom for them for several minutes when the subject was changed.

A student called Alice had drunk several glasses of wine during the first hour of the party, and she would look back on that night with embarrassment at something she told them while her tongue was loosened by the drink, a confession she wouldn't normally have told anyone. She hadn't even told her family. Still, she was glad she told them in a way, because it led to her getting some good advice, and changing her mind about the direction of her life in a way she thought would be good for her:

She said that the mention of kids and crime like assault had brought to mind her plans for the future, when she wanted to become a probation officer. When she was asked why, she said she felt an affinity with young offenders; she felt sure she'd be able to give them a sympathetic ear, because she'd done something she'd felt really guilty about for a while, so she felt she could identify with them and would be more understanding than some people might be.

"What? A lot of young offenders probably don't feel guilty about anything they've done!" Becky pointed out.

Alice still felt sure she wanted to be around them and help them.

A couple of students at the table were curious to know what Alice could have done that she'd felt so guilty about. One of them was nosy and intrigued enough to ask.

It turned out that that evening wasn't the first time Alice had done something she regretted under the influence of drink. Oblivious to the fact that Becky would be considered by most people to be a bit too young to be hearing such detail, possibly because she'd seen her in lectures listening to the tutors say all manner of things, she confided,

"A couple of years ago, I started going out with someone, and a few weeks later, he tried to persuade me to have sex with him. I wasn't sure it was a good idea at first, since I'd been going out with him for such a short time, and I wasn't sure I was serious about him, and I wanted to be before I had sex; but we went out one evening, and I'd had a bit to drink, and we started cuddling, and one thing led to another as they say, and I thought it would be fun and shrugged off the idea that anything bad could happen. Actually, nowadays I think he probably planned that he'd get me drunk so I wouldn't care so much about waiting before I had sex with him, because he kept buying me drinks; and it upsets me that he could be calculating like that. But I still think I'm partly responsible, because I could still make decisions.

"Anyway we started this physical relationship, and about six weeks later I felt sure I was pregnant. I found out I really was. I was worried, and I didn't want my education to be ruined by having a baby, so I had an abortion. I didn't like the idea, but I thought it would be for the best. Afterwards, at first I was just relieved, and I felt wiser than I'd been before I started going out with him, and decided to take more care in future by using contraception.

"My boyfriend split up with me soon after that, because I didn't feel like having sex for a little while after my abortion, and he got impatient and irritated with me for it, and I got annoyed and told him there were probably far nicer boyfriends out there.

"But anyway, just over a year later, I was at a friend's house, and her sister came in with a baby who was smiling and laughing and just learning to imitate funny faces people made. My friend's sister was having fun with him, and then asked me if I wanted to cuddle him. Suddenly I started feeling kind of contaminated, as if I didn't deserve to. I hadn't been upset by having had the abortion before then. But then I started thinking about how if I'd had my own baby, he or she would be doing things like that by then.

"Then I started feeling really guilty about having had the abortion, and thought of myself as a murderer, and I felt that way for months. Now I feel as if I want to be among other people who've done bad things, because I'll feel more at home, and I think I'll be able to be more caring than someone who's never felt as if they've ever done anything that bad themselves, who might be more judgmental. I'll know there were probably bad circumstances that led to them doing what they did, so they can't be held entirely to blame."

The other students were sympathetic. They were silent for several seconds. But some of them thought there were problems with Alice's ideas, and thought they ought to speak up.

"But some people deserve to be judged! Surely being judgmental can be good sometimes," said Amy, resigning herself to not enjoying the party any more.

"Yes!" said another student, Nathan. "I don't know how long your compassion would last after hearing about some of their stories, especially if you started feeling sorry for their victims! Some of their crimes might have been really gross!

And some of the offenders might be abusive to you, for all you know. How would you feel then?"

One of the students, Rachel, said, "You don't really need to feel guilty about having had the abortion. I know you said the guilt wore off. That's good. But I don't think you should ever feel bad; after all, I imagine you would have had it decently early enough that the foetus didn't feel any pain, and didn't even know it existed; after all, if it hadn't developed any parts of a brain by then, it wouldn't have had any consciousness.

"And if you had had the baby, not only might it have meant that you didn't have the time to become so well-educated, but if that uncaring boyfriend you used to have wanted to see the child sometimes, you'd have had to stay in contact with him for years and years whether you liked it or not."

Becky advised, "I don't think you should choose a career till you know what it's like to do the job from day to day. After all, you might go into it with high hopes, but if it's not the way you expect, you might quickly get fed up, and it would be a shame after all the training you might have done. If I were you, I'd have a look on the Internet for personal experiences of probation officers and their accounts of what the day-to-day realities of their job are like, and the kinds of problems they've had to face. You might be encouraged, but you might be put right off."

Alice thanked Becky, and said she'd do that.

A couple of days later, she did. She found out some things she hadn't known about before, and after a good think, she decided to change her career plans.

Those were wise words from Becky; but unfortunately, she wasn't wise enough to manage to avoid the unexpected trouble that was to befall her that evening. But then, some people much older than her wouldn't have done either. After all, it wasn't as if all of it could have been foreseen and planned for.

Just then though, there was nothing to suggest that anything out-of-the-ordinary was going to happen that night.

The Students Talk About Unpleasant Jobs, and Joke About Wacky-Sounding Ones

After Becky gave Alice her advice, Rachel said, "I think that's good advice! I've had jobs I had no idea I'd hate as much as I did! I did a gap year last year . . . well actually I had to have one because I failed my A levels, so I had to study more and re-take them before I could come here. My parents wanted me to get a job, to save up for university and to help them out with money a bit. They said I was old enough to be paying them rent, and that future employers might value me more if they had evidence that I could stick at a job. So I had a look around for what was available.

"I got a job in a fast-food restaurant, serving customers. But I hated it! Now I realise I'd be no good at that kind of work!

"For one thing, I hadn't realised how much we'd be required to smile and be friendly with customers; the management still wanted me to do that even though learning the job was stressful, so I didn't feel like smiling at all. It was really busy, and I kept making mistakes, because I couldn't cope with having to do several things at once like we were supposed to. I couldn't do them fast enough, and I'm clumsy by nature, so I felt as if everyone else there must be more efficient than me. The person training me kept following me, telling me things and asking me questions, expecting me to answer her and concentrate, while at the same time I was trying to serve customers and remember all their orders. I couldn't do it! It made me feel stupid and incompetent.

"One day my trainer complained to the manager that I was ignoring her, because I wasn't answering her or giving her attention while I was trying to simultaneously make drinks, hand out food and remember orders. I couldn't do that many things at once, and as well as that, I was feeling nervous because I was being watched and assessed for how well I could do the job, which was making me even more clumsy and forgetful than I normally am.

"I kept doing things wrong. I couldn't do so many things at once; I never smiled enough; I kept forgetting orders; I was too slow, and I wasn't good enough in other ways too. It made me miserable.

"They must have decided I was no good at the job, because they cut my hours down to the bare minimum after a few weeks; they must have been hoping I'd get fed up and leave.

"I couldn't sleep at night for worrying about what it would be like when I went in the next day. I felt like a failure, doing so many things wrong. I started to get really anxious. And while all that was going on, I was trying to help my sister whose boyfriend was beginning to get abusive; and my family's pet dog got ill, and I was worried it was something serious and that he wouldn't recover, and he'd have to be put to sleep. Thankfully he did recover, and my sister split up with her boyfriend in the end; but worrying about them and wondering what the best thing would be to do while those things were going on just added to all the stress. I think it was the worst time in my life.

"I left that fast-food restaurant. But my parents still wanted me to have a job, and I knew it made sense, because I thought it would be sensible to save up for university; so I got another one. But I didn't get on well with that one either!"

Nathan said, "Oh that's a real shame! It's a pity you couldn't find a job you liked. Hey, it would have been good if you could have got a job as a wine taster or something; you might have enjoyed that!"

Pippa said, "Oh I don't know about that; I've heard they have to spit the wine out once they've tasted it!"

Amy grinned and said, "At least if you thought some wine was repulsive, you'd have a good excuse to spit it out! You could spit it out with feeling, and then say to anyone who saw you, or the manager of the wine company if they were watching you, 'Don't be offended; I'm just doing my job!' "

They laughed.

One of the group was called Paul, but all the other students called him Prawn, because he'd told them that had been his nickname ever since his younger brother had been a toddler and had started calling him Prawn, perhaps because he couldn't pronounce the name Paul, or maybe just for fun.

He said, "I've heard there are some really wacky jobs around. It's a pity you couldn't have got a job as an official zombie, Rachel. Apparently the London Dungeons employ people to be zombies, and they just have to scare people!"

Rachel grinned and said, "Now scaring people, I think I could do!"

They all laughed again.

Prawn said, "Or maybe you could have got a job as a golf ball diver. I read on the Internet that there's a lake in London that gets so many golf balls landing in it after careless golfers accidentally hurtle them into there instead of along the course that there are actual divers employed to fish them out, and any one of them can find as many as a million balls a year!"

Amy said, "Wow, there must be a lot of careless golfers out there! . . . Well, either that or it's just the same few rich golfers with loads and loads of golf balls accidentally swinging them into the lake all the time! Imagine them standing there hitting a ball all day, and almost every time they do, it splashes into the lake and they say, 'Oh, whoops, it's gone in the lake again! I must try harder next time! Oh well, time to get another ball out of the bag.'"

Prawn continued, "I read that another weird job is a professional sleeper! I bet you'd have enjoyed that one, Rachel! They go around to hotels testing their new beds out, finding out how comfortable they are and how easily they can fall asleep on them."

The students giggled. Rachel said, "Now That sounds like the kind of job I'd enjoy!"

Becky grinned and said, "I bet everyone would enjoy it!"

Prawn smiled and said, "Apparently some other people have a job as a professional armpit sniffer! Well, I think they're called odour judgers, but they work for companies that make deodorants, and they go around sniffing the armpits of people who are using them to test them out, to find out if they're working!"

The students laughed again. Rachel giggled and then screwed up her face and said, "Oh yuck! I wouldn't fancy that one, thanks!"

Prawn said, "What about a job as a human scarecrow then? I read that one person really had a job as one. They had a cowbell they'd ring when birds came too close. I don't know what else they did."

Alice grinned and said, "Maybe they jumped up and down all day making silly loud noises, and things like that."

The students giggled. Pippa grinned and said, "I wonder if he had to go on a special training course in silly loud noise-making and frightening jumping dances first!"

Rachel said, "It sounds like a fun job; but knowing me, I'd get tired and fall asleep, and wake up with birds on my head! So much for being scary!"

They all laughed again.

Then Nathan said, "I read about a council in Scotland that tried putting sophisticated robot bird scarers that looked like birds of prey at the seaside to deter seagulls from landing around there. The robots were specially programmed to look menacing. They could flap their wings, turn their heads and make calls that sounded like birds of prey. But instead of being scared, the seagulls all ganged up together to fight them!"

The students giggled some more. Then Prawn said, "Alright, how about being a train stuffer, Rachel? I read that in Japan, they have professional train stuffers, or squeezers-on, who are paid to push people into carriages neatly at rush hour, when there are so many it's difficult to find room on trains."

Rachel laughed and said, "What would my mum say if I told her I was a train squeezer! And I'm not sure people would take kindly to me shoving them onto trains around here!"

Amy said, "Well, they probably do it quite delicately. The art of delicate shoving!"

Becky giggled and said, "There must be more to the job than just shoving people around!"

They all laughed again. Then Nathan said, "What would you call yourself if you were a train squeezer and a train spotter? A train spot squeezer, maybe?"

Rachel grinned, screwed up her face and said, "Oh yuck!"

Prawn said, "This might be more up your street then: How would you like a job watching paint dry? Apparently jobs like that really do exist! I read that some paint companies really employ people to do that, and give them stopwatches so they can tell how long it takes."

Rachel laughed and said, "Yes, that sounds like the kind of job I might be able to do, although I'm not quite sure: I can imagine falling asleep and rolling off the chair and hitting the thing that had been painted. If the paint was still wet, it might end up with an imprint of my head on it!"

Prawn said, "Alright, if you'd want something more exciting, how would you like a job as a professional thief? I read that some shops employ them to try to steal things and see if they can get away with it, so they can find out if their security systems all work properly."

Rachel smiled and said, "I'm not sure I'd like doing that . . . I mean, what if a customer saw me trying to walk out the shop with something without paying and did a citizen's arrest on me? What if that happened, say, fifty times a day? I'd be really used to citizen's arrests by the end of it!"

They all laughed.

Then Prawn grinned and said, "How would you like a job as a daredevil window cleaner then? I read that there are people who clean the windows of really tall buildings, who abseil down really big skyscrapers or dangle from bridges on specially-designed ropes to clean windows!"

Rachel smiled and said, "I think I'd find that job a bit scary! Even scarier than the ones I've had!"

Becky turned the conversation serious again by asking, "What other jobs have you had?"

Rachel said, "Alright, I'll tell you about them. Well, it was probably really silly of me, but after I left the job I told you about, I got another job in a fast-food restaurant. There didn't seem to be many other jobs going that I thought I'd be able to do, and I thought maybe I'd be better at it than I was before for having had the experience and training at the last place. But I did even worse!

"It had a drive-through section, and I was put on it one day not that long after I started there. There was so much I had to do at once, my mind ended up just going completely blank, as if it just couldn't cope. I mean, I had to stand at the counter taking orders from customers through a headset and talking to them, while I was processing their money through the till, at the same time as I was making the drinks they wanted, while I was packaging up what they wanted and passing it to them, at the same time as I was supposed to be listening to the manager giving me instructions through the headset and reacting to them . . . and I had to do all that really really fast! I just couldn't cope! I ended up feeling so confused, I just didn't know what to do first any more, or even what I was doing – I just couldn't remember everything any more, so I just gave up and stood there doing nothing.

"My manager saw that and moved me to a less busy counter. But I was no good at any job there. I was physically incapable of moving as fast as the job required me to! I just couldn't do anything with the speed and efficiency they wanted me to! They realised I was no good at packing food and drink quickly, so they started putting me on the till all the time; but I wasn't much good there either! Some people did it really well; they were friendly to the customers all day, always smiling, and they managed to encourage them to buy extra things to go with their meals. But I just haven't got the personality to be bubbly and smile and chat, while I was taking their money and handing out their change and things, especially while I was finding things so stressful.

"One day the manager called me into her office and told me I needed to smile and chat more. But I just find it really difficult to fake a smile; people have told me I look evil when I've tried! I did try to be chattier, but I just found it really tiring, because it just doesn't come naturally to me!

"Then I got another warning about how I needed to smile more and be more friendly to customers if I wanted to keep the job! I hadn't realised that was such an important part of it before I started working in those places! I never want to work with the public again now, at least in a job where I have to be cheerful. I don't think I'm any good at it at all!

"Then the manager asked me if I felt any more confident packing the food and drink quickly than I had before, and I didn't want to make myself sound too incompetent, so I said I thought I'd do alright. So she said she'd try me on the drive-through counter again! I panicked! I decided to leave right then and there, because I knew that if I went on the drive-through again, I'd either be so bad at the job I'd have a complete breakdown, or she'd sack me on the spot because she found out I was still no good at doing it!

"They call these kinds of jobs unskilled, and yet I couldn't even do the supposed least skilled bits of them well! You know, it's a bit demoralising!"

Becky said, "That's a shame! Maybe the people who labelled that work as unskilled never tried it!"

The others grinned.

Then Becky said, "I can imagine not being very good at that kind of job myself when I grow up!

"The thing is though, it might have looked to you as if everyone else in those places could do the job much better than you, but what if they took weeks or months before they got that good? For all you know, you might have got to be as good at the job as they were if you'd done it for as long as them. How do you know they didn't do it as badly as you did in their first week? And it might have looked as if they were doing it well, but what if inside, some of them were feeling stressed and thinking they were struggling with it? You wouldn't necessarily know."

Rachel said, "Maybe. But it's hard to imagine ever getting to be able to do the job any faster than I did; I just don't feel as if I'm physically capable of doing that!"

Becky said, "Maybe. But maybe you would have got better with practice. I know someone who worked in a fast-food place, and she said that when she first went there, she was slower than the others herself, and they didn't like that, but with practice, she got to be faster than them, and she enjoyed the job.

"Maybe not all places are as pressured as where you worked though; or maybe some people are just naturally faster and better at that kind of work than others. Maybe some people get an adrenaline buzz out of the challenge of having to do so many things almost at once and as fast as they can. It's funny what some people get adrenaline rushes from, like skydiving, or arguing!

"But it sounds as if you had more to do at once than was realistically possible where you worked. What if part of the problem was nothing to do with you at all, but it was that the restaurant should have been employing more staff and shouldn't have expected people to do so many things at once? They might have been expecting unrealistic things from people, or at least new employees who weren't used to working there!

"You've been blaming yourself for being too slow and clumsy to do the work all this time, but what if it was unrealistic of them to have expected you to do as much work as they did in so short a time, especially without even training you properly first? I mean, they should at least have found some way of simulating the amount of pressure you'd be under to do things quickly so you could get used to it before you had to do that for real, giving you advice as you went along so you could get better at the job before you had to actually do it! They shouldn't have expected you to be really good at it straightaway!"

Rachel said, "That's true! I feel a bit better now for thinking that! Thanks!"

The Students Tell Funny and Interesting Tales About Famous People's Gaffes and Failures

Nathan said, "Don't worry too much about failing at something. I read that quite a lot of famous people have failed at things, and done embarrassing things in front of people, and loads of people have got to hear about it or see pictures of it!

"Like there's that recent American president who's famous for getting his words muddled up for the world to see, saying things like, 'Our enemies are innovative and resourceful, and so are we. They never stop thinking about new ways to harm our country and our people, and neither do we.'

"And he condemned America's enemies as having, 'no disregard for human life'! And one day he said, 'I understand small business growth. I was one.' And talking about people who'd come to America since it was founded, he said, 'These immigrants have helped transform 13 small colonies into a great and growing nation of more than 300 people.' And he said, 'It was not always a given that the United States and America would have a close relationship.'

"Another thing he said was, 'Families is where our nation finds hope, where wings take dream.' And another one I remember hearing is, 'We had a chance to visit with Teresa Nelson who's a parent, and a mum or a dad.' And one more I remember is, 'Rarely is the question asked: Is our children learning?'"

Becky giggled and joked, "I'm not surprised that question's only rarely asked!"

Nathan said, "I also heard about a celebrity who had a tattoo behind one of her ears, and the press took a photo of it, but the picture showed she had loads of ear wax in her ear; so the photo got splashed over the papers, for everyone to see she hadn't cleaned her ears out recently! She must have been embarrassed!"

They giggled.

Pippa said, "I read about some famous people who failed at things they tried to do at first. Some of the things I read are quite surprising, although I can't be entirely sure they're accurate, of course, since I found them on the Internet and not in official biographies. But apparently the man who set up the Ford Motor Company, which is really successful today, tried starting five businesses before that one, but they all failed. Maybe he learned from his mistakes each time, I don't know.

"And apparently the man who started the huge supermarket chain Woolworths worked in a shop before he founded the business, and he wasn't allowed to serve customers, because his boss said he didn't have enough sense to do it well.

"And the man who founded the famous motor company Honda tried to get a job as an engineer with Toyota before he did that, but they turned him down, and he was unemployed for some time, so he started making scooters at home, and his neighbours encouraged him to start his own business. It gradually grew to be huge!

"And I read that Einstein was a late developer; apparently he didn't talk till he was four, and couldn't read till he was seven, and his family and teachers thought he must be mentally handicapped and slow. He was even made to leave school because of it, at least according to what I read.

"And you know how famous and respected Charles Darwin got to be in the end? Well, apparently when he was growing up, his dad and his schoolmasters thought he was of below-average intelligence, and too dreamy and lazy.

"There are loads of examples of people who did things badly or weren't well thought of before they succeeded well on the website I got this information from, like famous authors whose books got rejected by loads of publishers before they finally succeeded, and all kinds of people like that!"

Rachel said, "Well that's encouraging!"

Prawn, who knew he himself had a habit of being a bit lazy sometimes, grinned and said, "Charles Darwin was too lazy and dreamy when he was growing up? There's hope for us lot yet!"

The others tittered.

Pippa said, "Another website said that Isaac Newton's mum got him to leave school to help on the family farm, but he was really bad at the job, because he got so engrossed in making things and experimenting and studying things that he didn't pay attention to what he was supposed to be doing. Like he was supposed to watch the sheep, but he got engrossed in doing his own thing, and they strayed into a neighbour's field and started eating what was in it, and his mum had to pay the neighbour damages because of it. I suppose different people are good at different things in life."

The Students Talk and Joke About Jobs and Related Things Again

Nathan said, "Wow, it sounds as if there are a lot of jobs it's possible to fail at, and a lot of jobs you can do for years without liking them. I think it's nice that we've got the luxury of being able to spend a few years deciding what we really want to do in life, so we'll hopefully end up doing something we've been able to put quite a bit of thought into choosing, not like people who have to go out and work at whatever they can get, because they've got children or parents who need them to bring money into the home, or they need to get one of the jobs where they can work hours they can fit around the times when they have to look after their children, so they don't have the chance – at least for the time being – to be able to dither around thinking about what they want to do in life before they have to decide."

Some of the others agreed. But then Becky laughed and said, "I don't call studying here 'dithering around'!"

Nathan responded, "That's not quite what I meant. I meant we can just take time to think things over and make up our minds."

The students smiled.

Rachel said, "Mind you, some of us might decide we need to get temporary jobs to help us through if money gets a bit short."

Nathan said, "Yeah, true, but hopefully there won't be any urgency . . . Actually, if I do need a job, maybe I can get a job as a barman, and then maybe people will treat me to free drinks!"

Rachel laughed and said, "You'd better not drink too many of those if that happens, or you might start doing your job worse than I did mine! I can just imagine you ending up tipsy and saying to a customer you're serving, 'Oh, you wanted your drink in a glass, and not all down your front? Oh, sorry about that! Oh what did you say? You wanted beer, not whisky? Oh well, you won't mind that I somehow accidentally got it all down your front then if you didn't want it anyway!' "

The others laughed.

Then Rachel said, "Maybe if we both got a job in the same pub, the management would have a hard time deciding which of us was doing it worse! Mind you, I'm not a disaster everywhere I go. When I was doing my gap year, I did get a job I liked and could do better in the end, after I decided I wouldn't be able to stand serving fast food to customers again.

"I got a job cleaning the pavement around a shopping centre in the early hours of the morning with a scrubbing machine for a few hours. It was so much nicer being able to go around knowing there was no boss watching and criticising me, and no customers to serve at a speed that was beyond my capabilities! The only thing was, there were CCTV cameras all around, so I felt a bit self-conscious knowing I might be being watched by someone somewhere looking at the screen. Still, I'm sure they had better things to do than look at me all the time!"

Alice said, "I was watching a television programme once where a man was interviewed who went around picking up dog mess and emptying dog poo bins, and he actually said he liked the job! I don't know why; maybe he often got to chat to some nice people along the way, or maybe he enjoyed watching children play and other people having fun in the parks where some of the poo bins were, or maybe he got a sense of fulfilment out of cleaning the place up so it was nicer for people to be in; or perhaps he liked being out in the fresh air a lot . . . well, whatever fresh air there actually can have been when he spent so much time close to dog poo! Maybe it wasn't that last reason after all!"

The others giggled. Then Amy said, "I wonder what makes someone want to do a job where they have to unblock a lot of drains. I mean, it doesn't sound like a very nice job, does it, but I suppose if some people stick at it for years, there must be something in it . . . Or in the drains at least."

Nathan said, "My dad used to work in a factory that made drains, till it closed down."

Becky said in surprise, "A factory making drains?"

Then she blushed slightly and said, "Well, I suppose drains do have to be made; they don't just appear out of nowhere, do they. I suppose I just never thought about things that are mostly holes being made before; you think of digging holes, not making them, don't you . . . although I'm not daft enough to have ever thought people might dig drains . . . Well, I suppose people dig the holes to put them in in the first place . . . I mean the bits of them that are put in the ground anyway; but of course, people don't dig the metal bits, do they; they must make them . . . Well I mean, some people must dig to find the metal in the first place . . . well, that's to say the stone and stuff with the metal in it; but . . ."

The others giggled, and Amy said good-naturedly, "Yes, we know what you mean!"

Prawn joked, "You sound as if you've been breathing in everyone's alcohol fumes tonight, Becky!"

Then Nathan said, "I came across a website about strange things that have been found in blocked drains. It said one thing that sometimes gets found in them is books, as if some people take a book into the bathroom thinking they'll have a leisurely read of it on the loo, and then they get fed up of it, and decide it's so bad they just fling it down there!"

The others giggled.

Becky responded, "You'd have thought they'd only take a book in there in the first place if they knew it was going to be interesting, wouldn't you. I mean, how much time must these people spend sitting there? How much time does it take to go from thinking a book might be good to deciding it's so boring you just don't want it any more? Maybe these people are sitting there for hours or something! You wouldn't want to live with them, would you! When would you ever get in the bathroom yourself?"

Alice said, "Maybe the books are thrown down the loo by children though; maybe they sometimes throw ones belonging to other family members down there out of spite, or just because they think it's fun."

Pippa said, "It's strange what some people think of as fun, isn't it!"

Amy replied, "Yes; but even you might have thought that kind of thing was fun when you were little!"

The group giggled again. Then Nathan said, "I heard that people can go on tours down the sewers in some places. I've even heard of outings of schoolchildren going down there. Maybe some parents encourage them, saying things like, 'Yes, you go down there, and while you're there, you can see if you can find that book of mine you threw down the loo! It might take you a while – happy searching!'"

They grinned. Then Rachel said, "Maybe if the sewer tours are popular, it must mean some people think it's fun to go down there. I wonder what could make it fun! I suppose it might be all the stories a tour guide might tell about weird things being found down there, and sewer rats the size of small dogs frightening people who should be used to rats because they've been working there for years, and that kind of thing.

"Actually, I've been wondering if there are people who could make a lot of things seem like fun that most people wouldn't think of as fun, ever since I got rejected for another job I went for before I got the pavement-scrubbing job. It was a job in a stockroom in a clothes shop, that would mainly have been just unpacking clothes after they got delivered and hanging them up. A group of us went for the job and we were given a trial for an hour or two. Then the manager said she didn't think I was suited to the job because I was too quiet. She said she wanted people who could fit in better with the jolly chatty atmosphere she wanted in there, because work like that could begin to get boring, so it helped to have people who knew how to liven the place up and make the work seem more enjoyable so they'd be more likely to stick at it. I'd never dreamed a job like that would involve requirements like that. I suppose it makes sense.

"And it's far better that it's that way around than if there was a rule that said people weren't allowed to talk, although I suppose if there was, it might be something to do with stopping people getting distracted and losing concentration on what they were doing."

The Evening Begins to Go Downhill

Just then, a few social work students came to sit with them. They asked the psychology students if they'd like drinks, and if so, what they'd like.

Seeing so many people drinking alcohol around her, Becky was curious to find out what it was like. Her friends sometimes drank a little bit of alcohol around her, but they'd never have approved of her having any. So she asked if she could try a little bit of wine. She was envisaging someone allowing her to sip a bit from their glass, or them pouring a bit of theirs into an empty glass she had. But one of the social work students, Russell, possibly already a little bit the worse for drink, got her a whole glassful.

She coughed when she first tried it, but she carried on, and though she wasn't keen, she finished it, curious about what it might do to her – she'd heard so many people say they enjoyed drinking, or that it changed their mood in different ways.

She was asked what she thought of the wine, and she said she didn't really like it. One of the social work students, Kevin, said cheerfully, "Try a beer then!" He got her half a pint, somehow seemingly oblivious to the fact that she was only a child.

Normally the psychology students at the table would have advised Becky not to drink any more alcohol, but at the start of the evening they'd decided to let themselves go and drink enough to get tipsy, thinking they'd enjoy themselves more that way, and the amount they'd had to drink had made them less alert to the risks of what was happening, and less concerned about it than they would have been sober.

Becky wasn't keen on the beer either, but it seemed a shame to waste it, and she thought it would be impolite not to drink it since Kevin had paid for it; so she drank it all. She still thought it might be interesting to find out what it did to her.

But when they asked her what she thought of it, she admitted she wasn't keen on that either. Another social work student called Donna suggested she might prefer alcopops, saying it was possible to get blackcurrant or cherry ones and other nice flavours. She got one for Becky and she drank that too. So far, she didn't feel as if the drink was having much effect on her.

A Social Work Student Complains About His Course and Its Tutors

Kevin pointed to a man at the next table and said in a loud whisper, "You see him? He's one of our tutors. I don't like him."

Whispering when there was fairly loud music playing wasn't a good idea; no one heard him. Nathan told him so.

So he spoke up, probably more loudly than he should have done, saying,

"I don't like our course at all! We spend almost the whole time talking about how we can be more politically correct. We haven't learned a thing about child protection, or how best to help the different kinds of people we might meet. One of our tutors is better than the rest because she at least gives us interesting course handouts in the lessons. None of the others do."

It occurred to one or two of the psychology students that although Kevin might not have learned a thing about child protection on his course, he should at least know the basics already, such as not giving children alcohol.

Oblivious to their thoughts, Kevin continued, "Before we came here, some of us hoped we'd learn about what to do in difficult situations . . . you know, like how to go about dealing with child protection cases, what kinds of services social services can offer old people whose health is failing, the main duties of various kinds of social workers, how to help mentally ill people, how to advise parents of children who are difficult to control, and that kind of thing.

"But just about all the course is about is how we can make sure we've got politically correct attitudes to gay people and women and disabled people and black people and so on, so we don't discriminate against them somehow or have unfair attitudes to them. The tutors don't look for evidence first as to whether any of us actually do have politically incorrect attitudes to them; they just assume we've all got them, so we have to examine ourselves for them all day regardless. Even a black disabled lesbian would have to do that, although I suppose she might be also encouraged to examine herself to work out if she's got politically incorrect attitudes to non-disabled straight white males, possibly. I've never heard anyone be told to do anything like that though."

A few of the psychology students thought it was pretty strange that Kevin seemed to be concerned about child protection, and yet he hadn't seen anything wrong with Becky being given alcoholic drinks. One or two of them concluded that he either must be pretty drunk or rather stupid, or perhaps hypocritical. They thought it seemed he had more to learn about child protection than he might think, so it was a pity he wasn't learning anything about it at all!

They began to feel a bit guilty about the fact that they hadn't said anything about Becky being encouraged to drink themselves. But at first, apart from feeling more easy-going about the idea because of the alcohol they'd drunk, they'd thought Becky having just a bit of alcohol would be OK; and then, since she seemed to want it, they felt awkward about behaving like authority figures and telling her they didn't think she should have any more, although they thought they'd better do that if she carried on drinking.

Alice found things a bit ominous, wondering how sincere Kevin could really be about caring about child protection when he was happy to give a child alcohol. His concern sounded weird to her; but she thought that maybe he just didn't consider a child of Becky's age having a couple of drinks to be that serious. Then she remembered hearing someone make the puzzling remark that humans often have contradictory attitudes in their minds. It put her in mind of something a tutor had recently claimed about how people who've suffered a few hard knocks don't get bothered by everyday frustrations, because they seem trivial in comparison. He'd given the impression, rightly or wrongly, that he was speaking from experience; but this was a tutor who'd only a few weeks earlier casually told a few of them that he'd thrown his mobile phone across the room in frustration a few days before because he couldn't get something on it to work after a few attempts.

Then Alice reflected that Kevin had used the phrase, "some of us" when he was referring to some social work students' wish to learn about child protection, so that didn't *necessarily* include himself, although why he'd want to go into social work if he wasn't caring enough to be concerned about it, she couldn't guess.

None of the students got the chance to ask Kevin what the truth was, because he carried on talking without allowing anyone to get a word in edgeways. Oblivious to what they were thinking, he continued, "But our tutors haven't even got the attitudes they're trying to teach us to have, even though they pretend to have them! There's someone who's a bit deaf on our course, and one day, after a lesson on political correctness, a tutor got into an argument with her and told her straight, in front of everyone on the course, that she didn't think people who've got hearing difficulties should be social workers, because they're more likely to misunderstand what people say, and not pick up on clues in their tone of voice that they're lying about things.

"The woman with hearing problems said she hadn't ever wanted to go into the kind of social work where that type of thing might be a risk to anyone, and that besides, there were ways around the problem, such as going to see people with a support worker who could interpret what was being said into sign language for her, and discuss their opinions of it with her after the visits. She asked why she'd been accepted onto the course in the first place if the tutor had thought she shouldn't be a social worker. The tutor looked embarrassed and said there was a policy on the course of not refusing to accept people on the grounds of disability, since doing that would be politically incorrect. She herself had been one of the ones to make the decision to accept her onto the course, since she's the head tutor.

"The student with the hearing problem thought some of the tutors must be hypocrites who wanted to give the impression they were keen to support people with disabilities when they weren't really. She'd found the interview to get onto the course much easier than she'd expected, and didn't understand why, if they thought some people with disabilities weren't suitable, they didn't ask much more difficult questions that would show up difficulties people would have with doing the job so they could weed people who couldn't do it out and they'd be seen to have a reason not to let them on the course . . . Perhaps they aren't clever enough to have thought of any questions like that! Or maybe they are, but they slapped each other on the back congratulating themselves on their political correctness with every disabled student they allowed on the course, hoping they could somehow manipulate those students into giving up of their own free will before the end. I don't know."

The other students at the table were unhappy to hear about the attitude of some of the tutors. There was a pause in the conversation while they took it in.

Then the silence was broken. It was broken by what sounded like a plate that was dropped loudly, and also possibly broken, some way off in the room, just as a record ended. Or perhaps it was the record being broken, though it would have to have been broken in very dramatic style to have made such a racket, possibly along with the CD player it was on.

One or two of the students at the table jumped, but didn't comment; they were too preoccupied with thinking about what Kevin was saying.

"What's this about the tutor at the next table then?" asked Prawn curiously. He was sitting near Kevin, and had heard just enough of his loud whisper earlier and the tone of intrigue in his voice to feel sure a scandal was afoot. Perhaps he wouldn't have done if he hadn't had the unfortunate habit of assuming the worst about things. In this case though, some of the others soon got the same impression as him.

"He's one of the worst!" Kevin said. "I don't know what his proper name is; I bet I couldn't pronounce it if I did. Maybe he thinks we all couldn't, because he told us all to call him BJ. Well, I have heard one or two people call him something like Parrot before, or maybe it was Carrot. No, it couldn't have been! No parent would ever call their child Parrot or Carrot, would they!"

Some Humour Breaks Out as the Students Talk About Weird Baby Names

"I don't know," said Amy. "I've heard of parents calling their children strange names! I read about twins who were called Sid and Stan Still. Imagine if someone asked one of them his name while they were walking along the street together or somewhere and he said, 'Stan Still'! They might stop in their tracks, wondering what the matter was. And I heard about a girl called Blip, and another one whose parents called her Wrigley."

"All babies are wriggly," said Nathan with a smile.

Becky said, "I don't see why a name like Parrot or Carrot would be hard to pronounce . . . Well, that's unless the effort not to laugh while saying it would be hard. I bet it isn't one of those though!"

"I heard about a boy who was called Caige," said Pippa. "Why don't the parents of these children think about how embarrassed they'll be to tell people their names?"

"Who'll be embarrassed? The parents, when they start having to explain their naming decisions to other people, or the children?" asked Rachel, grinning.

"Probably both!" laughed Amy.

"I heard about one girl called Blue, and another called Green," said Pippa.

"I heard about one poor boy whose parents named him Hurricane!" said Nathan.

Amy said, "I heard about a boy whose parents called him Finch. Poor boy! Imagine all the bird jokes! For one thing, when he's old enough to go out with girls, I don't suppose he'll appreciate being asked by other boys if he's a bird himself!"

"I'd prefer bird jokes to the hurricane jokes!" said Prawn with a smirk.

The Social Work Student Complains Some More About His Course and Its Tutors, as Well as Some Bad Work Experience

Kevin said, "Our head lecturer's called Spam . . . Oh no, it's Pam. I forgot for a minute; I'm so used to a couple of people calling her Spam. Actually one calls her Scam. It's kind of appropriate, I think. That's partly because some of the lectures on our course just seem to be some kind of propaganda, not anything useful!

"Like one day, one of the tutors did a lecture all about how old and disabled people are treated so much better in Africa and India than they are in the West, because people in Africa and India all have family values and care so much more.

"Well that's bunkum! At least according to a few people I've spoken to, who've told me horrible stories about things that have happened to some people in some communities in certain parts of the world, like blind children being turned out on the streets by their families to make a living as best they can by begging in parts of Africa. Mind you, the person who told me about that didn't say so, but thinking about it, maybe that often happens not because of heartlessness but because their families think they'll be a burden to them all their lives if they don't learn to beg, because they don't see how they'll ever be able to work to support them through their hardships if they don't, which a lot of them really won't be able to, because it seems facilities aren't available to educate most of them in some countries, which makes blind people's chances of getting decent jobs even lower than they would be if they were educated. Still, from what I heard, it seems a lot of them are sent out to beg from a pretty young age.

"Also, I watched something on TV about how being born deaf is seen as a karmic curse in at least some parts of India, a punishment for sins supposedly committed in a past life, so some deaf people aren't treated well.

"In some countries in Africa, if a child's born with a disability, such as deafness or blindness or Downs syndrome, a lot of people think their family must have been cursed by an evil person, or else by their ancestors because of bad things one of the child's relatives must have done, or they can believe the birth of a disabled or deformed child is an omen of a calamity that'll befall the family, so they can think the product of the curse or omen – the disabled child – must also be evil or will bring bad luck, so the child can be feared and ostracised, or even suffer a lot of violence. They can even be killed. A lot of families are ashamed of having a disabled child because of other people's or their own opinions about why it happened. And other attitudes like that are quite widespread in certain parts of the world where I think most people aren't given a good scientific education that would reveal the real reasons for disabilities and illness to them.

"And it might be more common for old people with failing health to live with their families in the developing world, but that's probably partly because there aren't that many old people's homes around, and they might not be affordable to most people if they were; and besides that, old people often die much sooner than they do here, so a lot of families probably don't have to look after old relatives whose health has declined so much that they need a lot of care for nearly as many years as they would here. Several generations of families often live together in poor parts of the world anyway, probably partly because it's easier to afford to do that than for each of the children to buy or rent their own house. I'm pretty sure it isn't just because people are nicer out there."

Alice spoke up and said, "Things can't be as bad as you say it is for disabled people everywhere in Africa. I know a blind man from Nigeria who went to a primary school for blind people out there. Then he came here to go to a secondary school for blind and partially-sighted children, and he's lived here ever since. But that proves that they must have at least some facilities out there for blind people. Maybe a lot more good things than bad ones are going on for disabled people in developing countries, but the bad ones are just the ones you've heard about, because bad things often get more publicity than good ones."

Kevin said, "Maybe. But the fact that I've heard about bad things going on from several people proves things aren't as rosy as the tutor who gave that lecture about how people are so much nicer in those countries than they are here was trying to make them out to be. I first heard about some blind people being made to beg on the streets by their families in some poor countries from my old maths teacher at school, who used to work at a school for blind children in India. That in itself would have been bad enough for them; she was a short-tempered thing! She was a Christian, so it might have been a missionary school. Anyway, if you don't believe that what I've been talking about can be that widespread, look on the Internet and see what you find.

"But as for this tutor who lectured us about how people are so much more family-orientated and kind in countries like that than they are here, the first day we were here, she was complaining about some people having politically incorrect attitudes towards people from her country or something, and one of us suggested she could educate them about why their thinking was in error. The tutor got all indignant and asked sarcastically, 'Is it our role in life to educate people?' (She meant the role of people from her country who live here.)

"The person who'd suggested educating others thought afterwards that she should have replied by saying something like, 'Well, this is an educational establishment after all . . . at least that's what I was led to believe.'"

Kevin went on and on talking for the next several minutes, while the other students became more and more shocked and depressed by what he said. More than one of them wrung their hands under the table, almost forgetting they were at what was supposed to be a party, till a balloon fell onto Nathan's head. Someone had put up a few Christmas decorations in the room, hanging a few bunches of balloons from the ceiling. The balloon that fell down bounced onto the table after it had hit Nathan on the head, and then bounced right into Becky's food.

A few of the students laughed, but Becky wasn't pleased; she felt sure her food wouldn't taste quite so nice after it had had a balloon in it. Not that she'd ever tasted balloon – or at least, not very often, but she didn't like the idea of trying balloon-flavoured food. She flung the balloon over her shoulder without looking to see where it went. The people sitting opposite her saw it though; it flew over the heads of some of the people at the next table and landed right in the food of another student. He was perhaps a bit drunk, since he took time to lick all the food residue off it, both from his own food and Becky's, with a total lack of self-consciousness, and then he threw it on the floor.

Kevin paused for a few seconds when the balloon fell down onto Nathan's head, and then continued his sorry story as if nothing had happened, as if he was somehow used to balloons falling down from the ceiling and hitting people on the head around him.

He said, "Anyway, one day, we had a day of lectures about AIDS. In the morning, the tutors were lecturing us all about how we must be clear that HIV is different from AIDS, just in case we ever unfairly stigmatise people with HIV as having AIDS, or something like that – I can't quite remember what lesson they were trying to drum into us now! But in the afternoon, someone who'd had two husbands who'd both died from AIDS spoke to us; they were both haemophiliacs who'd caught it after having blood transfusions. I don't think that could happen now in this country, because they screen blood for diseases like that. But at first they didn't. Anyway, I smiled at one point, because the woman said, 'Forget the propaganda you heard this morning; now I'm going to tell you how it really is.' "

A smile crept across Nathan's face, as he thought of asking whether the woman was a bigamist who'd been married to both husbands at once, or whether she'd been married to them one at a time. Then he started feeling guilty for finding the thought so amusing, instead of feeling sympathetic towards the woman who'd lost her husbands, or feeling angry that the social work course was apparently a bit shoddy. He wondered what people would think of him for smiling, and felt embarrassed. But a few students around him were just as preoccupied, looking up to the ceiling, wondering if more balloons were going to fall down onto their heads, only half listening.

Suddenly though, they started giving Kevin their full attention again, when it was as if he suddenly remembered he'd been asked a question about the intrigue involving the tutor at the next table. Prawn had almost forgotten he'd asked it by then. But oblivious to that, Kevin answered it anyway. He suddenly looked surprised and sat up straighter, as if he'd just become alert to the fact that he was supposed to be answering a question.

He said, "Anyway, about that tutor BJ I was talking about: There's a Christian on our course who told us about something bad he said to her . . . Funnily enough we haven't had any political correctness training about respecting religious views, so perhaps they don't care if we disrespect people for those . . . or if they do that themselves.

"But anyway, the first essay we had to write on the course wasn't officially assessed, so the marks didn't go towards our course grades. The Christian doesn't think she should have done what she did now, but before she came on the course, she'd heard that political correctness is a very big issue on social work courses so she might be disapproved of for some Christian views, like the one that Christianity's a better religion than Islam, and things like that. She thought she'd take the opportunity to test the warning out, since she was curious about whether it was true. Since the essay wasn't counting towards her grades, she thought it wouldn't matter.

"So she wrote an essay about how children in schools would benefit if they were taught some Christian principles, like not having sex before marriage. She actually quoted the Bible for added effect. Her essay said there ought to be relationship counselling in schools, so teenagers learn that sex isn't something to be treated like just a bit of fun by people moving from partner to partner and things like that, since it could have bad consequences, including leading to heartbreak.

"Her essay was failed, and that tutor BJ had a discussion with her about why he failed it, where he actually said it was unfair of her to want to stop twelve-year-old girls in care from having sex if they wanted to; he said they should be allowed to, and she would be violating their rights if she wanted to stop them, even though all she was talking about doing was trying to educate schoolchildren about how having casual sex isn't a wise thing to do. She commented to us that she didn't know if it's just him who thinks that people shouldn't try to stop kids doing that, or whether it's some kind of politically correct ideological belief all the social work tutors have. None of us have ever felt like asking the tutors that!

"BJ's said other things like that too. Like in one lecture, he made me wonder if he'd make excuses for those criminal grooming gangs you hear about, by making the astonishing claim to us all that the reason there's a high rate of . . ."

Kevin suddenly stopped, looking at Becky, as if taking in for the first time how young she must be; and then he said, ". . . Ah, but that's not a topic of conversation to have at a party."

Then, disregarding the fact that in reality nothing he was saying was the kind of jolly cheery talk people might want to have at a party, and that people were probably feeling less and less like partying the more he spoke, he continued:

"Anyway, some of the tutors didn't like the Christian student after she wrote that essay. She didn't like them either, since she thought the course was as rubbishy as we do.

"She heckled the lecturers sometimes, shouting up if she thought they were talking nonsense, and stayed away from classes a lot of the time. She especially heckled BJ, telling him where she thought he was telling them useless things no one needed to know. The reason she especially heckled *him* was because although she thought a couple of other tutors did lectures that were like huge cobweb-like structures of complex-sounding but meaningless phraseology, and she said she had to admire their ability to string strands of rubbish together for so long if nothing else, at least they were on a topic vaguely related to social work, as far as she

266

could tell; his didn't even pretend to be; they were about dinosaurs from way back in history . . . I mean ancient psycho-logists from the beginning of the twentieth century, who didn't have much of a clue about how to help people, and loved inventing theories that were just wacky.

"But after she heckled the tutors, they liked her even less. She told us she both heckled and stayed away a lot because she was so stressed that the course wasn't teaching anything worthwhile. We tried to persuade her not to heckle them and to keep on the good side of the tutors, saying everyone knew the course was rubbish but it would at least be a qualification in the end, but she didn't seem to want to stop, for some reason. We nicknamed her Heckleback."

While some people in other parts of the room played student party games like 'Let's see who's the most daring', where they'd put things in their pints of beer like pepper, torn-up beer mat, vinegar, bits of cheese sandwiches and all kinds of things before drinking them, some of the students at Becky's table, who weren't observing closely but heard a lot of laughter, began to wonder if they were hard done by because they weren't really free to join in with whatever was going on in other parts of the room, but instead listening to Kevin's story. Still, it sounded quite interesting.

He continued, "At the end of our first year, we all had to go on work experience in social work departments and places like that. At first they gave Heckleback a placement where she hardly had anything to do, which wasn't even with social workers, so she didn't like that. She must have made herself even more unpopular by complaining, but they moved her to another place, with social workers who were trying to help old people who were becoming disabled.

"They'd actually been thinking of moving her to a day centre for disabled people, working in the kitchens, peeling carrots and things for their dinner. She said she wasn't keen on that idea, and our head tutor, Scam, accused her of objecting because she thought peeling carrots was demeaning, and scolded her for it, sounding absolutely certain that she was right about her accusation, when in reality, Heckleback just wanted to do something that was more related to actual social work, so she could learn stuff."

Kevin suddenly seemed to be weary from talking, poured the rest of his beer down his throat in one go, and offered to go and buy more drinks for everyone. He jumped up without taking orders or asking whether the others actually wanted them, and went to the bar. They waited in silent suspense, wondering what they'd get, and what the end of the story would be.

He came back with several glasses of beer. He put one in front of Becky as he put the others down. Becky was still slightly curious about what would happen if she drank more, and besides that, she worried that it would be impolite to refuse it, so she sipped it slowly, even though she'd have said she didn't want one if she'd been asked first.

A couple of years earlier, she wouldn't have worried in the least about being impolite; but she was increasingly conscious of the expectation that she should fit into the fairly grown-up world where people were apparently supposed to give an impression of being polite and willing to please, and careful about what they said so as to be considerate of people's feelings, even if they'd rather not be; and after all, Kevin had paid for the drink, so she thought it would be awkward to say she didn't want it.

Later she was to realise it would have been better if she had, not worrying about what might be considered polite by others.

Kevin sat down and continued his story:

"Do you remember what I said just before I got drinks? I hope so, because I'm going to carry on now, without telling you it all again before I do. On this work experience, at first Heckleback just went out once with a couple of social workers to observe what they were doing. She thought all the social workers on the team were nice people, but the team manager – well, not so much, to put it politely.

"But one social worker she went out with promised an old man he could have a few things to make his life more enjoyable, including regularly being taken to play the piano with someone; she'd asked him what he'd like to do if he could, and he'd said he'd love to be able to play a piano again somewhere, and even to have lessons. But afterwards, the social worker told Heckleback that though she'd told him they'd arrange for him to be able to do that, they never would, because the service wasn't one social services paid for people to have. Heckleback asked her why she'd given the man the impression that the service could be provided in that case, and discussed it with the other social workers on the team too, and they said they often did things like that.

"She asked the team manager why social workers would offer things to people that weren't really available for them through social services, and was told the reason they offered people services to make their lives more interesting they were never in reality going to get was that perhaps if about twenty people wanted them, social services would apply to the council to see if they could get funding for them. Like that would happen in this age of cutbacks! Some of the other social workers told Heckleback that they themselves had offered people things they knew they were never going to get, even taking them to visit day centres where old people could do activities and get companionship from each other, knowing they wouldn't be able to go there, because the transport to get them there would never be provided. It was just the policy to do that."

Becky and the other psychology students began to feel a bit gloomy. They'd been hoping to enjoy the party. But Kevin didn't seem to be going to finish telling them what happened any time soon, so they thought they'd better sit and listen to him.

Rachel consoled herself by thinking it was good practice for future years when she was listening to someone complaining on the therapy couch when she'd much rather be on holiday cruising in the Caribbean, or sunbathing in Harrods, or shopping in the park . . . Then she realised that should be the other way around. She mentally cursed the drink. Then she took another mouthful for consolation. Still, she thought the story was quite interesting, so she didn't really mind listening.

Kevin continued, "The team manager was in consultation with the tutors here, and it seems she was looking for faults in Heckleback's behaviour or personality, maybe at their request.

"One thing she said was wrong with her was that she was too quiet. One day there was a team meeting where the team was discussing whether they could get someone in sometimes to look after and clean up after a man who hoarded all his rubbish so his home was piled high with it, and he kept soiling himself and his bedroom, just leaving his poo to pile up, so the house seriously needed someone to clean it up. I don't know why the man behaved like that. Heckleback listened, hoping to learn something.

"At the end, the team manager criticised her for being quiet all the way through it and not joining in. Heckleback wondered what she'd expected her to say – was she thinking she should have recommended a particular person who could go in there and clean up after the man? She isn't from this area, so she wasn't familiar with anyone who provided that kind of service. She joked to us that there was someone she could have suggested, but that it probably wouldn't have gone down very well – the team manager.

"One afternoon, the team manager asked her to . . ."

Kevin was suddenly interrupted. "Don't expect me to do that because I won't!" yelled a loud voice.

They all looked around to see who it was, but they couldn't work it out, and they never got to find out just what it was the person wasn't going to do, because they didn't hear any more of the conversation.

Kevin said, "Oh, if only Heckleback had said that; she might still be here today!"

The other students at the table were intrigued. But it turned out not to be that exciting. Kevin explained:

"The team manager asked her to write a personality profile of herself, describing what she was like. The manager didn't explain why, and Heckleback didn't ask, just getting down to it obediently. She should have boasted about what she was good at in it, but instead, she was ultra-modest, barely mentioning her good points, but analysing her weaknesses, which made them out to be a fair bit worse than they really were. They weren't serious ones. Some of them were just trivial things like, 'I think some people might think I laugh off-puttingly loud sometimes.'

"The next day, BJ was there with the team manager, and they told her she'd failed the work experience and the course, and gave her a few reasons why. They weren't good reasons . . . in fact the team manager said almost all of what she was judging her on was what Heckleback herself had written in the personality profile she'd been asked to write. Then Heckleback realised it must have been some kind of trick; the team manager and tutors had clearly needed more ammunition against her, so they were hoping she'd provide it herself, which she did.

"When BJ told her she'd failed the course, she didn't protest. BJ asked why, saying most people would fight when they were told that. She secretly thought the idea of fighting to stay on such a rubbishy course as ours was laughable! But she didn't say that. She didn't care about failing; she was hoping to go into social journalism anyway, not social work. She'd gone on the course in the first place partly because she was hoping to find out lots of information about people's problems and ways of helping them that might come in useful in journalism, when the knowledge would help her do a better job of reporting on stories in an insightful way, and it would give her ideas about what problems could do with being publicised in the hope that people would be motivated to change things. But she'd barely found out anything of any use.

"She would have told them what she'd been thinking of doing with the course if they'd asked her at her interview before she went on it, but they didn't.

"The social workers on the team at her work experience were shocked when she told them she'd failed the work experience and the course. She told them about some of the things the team manager had said, and they couldn't understand it and didn't think they were true. One was that she was too formal with the administration staff. When she told one or two of the administration staff that, they were surprised, and protested to the team manager. The team manager quickly told Heckleback not to tell anyone else about what had been said to her by her and BJ, as if there was some official reason it just wasn't the done thing. Really, the team manager was probably trying to make sure she didn't end up looking bad, so she wouldn't have any more awkward explaining to do if anyone else protested. Heckleback didn't say as much as she could have to the others after she was told not to.

"BJ told Heckleback the tutors weren't going to tell the other students in her year that she'd failed, but instead that she'd decided to leave of her own accord to do other things. He probably said that because he knew there wasn't a very good reason for failing her, and didn't want to be faced with awkward questions. But he knew it would suit her, because she wouldn't want people hearing she'd failed either. So predictably, she didn't protest that she'd prefer people to be told she'd been failed."

Kevin sat back and stopped talking. Alice said, "I'm glad *our* tutors aren't like that . . . at least I hope they're not!"

Then Kevin said, "You're psychology students, aren't you? BJ gives us psychology lectures. I've never found out what earthly use they're supposed to be to us – he teaches us about Freud and similar early psychology, when – no offence – but they didn't really know what they were doing, did they."

Then he exclaimed, "Ugh! I've just had a thought! It never occurred to me till now, but Freud had a big thing about sex, didn't he; he thought a lot of problems had to do with not getting enough, or people wishing they had each other's bits, or stuff like that. I wonder if the reason BJ's so interested in Freud is because they share the same obsessions. Gross!"

Then he noticed Becky afresh, and became embarrassed that he'd spoken like that in front of a little girl. He said, "Oh, I'm really sorry. I shouldn't be talking about this."

Then he offered to buy them all another drink, and suddenly it penetrated his consciousness that Becky shouldn't be drinking alcohol. He said he'd get her a Coke. He got the drinks and sat back down, feeling remorseful about having given Becky a beer or two before and talking about sex. The others in the group caught the mood, and they all fell silent.

None of them knew it, but the evening was all set to go downhill from there.

Things Begin to Seem a Bit Creepy and Strange

Soon afterwards, the tutor Kevin had been talking about, BJ, came cheerfully over and clapped the social work students at Becky's table on the back, loudly saying, "Hello! Nice to see you here!" Becky got the impression he was a bit drunk.

Then he turned his back to them as if expecting them to clap him on the back in return. They didn't, and he asked, "Don't you like clapping people on the back? You're going to have to learn to like it if you want to go into social work!"

He didn't explain why.

The drink had had an effect on Becky after all. Normally she would have kept a question like the one that then sprung to her mind to herself, but the drink had made her louder and more impulsive than usual, and she asked the tutor, "Hey, are you the one who said you think twelve-year-old girls in care should be allowed to have sex if they want to, and it's unfair to try to stop them?"

BJ was surprised by the question, especially since it was being asked by a little girl. But he interpreted her curiosity as approval and eagerness to hear more, rather than shock.

He himself probably wouldn't have spoken the way he then did if he'd been sober; but he said, "No one needs to be shackled by the needless restraints of dogmatic ideas. We don't need to let things stand in the way of us having sex. Would you like to have sex?"

Perhaps he wasn't suggesting they had sex with each other; but that was the way it sounded to Becky, and it gave her the creeps. She was about to say indignantly, "No, I'm only ten!" But it occurred to her that he might not think that was a problem, since being twelve years old wasn't much older than being ten. So she just said no.

BJ pointed to a particularly good-looking man and said, "Would you be tempted by him?"

It's just possible he was merely making what passed for polite conversation in the broad-minded social work department, but Becky was shocked, and shouted, "No, he's my teacher!"

Donna must have got the same impression of what he meant as Becky, because she said with a slight sneer, "Careful BJ, your wife could walk in at any minute!"

Becky was really getting the creeps by then, and thought she'd better make some excuse and leave the table, having learned about excuses from some of the grown-ups she'd spent time around. She jumped up and said she'd seen a friend she'd like to talk to in another part of the room.

She nearly knocked over the remains of her drink in her haste to get up. Nathan, in an impressively quick single movement, reflexively snatched it up and poured it down his throat, only then remembering that *that* one wasn't alcoholic; so he felt less enthusiastic about having drunk it.

Prawn felt relieved it hadn't gone on the floor and been wasted though, and admired the speed of Nathan's reflexes, so he shouted, "Good save!"

Becky was walking away from the table when a man she didn't recognise, who'd had a bit too much to drink, stopped her and boomed, "Hey, how about a dance?"

Becky had never learned to dance, and didn't really like the look of the man, since he seemed to be a bit drunk, plus he looked about thirty years older than her; but she thought it would at least get her away from BJ, so she agreed, and he put his arms around her shoulders and began to sway with her, without the slightest effort to stay in time with the rhythm of the music. Whether he swayed because he was unsteady from the drink, or whether it was his idea of dancing, she never found out. It turned out he was even worse at dancing than her. He trod on her foot after a minute or so. She yelled out, and he apologised. But less than thirty seconds later, he trod on her foot again! She yelled at him again. Then she broke free of him, saying she wanted her feet to still be in one piece at the end of the song, before running away.

She sat down in another part of the room and looked back at him. He danced on his own for a moment. Then, as if he realised for the first time that no one was dancing with him, he looked hurt, shook his fist in protest, and lumbered off. Unfortunately, he wasn't looking where he was going and bumped into a couple dancing.

They yelled at him, and he apologised, swung around to walk off, staggered across the room with the momentum, and bumped straight into BJ's chair, knocking his drink all over him, and at the same time stumbling and falling onto his lap. He hauled himself to his feet and apologised, telling BJ he'd make it up to him on the dance floor, urging him to come and dance. He grabbed BJ's wrist and tried to drag him to his feet, encouraging him to get up. BJ thought he'd better get up if he didn't want to be minus an arm soon, so he got up, and the man dragged him off to dance. He put his arms tightly around BJ's waist and swayed with him.

Becky crept nearer to get a closer look.

BJ didn't enjoy dancing with the man, and struggled, trying to break free. But as if the other man thought he'd let one get away already and it wasn't going to happen again, he held him tighter.

Becky thought she heard someone shout mockingly from the table she'd been sitting at before she moved, "What's the matter BJ? All those lessons you've taught us about political correctness, and now you're trying to get away as if you're embarrassed to be thought of as gay because you're dancing with another man?"

But then, as if the other man hadn't realised BJ was male, and suddenly became aware of the fact, he himself stepped backwards and bellowed, "You're a man! How dare you masquerade as female and make me dance with you, you dirty wretch!" He slapped BJ hard, first on one cheek and then on the other. Then he stormed off.

BJ stumbled back to his seat, looking as if he was feeling sorry for himself. Then he knelt down and loudly wailed, "Oh, to the gods of drink! Let me suck the carpet, and make the drink that got spilled on it rise up into my mouth, unpolluted by carpet fluff and dirt!"

The people at the surrounding tables weren't sure whether he was joking or being serious. Most of them thought he was probably just joking; but some thought that maybe he really meant it.

Then he lay down, as if he intended to suck the carpet for real, although it might have just been that he was losing control of his muscles a bit because of the amount of alcohol he'd imbibed; or maybe he was just being theatrical. That wasn't like him, as far as the social work students knew; he normally kept a professional demeanour in front of students. Perhaps he'd managed to drink a few more drinks than he should have done before the last one he'd been trying to drink had got spilled. Just why a professional tutor had allowed himself to get into such a state in front of students he was responsible for teaching, it seems no one ever found out.

A caring first year sociology student called Lisa, who thought that maybe he'd really meant what he'd said about sucking the carpet, went over to him and told him it would be far better if he had another drink instead, and offered to get one for him. Then a thought struck her. She'd recently begun to learn about other cultures in her sociology classes, particularly those in the developing world. Well-meaning but misguided, she said hesitantly, ". . . Unless calling on the gods to help you suck spilled drink out of the carpet is a special ritual where you come from or something, in which case I'll respect your right to carry on."

At that point, BJ's training or ideology should have prompted him to admire her for attempting to be politically correct, even though she'd got things wrong. But he seemed to have forgotten all about it. Perhaps it was the amount of drink he'd managed to get down him on the inside, as opposed to the one he'd recently had knocked down him on the outside; or perhaps he was fuming from being slapped in the face by the drunken dancing man, so it didn't take much for his anger to turn into rage; but whatever the reason was, it seems he wasn't thinking straight just then. He leapt up and roared, "You racist! This is what you're going to get for insulting me like that!"

He made as if to hit her. She quickly put her arms up to defend herself. She was holding her drink at the time. What BJ actually succeeded in doing was knocking it out of her hand; it flew towards him and hit him slap bang in the chest, spilling all down him.

Lisa went away quickly. BJ sat down and suddenly felt ashamed of himself. He said, barely heard by anyone, "Sorry; I often fantasise about knocking students' heads together when I hear them saying ignorant things, and the drink must have robbed me of my impulse control and made me feel like actually doing something like it! Plus I was still upset after that man hit me! I know I shouldn't have let things get the better of me."

But he wasn't left alone to reflect on his misdeeds for long. A merry philosophy tutor came by holding a drink. He stopped in front of BJ and said, "I see you prefer to wear your drinks than drink them. Here, have mine; I don't like it."

With that, he threw it over BJ's head. Whether he did that because he was drunk, or whether he'd seen BJ nearly hit a student and was angry with him, or whether he always behaved like that just for fun, no one knew.

Becky heard someone joke, "Is that an example of the kind of new philosophies they invent in the philosophy department nowadays? And they don't just sit around discussing them as I thought; they act on them? He must be testing out whether it works – the grand philosophical theory that drinks are best worn!"

Not long after that, BJ's wife walked in. She saw him covered in various kinds of drink, and suggested he go and clean himself up, which it seems he did. He walked out of the room anyway.

Becky had sat at a little table on her own, worried about what kind of people she might find herself sitting with if she went and sat with anyone she didn't know. But a drunken student came up to her and asked if she'd like to dance.

She said, "No thanks! My feet still haven't quite recovered from being trodden on by the last person who wanted to dance with me!"

The student bellowed, "Oh dear, poor you! How about bathing them in beer! I'd like to bath in beer! It would mean I could drink it all afterwards! Go on, give your feet a nice bath in beer!"

He had a pint of beer with him, and made as if to tip it over Becky's shoes. She yelled, "No! I don't want my shoes to get all wet!"

The student said merrily, "Well, take them off then. Go on, take your shoes and socks off and put your little feet in my pint of beer! I'm sure it would do them the world of good!"

Becky wasn't so sure, and wondered if he'd happily drink his beer afterwards if she did. She said, "No thanks. I expect they'll get better soon anyway."

The drunken jolly student loudly said, "Then pour it down the inside of you! I'm sure it would help the process along – make you feel tons better!"

As he said that, he held his pint in front of Becky's face and tipped it a little as if to pour some in her mouth. She got hold of it and pushed it upright again, shouting, "No! I don't want any beer, thanks. I'm only ten years old; and besides, I've already had some."

"Oh, sorry," said the student, and blundered off.

Becky's Mum Panics, and Comes to Take Her Home While the Party Continues

Some time later, Becky would look back and find that funny; but at the time, she thought it was a bit scary. She'd never been to a party where things like that happened before. She worried about what would happen next. Her head was starting to spin, and some things that had happened had given her the creeps.

She began to feel alone and vulnerable, and wished her mum was there. Luckily, she always carried her mobile phone with her. She got it out to phone her mum.

As she did, two girls from her department sat down next to her. They were people she said hello to and chatted a bit with sometimes, but she didn't know them well. She still wanted to go home, so she phoned her mum and said she didn't feel well and was scared something bad would happen because the room seemed to be full of yobs and creeps, and she wanted to go home right away.

Her mum was worried, and promised to jump in the car right then and come and get her. She began to feel guilty about having left Becky there alone. She kept telling herself as she was heading out the door that she should have known better, and that she was stupid for not staying with her. She'd been lulled into a false sense of security because Becky had spent several evenings out with her friends before and nothing bad had ever happened, and also often wandered around the psychology department on her own to look at books and papers hours after classes had finished and never come to any harm.

Becky's mum had assumed that no one would misbehave with several tutors at the party, and that students and tutors doing things like psychology and social work must be nice people who could be trusted to be responsible and caring. Her heart was beating fast with anxiety as she jumped in the car.

Meanwhile, after Becky finished speaking to her on the phone, she suddenly felt very sick. She rushed off to the toilet and was sick a lot. She longed for her mum! She began to cry.

But soon, she found she felt much better for having been sick. She stopped crying, washed her face, and went back into the party.

She wandered around till she came to a table where there were about four young men laughing and chatting.

One of them, wondering why a young child was there, and thinking she must be the child of one of the university staff or a mature student, said to Becky, "Hello, have you lost your mum?"

Becky said she was waiting for her mum to come and get her.

The man seemed kind, and said, "Come and sit with us while you're waiting for her if you like. We're philosophy students."

The men all had pints of beer, but they were drinking them at a leisurely pace, and didn't offer her any.

Becky sat down, and they asked her about herself. They were impressed when she told them she was doing two degrees.

Then one said, "We're studying Socrates on our course at the moment. Have you heard of Socrates, Becky?"

She said she'd heard the name, but didn't know much about him.

He said, "He was an ancient Greek fella who they put on trial and poisoned for asking politically incorrect questions. They did that to people in those days. I think in some countries they still do."

At the mention of political incorrectness, thoughts of BJ sprung to Becky's mind, and she shivered and started to look uneasy, wondering if he was still around.

"Don't tell her gory stories John!" said another philosophy student at the table, assuming Becky was looking uncomfortable because she didn't like hearing about people being killed.

John apologised to Becky. Then he said to her, "Anyway, this Socrates used to ask a lot of questions, and he had a style of asking questions that made him famous because he upset some powerful people by using them to win arguments with them. We're studying the kinds of questions he asked and practising his techniques on each other.

"It's called Socratic questioning. It's where you can win arguments or make another person really think about what they're saying if you know they've got an opinion that you don't think is right. You ask them questions that require yes or no answers or other short ones, about things that are related to their opinion in some way but that you feel sure they'll agree with you on, because they make good sense, and you ask if they agree to things that are closer and closer to the opinion they said they hold that you disagree with, but that you still think they'll agree with, till it gets to the point where if they agree with the latest thing you're saying, it'll end up as if they're arguing against their own point of view, since they won't be able to believe both that and the opinion they said they had before, when they think about it, so you can show them they're wrong.

"Shall we try it on you? I know, Becky, pretend to be a dictator of a country with evil plans to conquer the world! I'll ask you questions to make you really think about your evil schemes to see if I can make you change your mind."

Becky thought that could be fun, so she agreed.

John asked: "So, you want to take over the world, do you? . . . Now, I know you think war is a good means to that end. But tell me, what would you value most in an ideal world, war or peace?"

"Peace," said Becky.

"Do you value your own people and think their lives are precious?" asked John.

"Of course I do!" said Becky.

"Well, Miss Dictator, how would you feel if trade links were increased with other countries so they wanted to import more things from yours, and that created more employment for your citizens, and your country made a lot of money?" asked John.

"I'd love it!" said Becky.

"So let's see," said John, "You think the lives of your subjects are precious and valuable, and you think peace is better than war. You think it would be great if lots of people were employed in trades that made your country rich because people in other countries were buying lots of its goods.

"So wouldn't you have to agree that squandering the lives of a lot of your people in military campaigns to take over the world, causing a lot of suffering and death that meant that those precious valuable people wouldn't be around to work to make your country rich, which would also make people in other countries too upset with you for invading them or countries they heard about you invading to want to buy anything from your country, would be against your best interests and what you truly believe in?"

Becky realised she'd been entrapped by her own answers into not having many options other than to either look bad by contradicting them by saying she still wanted to take over the world despite everything she'd just said she believed, or admitting John had won the argument. His demonstration of the technique on her had also clarified to her how it worked. But she wanted to carry on playing the game and win the argument. So she said:

"Well, I'd normally say yes, but this country's getting so full of people, I want to make them join the army so they go away. I'm just beginning to think some of them aren't as valuable as others, because they get on my nerves, because when I'm driving through the city, I'm always getting stuck in boring traffic jams; and when I go for a nice peaceful walk in the park, it's full of people, all wanting to go on the swings when I want to go on them. Herds of grown men queuing up in front of me to go on them! I can't get near them for hours!"

Another student at the table, Sean, said, "Hang on, are you a modern dictator or an ancient Greek one? If you're an ancient Greek one going through a city full of cars, I think there's something the history books aren't telling us!"

They all laughed.

Becky began to enjoy herself again. The philosophy students at the table were a friendly bunch, and soon she was joking around with them.

Meanwhile, her mum was anxiously driving to the university, wondering what was going on after the worrying phone call Becky had made. She parked her car as quickly as she could, charged into the university, and ran up the stairs to where the party was.

She shoved the door open and looked around. Then she saw Becky sitting with a group of merry students, laughing her head off.

She went up to her and said in surprise and a little indignation, "Rebecca! You phoned me up saying you were scared to stay here and you wanted me to bring you home. How come you said that when you're enjoying yourself so much?"

Becky told her she hadn't been enjoying herself when she'd made the phone call, but since then she'd met some nice people.

Her mum asked if she'd been drinking, saying she didn't look very well.

Becky said she'd had a few drinks, and been sick a lot not long before, but that she'd felt better after that.

Her mum said, "I think I'd better take you home! I don't want you to be sick again around here, and anyway it's way past your bedtime."

Becky protested, saying she'd begun to have a nice time again. So her mum said she could have a few minutes longer, and sat down with the others and chatted with them for a while.

Becky was very unsteady on her feet when she got up to go, which made her mum wonder just how much she'd had to drink.

In the car on the way home, Becky told her all about the party.

Her mum was shocked. She started wondering if Becky was safe at the university, and for a moment wondered if she ought to be transferred to another one. But then she reflected that Becky had always been safe up till that evening, and that she often went around in a group of friends she herself had met by then and liked and trusted; and also, the people who'd caused the trouble weren't from the psychology department, and perhaps some weren't even at the university and might not be seen there again.

But she decided to keep a closer watch on Becky from then on, phoning her up more often to see how she was. And she told Becky that if ever she was approached by anyone who worried her like the people who'd given her the creeps at the party, she should phone her up immediately and start walking away while she was on the phone, and then go and find one of her friends or a tutor she trusted, or go and strike up a conversation with someone else till the worrying person went away.

Thankfully, Becky didn't see any of the people who'd made her feel nervous that night again throughout all her time at the university, except for just seeing BJ in the distance a few times.

Becky's mum thought Becky might be dehydrated after having been sick and drinking alcohol, so she gave her three cups of water to drink before she went to bed, in the hope that it would prevent her from waking up with a bad headache the next morning.

The next day, Becky felt a bit shaky and ill, but not too bad. And it was the weekend, so she had time to relax and recover.

Becky Comes In For Some Unfair Criticism

When Becky went back to university on Monday, it was the last week before the Christmas holidays.

When she went into the psychology department, one of the senior tutors who'd helped organise the party met her and asked if she'd enjoyed it. She said she hadn't really, apart from some bits here and there.

The tutor seemed disappointed, and asked her why she hadn't liked it. Becky didn't want to tell the story of what had happened, so she just said it wasn't her scene. Then she turned and walked away quickly, because she didn't want to disappoint him further if he asked her any more about why she didn't like it and she couldn't think of anything to do but to tell him just why she'd found some of it so awful.

The next day when she went to her classes, she noticed she was getting looks of disapproval from some people she didn't know that well, but didn't know why. She said hello to a few people, but they didn't answer and turned their backs on her.

In one class during the afternoon, the students were split up into groups of half a dozen for group discussions. The idea was that afterwards, a spokesman from each group would tell everyone their group's thoughts on something they'd all been asked to discuss, and then everyone would discuss what the spokesmen said.

As Becky was deciding who to sit with, two young women she didn't know well went past her, and she heard one say to the other, "She won't want to sit with us; we're probably too creepy and yobbish for her!"

Becky sat with some of her friends, but wondered what the others had been talking about. After the lesson, she found them and asked them.

It turned out that the two girls who'd sat next to Becky just before she'd phoned her mum at the party to beg her to take her home had overheard Becky telling her the place was full of creeps and yobs, and thought she was referring to everyone there. Then Becky had jumped up and walked away without saying hello to them or anything. She'd actually rushed away to be sick, but the girls had thought she was snubbing them, supposing she must think they were creeps and yobs along with the rest.

Then they'd spread it about that Becky thought all the other students there were creeps and yobs. The two girls Becky was confronting right then had believed them and been offended.

Becky was upset. She worried she was going to lose friends, and that most people there wouldn't like her any more, all because some girls had misunderstood what she'd meant and spread a rumour about her.

She cheered up a bit when she told a sympathetic friend called Kirsty about it, who half-jokingly suggested she could set the record straight by hanging a sign around her neck saying, "No, I didn't mean all psychology students are creeps and yobs." Becky joked that she might just do that.

Another friend she told, Jasmine, tried to cheer her up a bit more by saying, "I know it's not nice to have rumours spread about you. One thing that comforts me sometimes when people make unfair accusations against me is a saying I read on an Internet forum once: 'Opinions are like . . .' well never mind, but basically it means everyone's got an opinion, and a lot of them are just brainless and cruddy. Sadly, I think false accusations and misunderstandings where something bad gets spread unfairly are just part of life."

To Jasmine's disappointment, Becky wasn't cheered up by that at all. In fact, she looked more unhappy than before. Later Jasmine looked back on what she'd said and realised that though she'd started off with cheering intentions, she'd got sidetracked slightly, and the second half of what she'd said in particular hadn't been cheerful at all, so it was no wonder it didn't make Becky feel better.

Still, Becky replied that she was at least a bit reassured that she wasn't the only one that things like that had happened to.

Then Jasmine said, "I know you might not feel like it at all, and you've got the right to be angry with those girls who spread the rumour about you, because it's rotten of them to have said nasty things about you behind your back, but you might be able to stop them spreading them some more if you say something to them that makes them feel better about you; I think it can often help calm bad feelings down if people apologise; you wouldn't have to say you were sorry for anything you did; you could just try saying you're sorry if they got upset by what you said, or what they thought you said, and then explain that they misunderstood it, and tell them what really happened.

"I think that would be better than being angry with them. I've angrily argued with people before and denied I said things people thought I said, only to find out weeks later that they still believed I said them, so it was a waste of time! Maybe behaving as if you're concerned because it seems they were upset by what you said, and saying you're sorry about it, works better.

"I'm thinking of trying that myself in future anyway. It won't always be easy, especially since if you suddenly hear an unfair accusation against you, I think it's just instinct for adrenaline to kick in and make you want to shout and get angry. But trying to calm down and behave as if you're sorry they've heard or that they think something about you that must be making them feel unhappy might have better consequences."

Becky had a think about that, and decided she might give it a try. But she said, "I wish people wouldn't spread stories about people behind their backs. Why do they do it? If they had a problem with something I said, they should have spoken to *me* about it, and I could have explained what really happened already, and we'd *all* feel better by now!"

Jasmine said thoughtfully, "I don't know why so many people prefer to talk behind the backs of people they think have offended them instead of clearing things up with the people themselves; maybe it's cowardice, or nervousness about what would be said back to them; maybe it's sometimes spite; maybe they sometimes think it makes for an entertaining story and they enjoy telling it; who knows! I don't like it any more than you. And some people seem to be eager to believe the worst about people, but not nearly so eager to find out the point of view of the one they're hearing nasty stories about! It's a shame."

Becky went away feeling comforted a bit for the understanding that had been shown her. And some people apologised to her for believing the rumour when she told them what had really happened. She spoke to the girls who'd spread the rumour in the first place, and they were embarrassed to realise they'd misunderstood the situation so badly.

But that wasn't the end of the upset for Becky.

It was nearly the last day of term, and there was a holiday atmosphere in the place. But Becky wasn't going to be allowed to enjoy it for long. Her personal tutor told her he wanted to see her in his office. Personal tutors were assigned to each of the students so they could go to them if they had any problems, especially with the work.

Becky was thinking of suggesting to him that one of the tutors could do a lecture on the psychology of rumour-spreading and why it's not a good idea. But soon she realised he was in no mood to discuss any suggestions she might have about improving the course.

He'd told her to come to his office at ten o'clock. He hadn't told her why. She got to his door just before ten. But she heard people talking in his office. She thought they might be talking about something important, so she waited till she couldn't hear them any more. She wasn't trying to listen to what they were saying; she just assumed it would be something to do with staff matters she wouldn't be interested in and that wouldn't be anything to do with her.

She hung around outside for about five minutes, thinking she ought to wait. Finally, she couldn't hear the voices any more, so she thought they must have finished their conversation, and knocked.

"Come in!" said the voice of her personal tutor.

She went in. He looked at her sternly and said, "You're late!" He seemed to be in a worse mood than usual.

The person he'd been talking to left the room.

Becky said, "I got here on time; it just sounded as if you were having an important conversation, so I waited outside."

"I don't want excuses!" her personal tutor said. "Now sit down and listen to what I have to say!"

"I'm not making excuses!" Becky protested indignantly.

Her personal tutor said more sternly and with a note of impatience, "Just sit down and listen! I've got something important to say to you!"

Becky wondered what it could be. It sounded serious. So she sat down without another word.

He told her he'd received complaints about her. He said a few different people had complained about her behaviour at the party. One was one of the head tutors who'd organised it. It turned out that it was the one who'd asked Becky if she'd enjoyed it a few days before. He'd complained to her personal tutor, saying he'd seen her there with a big plate of food that got refilled after she'd finished it, and he thought she was ungrateful to have gobbled it all up, only to say she hadn't liked the party later when he'd asked her if she'd enjoyed it, when they'd put a lot of effort into organising it. And he complained that Becky had just turned and walked away when he was asking her about it. He said he thought she was very rude, just turning and walking away when he was talking to her.

Becky was upset, and said she'd enjoyed the food; it was other things she hadn't liked, and she'd only turned and walked away so as not to have to answer awkward questions that would have let the tutor know just how much she hadn't enjoyed some of the party.

She protested, "Why do people ask others if they enjoyed something if they're going to be annoyed about the answer if it's not what they want to hear? He shouldn't have asked me if I enjoyed it if he only wanted to hear me say yes!"

Her personal tutor said, "He's not the only one who's complained. BJ from the social work department says he saw you accepting drink after drink, never going up and getting rounds yourself, or thinking of the money others had to spend on you and refusing their offers out of politeness."

Apart from the fact that Becky hadn't actually wanted some of the drinks she'd been given, but in reality had thought she ought to drink them out of politeness after she was given them, she thought it was strange and interesting that BJ hadn't complained about her drinking alcohol underage, but just about her not paying for the drinks she got – and in fact not going to the bar to get some herself! She thought, "Does he think it's perfectly OK for underage girls to drink as well as have sex? Doesn't he realise it's illegal for kids to buy alcohol at a bar in this country, or for anyone to sell it to them?"

She said to her personal tutor, "Oh how could I have gone up and got drinks when I'm way below the age people are allowed to buy drinks in pubs?"

"I'm sure BJ was thinking about non-alcoholic ones!" said her personal tutor sternly.

Becky told him she thought it was a bit hypocritical that BJ of all people should have complained about her, since he was the most badly behaved one there. She began to tell her personal tutor what he'd done; but he stopped her and said sternly, "I can't believe that!"

She urged him to go and ask some of the students in the social work department what BJ was like, and what he'd done, since some of them would have seen him at the party too.

Her personal tutor said sternly, "I'm not going to go asking students to tell tales about their tutor! I don't listen to hearsay and rumours, and you shouldn't be asking me to!"

Becky felt stung into anger, and said sarcastically, "But you listen to tutors telling tales about students! Are you saying you think it's just rumour and hearsay when a student says something bad about a tutor, but you believe it immediately when a tutor says something bad about a student?"

Her personal tutor snapped, "No of course that's not the way it works! And even if a tutor did misbehave a bit, it wouldn't change the fact that you misbehaved yourself, or make it any more excusable."

Then he said, "Rebecca, I'm disappointed in you. I hear you drank quite a bit of alcohol at the party. We put special trust in you when we let you come on the course; we wouldn't normally let someone as young as you come to university. We were hoping you'd behave yourself. We think you've let us down badly."

He didn't want to hear her explanations as to why she'd drunk the alcohol, thinking they were just excuses. He told her to go away and seriously think about what he'd said.

She left his office crying, scared they'd throw her off the course like the social work tutors had done to the politically incorrect Christian who'd heckled them. Then she started wishing she was far away.

She went home and told her mum she was fed up of university and thought it would be better if she left.

Her mum asked why, saying that only a short time ago she'd been enjoying herself.

Becky told her what had happened. Her mum wished Becky had never gone to the party.

She said she'd go and speak to the personal tutor for Becky, and remind him that Becky was young and inexperienced, and couldn't be expected to get everything right and to know how to deal with things that had never happened to her before, and she deserved another chance. She said that if the personal tutor started saying anything about throwing Becky off the course, she'd point out to him that surely the tutors who'd seen a child as little as Becky drinking alcohol and yet had done nothing to stop her at the time were more at fault, and that if he threw Becky off the course, the story – including that detail – would likely appear in the press – she'd do her best to make sure it did.

She went to see the personal tutor the next day. She was ready for an argument, but he assured her that Becky wouldn't be thrown off the course, saying he hadn't even realised Becky was worried that would happen. He'd just thought she was crying because he'd told her off. He said that they were willing to overlook what had happened, as long as Becky didn't behave like that again.

Chapter 11

Becky's Friends Try to Cheer Her Up With Some Comedy, and They Have a Bit of Serious Discussion Too

It was the last day of term, and the students hardly did any work at all. Becky met up with a group of her friends. She was glad to be among them again. She told them about everything that had happened. They were sympathetic, and tried to cheer her up and reassure her.

Becky wondered how she could ever work with her personal tutor again when he thought such bad things about her and hadn't wanted to listen to what she'd said. One friend, Wendy, suggested she might be able to get reallocated to another personal tutor, but Becky said hers had probably told all the tutors what he thought of her, so they'd all believe she was as bad as he did. She felt miserable and started crying again.

One of the friends, Mya, said sympathetically, "Aww Becky, don't cry. Come on, they might have nearly forgotten what happened after the Christmas holidays."

Then she said with a mirthless smile, "Besides, isn't psychology partly about learning from mistakes and changing so you can make better decisions in future? You could tell the tutors you've put the psychological principles they've taught us into operation, and you've changed and will never make those mistakes again! That'll please them, if they feel as if you're complimenting them!"

But Becky was still crying. She said, "But it wasn't my fault!"

Her friends said they knew that, but that if a tutor mentioned it to her again, she could at least tell them she'd learned a lesson and promise that she'd be behaving differently in future. To that, Becky heartily agreed! She fully intended to stick with her friends from then on, and never go to any more psychology department parties!

She said she thought it was strange that one of the people who'd complained about her behaviour most was BJ, the one who'd misbehaved the most at the party!

Her friend Kirsty joked, "Perhaps he was just jealous that you got to drink your drinks, when he only got to wear most of his."

Becky smiled a bit at that.

One of the friends, Suzy, tried to cheer her up by saying, "I found some funny acronyms on the Internet the other day, that pretended the letters of certain words stand for things they don't really. I didn't find any about university, but I found some about teachers and education.

"According to those, the letters of the word 'school' stand for 'sucking children's hope out of life', or 'sucking children's happiness out of life', or 'seven crummy hours of our lives'.

" 'Maths' means 'mentally affected teacher harassing students', or 'mental abuse to hapless schoolkids'. 'Class' means 'come late and start sleeping'. 'Homework' means 'half of my energy wasted on random knowledge'. 'Test' means 'tormenting every student tremendously'."

Becky grinned.

Then Suzy said, "I found some anagrams too. One said the word schoolmaster makes the anagram 'the classroom'."

Another friend, Bonnie, said, "That's interesting. I read some anagrams on the Internet not long ago as well. There are some funny ones! And some more of them are appropriate too! I read that the words 'a shoplifter' can be made into the anagram 'has to pilfer'."

One friend, Scott, grinned and said, "That's actually *more* appropriate than the word shoplifter, because it describes what they do, while the word shoplifter makes it sound as if people who shoplift have massively long arms, and they're putting their arms as far as they can around a shop, and with a huge effort, lifting it high into the sky . . . or at least out of the ground. Imagine someone not just stealing from a shop, but taking the whole thing home with them!"

The others laughed. Then Bonnie said, "I found lots of other interesting anagrams too. I didn't check them to find out if they really make the words it said they do on the website I found them on; but they sound pretty accurate. It said the words 'the eyes' can be turned into the anagram 'they see'; and the words 'a telescope' are an anagram of 'to see place'. The word astronomer is an anagram of the words 'moon starer', and the word 'astronomers' is an anagram of 'no more stars'."

"If there were no more stars, there'd be no more astronomers!" quipped Scott with a grin.

They laughed again.

Then Suzy smiled and said, "That's true. Here's an appropriate one for this time of year: The word 'Christmas' is an anagram of the words 'trims cash'. And here's another appropriate one: the word 'listen' is an anagram of 'silent'. And 'election results' is an anagram of 'lies – let's recount'."

They giggled, and Kirsty said, "I heard an interesting anagram once! Apparently 'eleven plus two' is an anagram of 'twelve plus one'."

"Wow, isn't that amazing!" said Mya.

Then Bonnie said, "Here are some other appropriate anagrams: 'Animosity' is an anagram of 'is no amity'. And 'the Morse Code' is an anagram of 'here come dots'."

Bonnie grinned while saying, "And there are some that might be appropriate in certain situations but not others: I read that the word 'conversation' is an anagram of 'voices rant on'. 'Father-in-law' makes the anagram 'near-halfwit', and 'mother-in-law' makes the anagram 'woman Hitler'!

"There was one that reminded me of school dinners: 'Semolina' makes the anagram 'is no meal'. Oddly enough, the word 'funeral' is an anagram of 'real fun'."

Scott chuckled and said, "Well I don't think school dinners were ever bad enough to cause any funerals! But I do remember that song, 'Hate school dinners, hate school dinners, burned baked beans, burned baked beans, soggy semolina, soggy semolina; I feel sick; bucket quick . . .'"

"Yes, I seem to remember singing a song a bit like that too!" interrupted Kirsty, laughing. "I never knew of a pupil who actually felt sick after eating a school dinner, but I remember being told off and sent outside the door as a punishment when I was about five for refusing to eat a bit of fatty meat! School staff did some weird things sometimes, looking back, didn't they! We all used to be glad when the holidays came around at our school."

Bonnie knew even more anagrams! She said, "I used to be glad when the holidays came around too. I read that the words 'vacation times' makes the anagram 'I'm not as active'. And typical of what often happens on holidays in this country, the words 'heavy rain' make the anagram 'hire a navy'."

Scott laughed and said, "I've been on holidays that have been spoiled because it's rained a lot, but the rain's never been as bad as that!"

The friends chuckled.

Bonnie said, "Yeah OK, perhaps that would be a bit of an exaggeration. Anyway, interestingly enough, the words 'the countryside' are an anagram of 'no city dust here'. And the words 'the detectives' are an anagram of 'detect thieves'.

"And there are a couple more I can remember that made me smile: 'Darling I love you' is an anagram of 'avoiding our yell'. And 'the public art galleries' is an anagram of 'large picture halls, I bet'."

Suzy said, "I read some anagrams of people's names once. The name Daniel is an anagram of the word 'denial'. And the name Josephine is an anagram of the words 'join sheep'."

Becky laughed and said, "That's my grandma's name!"

Jasmine, who'd tried to cheer Becky up a few days earlier, not entirely successfully, was with the group of friends, and she said, "I found some anagrams of countries' names on the Internet once. There are lots! Scotland is an anagram of 'cold ants'. Kind of appropriate!"

They chuckled, and then Jasmine continued, "Northern Ireland is an anagram of 'internal red horn', and Ireland is an anagram of 'real din'."

They laughed again, and a few other students came to listen in, wondering what they were finding amusing. Jasmine continued, amid more laughter:

"I read that the country name Namibia is an anagram of 'I am a bin'. Panama is an anagram of 'am a pan'. Poland's an anagram of 'old pan'.

"Lithuania's an anagram of 'I hail tuna'. Singapore's an anagram of 'sip orange'. United Arab Emirates is an anagram of 'but I'm in a desert area'. Thailand's an anagram of 'a thin lad', and Germany's an anagram of 'gray men', and 'my anger'."

Scott asked with a grin, "How do you remember all these?"

Jasmine replied, "I don't know, but I can remember some more:

"Columbia's an anagram of 'I mob coal'. Guatemala's an anagram of 'maul a gate'. Mauritania's an anagram of 'aim at a ruin'. Honduras is an anagram of 'sour hand'. Madagascar is an anagram of 'mad car saga'.

"Bangladesh is an anagram of 'bag handles'. Pakistan's an anagram of 'ask paint'. Mongolia's an anagram of 'in a gloom', and El Salvador's an anagram of 'sad overall'.

"Spain is an anagram of pains. The United States of America is an anagram of 'fears education at times', and also 'atomic tests are fun idea'. And United States is an anagram of 'I eat students'."

Scott giggled and said, "Maybe there are some tutors here who do that!"

Becky said, "Yeah, like some of the ones at the party the other night!"

She'd been having a laugh, but then she began to look gloomy again and said, "It's a lot more fun being here in this lecture theatre with you lot than it was at the party! . . . Well, some of it was fun, but some of it wasn't!"

Mya said, "Maybe you're having more fun here because you're with people you enjoy being with now, who are talking about things you like talking about. Also, it might help that people aren't full of drink! It's funny how so many of us automatically want alcohol at parties, as if we think we just can't enjoy ourselves without it, or that we've got no personality or sense of humour till we've had a drink, and then suddenly, whey hey! They'll somehow materialise!"

The students chuckled.

But then Becky said, "I'm annoyed with that tutor who asked me if I enjoyed the party and then got upset with me and complained to my personal tutor when I said I mostly didn't! I mean, how can I have enjoyed a party like that? Well, the whole of it anyway. And I thought psychology tutors especially would be supposed to want to care and understand!"

One of the most talkative students in the psychology department, Catherine, had joined them, and she said thoughtfully, "It does sound daft that he asked you if you enjoyed yourself and then complained because you gave him an answer he didn't want to hear! I agree it's not fair, and it wasn't nice of him to complain about you to other tutors! But a few things like that have made me realise that it seems that when people ask that question, they're not really asking it because they genuinely want to know if you enjoyed yourself or not, even if it sounds as if they do. I think people ask because they're hoping to hear something that makes them feel cheerful, and they assume you'll say yes, or they want to feel appreciated if they've done the thing they're asking if you enjoyed, or they just want to start a conversation and they think asking that's a good way of doing it, or they ask for some other reason like that. I think a lot of people who ask that aren't really looking for honest opinions of what you think.

"I remember someone recommended me a book to read once, and I did read it but I didn't like it. Afterwards they asked me if I'd enjoyed it. I told them I hadn't. They asked me why, but I wasn't keen on saying, since I knew they'd be disappointed. But they kept asking me to tell them. So after they'd done that a few times, I explained why, and they got a bit upset and started criticising me, saying I should have been focusing on what I could get out of it while I was reading it, instead of on what was wrong with it, as if it was my fault I hadn't enjoyed it, and I just wasn't being grateful or doing things properly.

"I realised that when people ask you if you enjoyed something, it sounds like a question that's looking for a yes or no answer, but it isn't really one at all. At least, that's the way it seems to me. Your instinct will likely be to give a yes or no answer, or something in between; but actually, if you didn't enjoy it, I've come to the conclusion that it's best to answer a totally different question, one they didn't actually ask, but which you can at least answer in a positive way, so they get what they want – the feeling of being appreciated or pleased.

"I'm talking about a question that doesn't even require a yes or no answer, but is something like, 'What is there about that situation I can be grateful for?' And, you know, you imagine they just asked you to tell them that.

"That way, even if you didn't like ninety-five per cent of a thing, if there's still even just a bit of it you did like, you can talk about that, and they'll assume that means you did enjoy it, or else get distracted from the question they just seemed to be asking about whether you enjoyed the whole thing, and feel pleased you're talking about the thing you liked . . . Well, that's the theory anyway.

"So for example, if someone gave you a cake and you thought it was grossly over-sweetened, and they asked you if you enjoyed it, if you liked the texture of it, or it looked pretty, you could comment on that, rather than saying, 'No, it was way too sweet!' or, 'No, it was rank, and I wish I didn't feel as if I had to eat it out of politeness in case you didn't approve of me leaving it.' "

Catherine grinned as she said that. Then she continued, "Or if there isn't anything you like about it at all, maybe you could say something like, 'It's nice of you to offer it to me. Thanks', so at least you show you're appreciating that they were trying to be nice. You might not *feel* appreciative at all – in fact, you'll probably wish they hadn't given it to you. But even if you don't feel grateful at all, you can still understand with your mind that they were trying to be nice, so you can still thank them for offering it.

"After all, if they offered it to you, it means they were giving up the idea of eating it themselves, and they might have liked to do that really . . . Well, it's possible they gave it to you because they didn't like it themselves but didn't want to waste it; but chances are they'll have given it to you even though they did like it themselves."

Scott said, "Hiding what you really thought of it would only work if they gave it to you as a one-off though. If they ate that cake often, then giving the impression you liked it could mean they gave it to you again and again after that!"

Catherine said, "Yeah, I suppose so. I was just thinking that the problem with saying what you really think is that –

at least with people who are a bit sensitive – you could end up in an argument. At least, that's what happened to me. Even if you just um and ah because you're not sure what to say because you didn't like what they gave you, and they pick up on the fact that you can't have enjoyed it, and they ask you why you didn't, and you're reluctant to say, and they keep asking, chances are it's just a spur-of-the-moment curiosity, and they don't want to know the answer even though they think they do."

Becky hadn't expected a psychology lecture so near the end of term, and especially not from one of the students. She began to feel a bit tired, and sat down. Still, she was quite interested in what was being said, and felt a bit soothed by it, so she listened quietly as Catherine continued, without batting an eyelid:

"I mean, I'm not saying that'll always happen. Some people might be genuinely interested in the reasons you don't like a thing. But I think with a lot of people, it's best to just try to think of something nice to say instead of telling them what you really think.

"It's not easy to do, because, at least in my experience, when you get asked a question, the brain just instinctively starts trying to think of the answer to that particular question, and if it's a yes or no question, the brain will be asking itself whether the answer's yes or no, instead of thinking about it in a different way, like, 'What can I say that's nice?' And if you don't like a thing much, it's hard to suddenly think of things you do like about it on the spur of the moment when you're put on the spot, and you didn't expect the question. But maybe it's possible for people to train their brains to instantly translate the question, 'Are you enjoying this?' into, 'What about this situation can you be grateful for?' I don't know, but I think it's worth a try.

"Maybe it would be easier if people go around thinking of what they can be grateful for as they go along, so they've already got an answer if someone asks them if they're enjoying themselves and they're not really. Mind you, that might not be all that easy when they're concentrating on doing other things. It might be worth a try though.

"I was on holiday with my parents once, and I wasn't enjoying myself most of the time, but there were a few things I liked, and my mum asked me if I was enjoying the holiday, and instead of answering the question she'd asked, I commented on one particular thing I'd liked, and we had a bit of a joke about it and then moved on to a different subject; so the fact that she didn't say, 'Yes but have you been enjoying the holiday as a whole?' proves that she wasn't really all that interested in the answer to that particular question, but she just wanted to hear something nice or appreciative.

"Mind you, that doesn't always work. I remember I went out for an evening with someone who'd invited me to a church service where I think a couple of people were being baptised or something, and afterwards, there were a lot of nice nibbles to eat. I thought the church service was boring, and I got fed up of it, but I did like the food. It was nearly time to go home when someone asked me if I'd enjoyed the evening. I knew they might be disappointed if I told them I hadn't liked the church service, so I thought that at least I could praise the food. So I just told them I'd really liked the food. Unfortunately, I got the impression they went away thinking, 'You sound like a shallow greedy pig! All you care about is the food! Don't you realise something much more important went on here tonight?'

"So you can't win them all! I don't know whether I'll ever work out how to get things right all the time. I'm still trying to work out what's best really."

Kirsty asked, "Would you do that kind of thing with us too? So if one of *us* did something for you and then asked if you'd enjoyed it, would you still try and make it sound as if you did, even if you didn't?"

Catherine said, "Oh no, I know I can just be myself and say what I think with you!"

She grinned mischievously and joked, "No, if one of *you* lot asked me if I'd enjoyed something I hadn't, I'd say, 'No it was rubbish!'"

The others giggled, and a few said sarcastically, "Thanks!"

Becky's friend Luke was part of the group, and he said, "This stuff reminds me of something that happened to *me* once. I read in a book recently that when a woman asks a question like, 'Does this dress make me look fat?', she likely doesn't want an honest answer. I've heard some people say that too, advising people to lie when they're asked a question like that, so as not to upset the person who asked it. I don't know how true it really is that women don't want an honest answer to the question, but I remember I had an argument with my mum one day because we were in a shop buying my school uniform a few years ago, and she wanted to buy a dress, and she tried one on and asked me, 'Do you think this dress makes me look fat?'

"I didn't want to lie. After all, if she'd bought it, other people might have thought she looked fat in it and slagged her off behind her back about it. I just assumed she wanted an honest opinion. So I said, 'Well you're fat anyway, so I don't suppose the dress could do anything else; but some dresses would do more to hide it.'

"She got angry, and said, 'So you're accusing me of being fat? You can be very rude sometimes!'

"I was annoyed, because I'd only been giving her an honest opinion. I think the annoyance made me raise my voice and sound annoyed, and I said, 'I was only telling you what you asked me to tell you! If you didn't want me to tell you if you look fat, why did you ask if you look fat?'

"My mum said angrily, 'Don't talk so loud, or the whole shop will hear!'

"If anyone in it hadn't heard what I said, but heard her say that, they must have wondered what juicy thing they'd just missed! Anyway, because she'd told me to talk more quietly, I whispered the next thing I said in an angry loud whisper, to exaggerate talking quietly; but so she'd hear it, I put my face close to hers.

"She didn't like that! We argued for a bit longer, and then she told me I was being no help whatsoever, so I should just go away. So I did.

"A few days later, I overheard part of a conversation where she complained about what I'd said to some other people in the family; but she didn't tell them everything that happened, judging by what I heard; she just told them I'd said she looked fat, and that she was upset because I'd put my face right up close to hers to say it. She made it sound as if what had happened was that I'd just walked up to her suddenly out of the blue, shoved my face in hers, and bawled, 'Mummy, *you're* fat!'

"I was annoyed about that. Really, when I'd put my face up close to hers, it was just like a sarcastic flippant gesture, exaggerating what she'd told me to do, like once when me and my sisters were kids and we were having a play-fight in the car on the way to somewhere one day, and she said, 'Keep your hands to yourselves!' So we stopped play-fighting; but then she offered us a sandwich each. I said I'd like one; but because she'd told me to keep my hands to myself, when she held it out, I leaned my head forward with my mouth open for her to put it in that. She wasn't amused! She asked me why I'd done it, and I said, 'You told me to keep my hands to myself!'

"Anyway, the book I was reading that mentioned the issue of dresses and looking fat in them said that when a woman asks if she looks fat, she's not really asking for an honest opinion; chances are she'll just want reassurance that she looks attractive, or at least not ugly. It said the best way to answer a question like that is to say something like, 'Well, you might not look like one of those fashion models in magazines, but they're airbrushed to make them look better than they really are. To me, you look nice enough! I like you all the better for looking natural.'

"Mind you, there might be women who *do* actually want an honest opinion, because they want to buy the thing that makes them look their best. And they might not like it if they think you sound insincere. Maybe you could say something like, 'I think there are other dresses that would look more flattering on you' . . . that's if they haven't already bought the dress when they ask you!"

Suzy said, "That sounds a bit like something I heard, about how when most people ask how you are, they're not really all that interested in knowing; they might be asking because they think it's polite, or to start a conversation, or because they assume you'll say you're well and they'll be happier for hearing that, or they're trying to be friendly, or whatever. I've heard people say that most people don't answer honestly when they get asked that question, but just say they're fine, because they assume the person asking doesn't really want the details of how they are, or they don't want to tell them something that sounds depressing or as if they're a complainer or something.

"And if you did say you weren't feeling that good, after someone asked the question when they were just passing you in the corridor or something, and they weren't that interested in knowing the answer, they'd probably think it would look heartless if they said, 'That's a shame. Bye.' So they'd probably think they had to ask why you weren't feeling good out of politeness, or they might ask out of a spur-of-the-moment curiosity, but then decide they'd rather not know when you started telling them."

Becky's friend Shirley was there with them, and she said with a smile, "Imagine if someone asked you how you are, and you said something like, "I'm not feeling too good; I'm really stressed out at the moment because I've got more work than I think I can handle; and I bruised my arm last week and it still hurts when I touch it; and I've got painful blisters on my feet from where I went for a walk yesterday in new boots; and my parents keep arguing and it makes me feel depressed; and I got a bad haircut from the hairdresser and it annoys me every time I look at it; and I've just been diagnosed with diabetes by the doctor, and he told me I shouldn't really be eating chocolate, and that's annoying, because I love chocolate!'

"They might go away wishing they'd never asked, and say to people, 'Never ask her how she is; she'll tell you all her problems, and you won't get away for the next five minutes!' That'll prove they didn't really want to know the answer when they asked the question."

Becky's friend Sharon had been there all the time, but hadn't said much till then. But then she smiled and said, "I expect a lot of people do want to know the real answer though. But if you didn't want to say you were fine when you weren't, or tell them what was wrong with you, maybe you could try confusing them instead for fun. Like when they ask how you are, you could say, 'I'm feeling a bit purple today; well actually, not purple as such; more a mixture of blue, grey, pink, orange, green and purple.' It would be funny to see their reaction!"

Kirsty smiled and said, "Yeah, but instead of going away and telling other people not to ask you how you are, they'd be telling them you were mad!"

The friends giggled, and Mya said, "That reminds me of a story someone I know told once: She said a cleaner in the place where she used to work was reading the Bible before she came to work one day as she always did. She was reading something from one of the psalms in the Old Testament. I don't know who it was really referring to, but it says God will cover you with his feathers to protect you from harm. She interpreted that as a promise for everyone who believes in him.

"She was on the way to work when some muggers stopped her and demanded she hand over her bag, grabbing hold of it. She said, 'You can't do this to me! I'm covered with feathers!'

"They ran away, shouting to each other, 'She's mad!'

"She came into work and excitedly told everyone what had happened."

The friends laughed.

Becky felt calmer for hearing the things her friends said.

Then Luke said, "Come on, let's go for a pizza."

They went out and had a nice afternoon. Her friends managed to cheer Becky up, and soon she was feeling much better.

When she came back to university after the Christmas holidays, Becky found that everyone was being nice to her again, as if they'd all put what happened behind them.

Soon she was quite happy there again, though she never shared any confidences with her personal tutor from that time onwards. Relations between them did improve though, and soon he was praising her work to her mum and other tutors.

Chapter 12

Fun At Christmas

Becky had a nice Christmas. A few days after Christmas Day, a friend called Jane from university invited her to visit her house for the afternoon, where her family were going to play games and then have tea.

Jane had a brother two years younger than her, Tony, and a sister of about fourteen called Teri. They were there, plus her parents, and her mum's parents, who Jane called Granny and Grandad. They were a merry lot.

They liked to make up zany games to play. They called the first one they played School Challenge. They took turns to challenge the rest to think up questions that were the same, but could be asked in two completely different school subjects they chose.

Jane started. She asked, "What test question could be asked in both psychology and maths?"

They all thought about it for a minute, and then Jane's mum suggested, "How about, 'If eighty-five per cent of the population of Britain was depressed, how many psychologists would it take to give them all two hours of therapy in a week?'"

They smiled. Then Grandad said, "If eighty-five per cent of the population of this country were depressed, I think it would be time for mass emigration to a sunnier climate!"

They chuckled. Tony said, "The trouble is that people live in most of the sunny places in the world already, so there might not be room for us all."

Becky joked enthusiastically, "Perhaps they could be persuaded to swap with us! We could all go and live in their nice sunny climate, and they could all come here."

They smiled. But Jane's mum said, "Not all sunny climates are nice all the time though; in some they get hurricanes and other destructive weather, and there are venomous snakes and other dangerous creatures."

Tony said, "We could swap with Spain! I think it's nice there, isn't it?"

Then Teri said, "But what if there was a horrible law of nature that said that if there were enough British people in one place, it would automatically go cloudy and rainy above them a lot of the time wherever they were in the world, because the climate here would follow the people who normally lived in it wherever they went!"

Granny said, "That wouldn't be so bad in a place where there was normally drought."

Becky said, "Imagine if even the places with the worst droughts would go rainy and cloudy if ever there were a thousand or more British people there at the same time! People in those places would beg us to come out to make it rain. Their governments would pay us.

"Imagine if a thousand British people were employed to constantly go around the world so it would rain; they'd spend a few months in Africa touring the deserts and other places that don't get much rain, and then they might go to the Australian desert, and then to other places; and if they always went at the same times of year, there would get to be new rainy seasons at those times of year there. So schoolbooks would get to say things like, 'Australia has a rainy season in June.' But then if the British stopped going and refused to go back, the books would have to be rewritten."

They smiled. Then it was Becky's turn to suggest a question. She said, "What about a question that could be asked in both chemistry and English literature?"

"Ooh, that's mean!" laughed Jane.

They thought for a minute, and then Jane's dad suggested, "What did Charles Dickens say when he accidentally split the atom while going about his daily business?"

They laughed, and Granny said, "Um, 'Ouch!' "

Tony grinned, and then said, "Hang on, would it even be possible to split an atom by accident while going about your business? How do you split an atom anyway?"

Jane's mum scratched her head in thought, and then asked, "Hey, wouldn't splitting the atom be physics, rather than chemistry? Or would it be both? I suppose it could depend on whether it was an atom of a chemical that was being split, or if chemicals are used in the process of splitting them. But yeah, how would you split one?"

Jane said, "I expect you'd need a lot of specialised equipment. I can't imagine Charles Dickens needing to use equipment like that."

Becky joked, "I don't know; who knows what he got up to while he was contemplating what he was going to write next!"

They all laughed.

Tony had a turn in the game next, and asked, "What question could be asked in both biology and computer studies?"

They thought for a minute, and then Becky said, "How about: 'If a computer was invented that was just as intelligent as a human, would it need a human brain to help it work?' "

Granny said with a smile, "It wouldn't want mine, for a start! I don't think it works quite as well as it used to."

Becky said, "Hey, just imagine if they could make artificial brains for people whose brains were wearing out, just as they make artificial hips and things. Imagine if a person had their brain filled with computer chips! Imagine what they'd be able to do then!"

Teri said, "Wow, maybe they'd be able to do thousands of calculations in seconds, like some computers can!"

Grandad said, "Yeah, and maybe someone would have to press a button on their heads to shut them down when it was time for them to go to bed at night!"

They laughed.

They played the game for another half an hour or so, and then they played another one, where people had to say things that could be answers or punchlines, and the others had to think of questions or jokes that would go well before them. There was usually a few seconds' pause while people thought, but no one thought it mattered.

Granny started. She said, "A sock, a loaf of bread and a maggot."

Jane's mum said with a smile, "What did the cleaner find when she opened the doctor's fridge?"

They giggled, and Jane's mum told them all that when Tony was about five, one day she'd found one of her shoes in the fridge. She felt sure he must have put it there, though why, she had no idea.

They all grinned. Then it was Tony's turn. He said, "The chemist went red in the face and said, 'Don't be so rude!' "

Teri laughed and said, "Oh I'm sure I've heard something like this. A man went into a Chemist and asked, 'Have you got something that can stop me wetting the bed?' "

Granny said with a grin, "Oh, wouldn't it be awful if chemists really did behave like that!"

Grandad's turn was next, and he said, "A pigeon on drugs."

Jane's mum said, "What gets high in the sky and then comes down with a bang?"

Then Becky had a turn, and said, "A newspaper from 1895."

Grandad said, "What did my local chip shop used to wrap chips in when I was a child?"

They chuckled.

Jane had a turn and said, "A haggis on the head."

Her mum teased, "What did Jane always like going around with when she was a child?"

Everyone burst out laughing at the thought.

They carried on playing that game for a while, and then they played a couple more. Then they had a nice big tea, with quite a lot of cakes and other yummy things.

But in the middle of it, Becky made a complaint. No, it wasn't about the tea. Or any of Jane's family.

She said, "A few times, I've asked for things for Christmas from a couple of people in my family, and ended up with things that are almost the opposite in some ways from what I asked for! One thing was when a couple of years ago, I told one person I wanted a mixture of sweets, and said I especially liked Jelly Babies. They just got me a big box of Jelly Babies, which was nice enough, but I'd asked for a mixture of things, so to get me one single thing was almost the opposite of what I asked for."

They sympathised. But then Jane's granny said, "Well, at least you got something you enjoyed. Imagine if you'd just got a load of empty sweet packets instead as a joke present! My dad had three brothers, and he didn't like one of them. One Christmas, he got a present from this brother shaped like a football. He was really excited, thinking it was one. But when he opened it, he found it was a cabbage! His brother had given it to him for an unkind joke!"

Tony said, "Hey imagine if footballers trying to play an FA Cup final were given a cabbage instead of a football. Imagine if they all loved raw cabbage, so they just stood around in a huddle for ages, sharing it between them and eating it, and when they'd finished they asked for a real football, but were just given another cabbage, so they ate that too. A hundred thousand people might have gone to watch them, and millions might be watching on telly, but all they might see for over half an hour would be all the footballers standing together chomping on cabbage.

"And imagine if whenever they finished one and asked for a real football that time, they always just got given another cabbage and decided to eat that, so for the entire ninety minutes, they were just standing together eating cabbage, till they got through about ten of them!"

Teri grinned and said, "Eek! Wouldn't that make it a bit windy on the pitch? I mean, wouldn't eating that much cabbage do one or two unfortunate things to their digestive systems?"

They laughed, and Jane's granny said good-naturedly, "Oh stop it!"

Jane's grandad said, "I suppose if people went to watch an FA Cup final and just saw the footballers standing together eating cabbage, that would be the opposite in some ways of what they'd hoped for; I mean, they'd have been hoping to see them running around scoring goals, and instead they'd see them just standing together . . . But then if the amount of cabbage they'd had really did do dramatic things to their digestive systems, they'd possibly get the runs afterwards instead, when hopefully no one was watching at all."

They giggled and made faces, and Jane's granny told him off in an exaggerated way, while laughing herself, saying, "Grandad! You should know better than to say things like that, especially at the tea table!"

Grandad apologised with a smile.

Then Jane said, "Sometimes in the kitchen in my student halls of residence, I open the fridge, and someone's left some vegetables in there for longer than they should have done, and they're beginning to go rotten. Maybe they bought them and then couldn't be bothered to cook them, or maybe they're eternal optimists who keep thinking they'll last longer than they will. It's not very nice. But it makes me think: You know that slogan, 'A dog is for life, not just for Christmas' that they started publicising because a lot of dogs were being abandoned not long after Christmas, after some people seemed to think it would be cute to get their kids a puppy for Christmas, not thinking about how it might be when they turned into big dogs that might be naughty and a handful to manage, and need expensive vet's treatment because they'd need vaccinations and they might get ill, and they'd need to be taken for walks every day even in the cold and the rain and the snow and high wind and so on?

"Well they could publicise a slogan that would be more or less the opposite of the puppy one: Maybe they could put it in adverts on the telly or put it up in vegetable aisles in super-markets, and it could say, 'A cabbage is for one or two weeks, not for life!' Imagine someone thinking they could keep a cabbage for the whole of their lives!"

They grinned.

Then Grandad said, "That's a bit like what Becky said earlier about getting presents that are in some ways the opposite of what you want. I can feel an idea for another game coming on: Suggest Christmas presents that are almost the opposite of what a person asked for, but not in an obvious way. I can think of one already: Imagine someone asks for one of those bread-making machines, because they like the taste of freshly-made bread much more than shop-bought bread, and they think they'll be able to make it taste like it in a bread-making machine; but the person they ask for one thinks, 'Oh, they like bread', and buys them a loaf of bread instead, thinking that's what they want."

Jane said, "I actually read on the Internet that someone really did get a loaf of bread for Christmas once. I was looking at a web page about the worst Christmas presents people had ever got. I think someone else said they got a bag of onions. Some things are nice to have in your ordinary everyday grocery shop; but at Christmas, you want something a bit special, don't you."

"Well, it could be worse," said Jane's grandad with a grin. "Imagine if someone was going shopping and asked you if you wanted anything, and you asked if they could get you a loaf of seeded bread, and they came back with a loaf of bread without seeds in it, and when you told them you'd wanted bread *with* seeds, they said there was no need to worry, and went and got some seeds from their greenhouse, and said you could just sprinkle those on your toast."

Jane giggled and said, "I don't think that would be very healthy!"

Teri laughed and joked, "No, imagine if it was a variety pack of seeds, and you ate them, and a flower garden and a vegetable plot started growing inside you, and you ended up with carrots growing out of your ears, tulips growing out of your mouth, a pea pod hanging down from each nostril, daffodils sticking out from your eyes, and a Brussels sprout sprouting out of your belly button!"

They giggled, and Jane's mum said, "Somehow I don't think they'd make it that far! The seeds would probably just give you a tummy ache, because seeds really need to be cooked before they're alright to eat."

Jane asked, "How come birds can eat them without cooking them then? It seems they must have stronger stomachs than humans! So much for the idea that we've got the advantage of millions of years of evolution!"

"Yes, but we've got lots of other advantages," said Jane's dad with a broadening grin. "I mean, it's just as well birds can eat raw seeds, because they can't cook . . . And I don't mean they're bad at it, like I might mean if I said a human couldn't cook; they literally can't do it, can they. I mean, can you imagine going outside and seeing a family of little birds making a seed pie and putting it into a little solar-powered oven you saw some scientist birds inventing the other day?"

They all giggled, and Jane said, "Wow, that would be cool!"

When it was time for Becky to go home, they gave her some cakes to take with her. One had nuts in. Jane's mum said, "There you go. One of those is a nutty cake. Maybe one day you can make one yourself, and pretend you're a really clever squirrel, who's not only learned to gather nuts, but learned to make cakes with them too."

Becky giggled. She'd had a lovely day, and she went home happily.

When she went back to university, she felt a lot more cheerful than she had when she left for the Christmas holidays. She met up with all her friends again, and they had more good times.

Acknowledgements

Here are some books and podcasts where a bit of the advice and information Becky and others pass on in this book was acquired.

Chapter 2

Child discipline: *Parent in Control* by Gregory Bodenhamer.

Marriage problems: *The Divorce Remedy* by Michele Weiner Davis; *When Love Dies: How to Save a Hopeless Marriage* by Judy Bodmer.

Chapter 3

Auctions, sales tactics and getting help in a crowd:
Influence: Science and Practice by Robert B. Cialdini.

Chapter 9

The story of the Cambodian Immigrants in therapy:
Therapy Ghostbusters, from the podcast *Invisibilia*, season 9.

The story of the horrible card game played in class:
Absolute Power, Green Triangles, from the podcast *The Story Collider*, season 7.

About the Author

Diana Holbourn has written self-help articles and is the author of *The Early Life of Becky Bexley the Child Genius* and other books about the same character. Taking short psychology courses, working on a helpline and reading psychology books has prepared her for writing the self-help information that appears as part of the story in the Becky Bexley series. Diana lives and works on the south coast of England, where the sun shines ... sometimes.

For more about the author and her books, visit:

www.DianaHolbourn.com

Other books in this series
Becky Bexley, Book One

Even from the moment she was born, it was clear that Becky Bexley was not like other children. Her family were shocked by her behaviour!

Just a few years later, and she's in secondary school, often seeming wiser than her teachers. She does her best to help people, whether they like it or not. She has advice for her teachers when they want to give up smoking, gives a boy advice he uses to stop himself being teased, and even gives the headmaster some advice on improving the school's anti-bullying strategy.

She helps people outside school too, including rescuing her mum from a con artist. She even gets to go to the White House, where she ends up giving the president advice about his behaviour!

He invites her to help some politicians with the depression they have. But will a few tactless remarks she makes and their own fierce disagreements unwittingly stirred up by some of the insights she tries to pass on ruin her efforts?

Becky's advice is based on genuine therapy techniques and psychological research, and the books in this series combine humour with handy information.

Becky Bexley, Book Three

Child genius Becky Bexley entices a group of her fellow university students to play a rowdy game in class for fun one day that has worried tutors coming to investigate what's going on.

On another day, she and a group of other students have a long long discussion where they talk about such things as world leaders taking foolish risks, false rumours, and interviews with transsexuals, and they tell stories about scams and broken friendships.

The discussion often becomes humorous though, as they tell each other funny news stories, make up jokes, and think up wacky ideas for fun.

Printed in Great Britain
by Amazon

25315093R00189